without warning

also by eugenia lovett west

the ancestors cry out

without warning

eugenia lovett west

thomas dunne books

st. martin's minotaur

new york

THOMAS DUNNE BOOKS.
An imprint of St. Martin's Press.

WITHOUT WARNING. Copyright © 2007 by Eugenia Lovett West. All rights reserved. Printed in the United States of America. No part of this book may be used or reproduced in any manner whatsoever without written permission except in the case of brief quotations embodied in critical articles or reviews. For information, address St. Martin's Press, 175 Fifth Avenue, New York, N.Y. 10010.

www.thomasdunnebooks.com
www.minotaurbooks.com

Library of Congress Cataloging-in-Publication Data

West, Eugenia Lovett, 1923–
    Without warning / Eugenia Lovett West.—1st U.S. ed.
        p. cm.
    ISBN-13: 978-0-312-37113-5
    ISBN-10: 0-312-37113-6
    1. Widows—Fiction. I. Title.

PS3573.E818W58 2007
813'.54—dc22
                                                        2007033537

First Edition: December 2007

10 9 8 7 6 5 4 3 2 1

To wonderful family and friends

prologue

The automatic people mover at a JFK terminal was crowded with passengers booked on the long New York–Hong Kong flight. As the steel ridges inched along, a young woman shifted a heavy backpack and took the hand of a small girl who was trying to run ahead. Four Chinese businessmen wearing dark suits and carrying briefcases stared blankly at the ads that lined the echoing walls.

No one paid attention to the jogger weaving his way through the line—there was always someone in a hurry at airports. He paused as he reached the four men, then ran on.

A few seconds later, the tallest of the Chinese stumbled. He put his hand to his chest, coughed, and fell forward onto the moving steel. The small girl pulled at the woman's hand and pointed. "Look, Mumma. Red paint. The man is spilling his red paint."

part one

one

Monday, June 2

Connecticut

There was no warning siren. No message flipping across a TV screen. The stripping down began on one of those perfect June days created for outdoor weddings and graduations. A day for celebrations, not loss.

At noon, my godmother, Caroline Vogt, had arrived for lunch on my terrace overlooking the Connecticut River—a detour on her annual migration from New York to her Newport "cottage." Caroline was seventy-four. She had been divorced four times. Her voice sounded like a tuba filled with gravel, her tongue was razor sharp, but she was the closest thing I had to a mother and I adored her. She had always called me darling girl and over the years we had worked out a system: She was free to speak her mind. If I didn't take her advice, no hard feelings. The system hadn't worked today.

As the black Mercedes disappeared down the drive, I ran upstairs, threw the linen shirt and slacks on the floor, and yanked on ragged work jeans. Picked up my gardening tools and rushed out to work on the herbaceous border I was copying from an English magazine.

"I am not, not, *not* a clinging mother," I muttered, plunging the shovel into clumps of hard roots. Caroline had come to hit a nerve and she had succeeded:

"Pay attention, darling girl. You're forty-seven. You survived losing your singing voice. You've done a superb job with those hunks of boys, but now they're off to college. They're men. Let them go. You've got the money, the time, the energy to move on and do something important. Don't drag your feet. Do it."

For more than an hour, I dug and made piles of dirt until my shoulders burned. Finally I straightened and pushed back my hair with a sweaty hand. I should have said, "Give me a break, will you? I work in a soup kitchen. I raise money for the children of 9/11 firefighters and disaster victims. There's Lewis, don't forget. Tomorrow I have to go to London with him."

O'Hara, our black and tan Jack Russell terrier, was sniffing in the tall grass by the tennis court. Last week he had appeared with a baby rabbit in his mouth.

"Come," I said, and started down the path that led to the front of the house. The sun had shifted to the west; the birds in the old maples were busy feeding those hungry little mouths. I stood still, muscles aching, and looked at the old fanlight over the door, the antique carriage lamps. This was my nest, safe— so far—from anthrax and bombs. I loved every uneven ceiling and iron latch.

The old part of the house was built in 1798 by a local shipowner. Yellow clapboards, with original wide floorboards. Windows that had to be propped up with sticks. We had come here ten years ago when Lewis was made the CEO of Galbraith Technologies, a leading high-tech company, but this was still known as the Sterling place. We had kept the original four rooms and added an all-purpose wing: kitchen, living and dining space, mudroom, and the long flagstone terrace.

"There you are." Our caretaker, Mrs. Gates, was coming down the steps. In winter we put our cars in a nearby barn with an apartment above for Mrs. Gates, a round-faced, cheerful widow, far more friend than employee.

"Just down in the garden."

"I cleared up the dishes and did some ironing. Can't believe the quiet around here. No mess. No dirty clothes."

I winced. "We'll get used to it." My two sons had been day students at a nearby prep school. Boarders had flocked here for weekends; the mudroom was still filled with lacrosse sticks, soccer balls, hockey pucks. Jake had finished a year at Brown; Steve would be a freshman at Harvard. Last week they had gone off to their summer jobs, Jake to a radio station in San Francisco, Steve to a ranch in Montana.

Mrs. Gates shook her head. "Not much for me to do anymore. I'll be going along; my sister's grandchildren are coming for supper. What time are you off tomorrow? London again, is it?"

"London, back Thursday night. Three days and two nights. I could have used the time here, putting in the new border."

Mrs. Gates made a clucking sound. "Good for you to get away, is what I say. Fly off in a private plane. Dress up like one of those high-paid models." The Streat choice not to live like industrial royalty was an ongoing joke between us.

"Model—tell that to my brother. He says I've got hair like a horse's mane. A messy chestnut mane."

"Well, a model would kill for your eyes."

I smiled, remembering my old nurse Biddy McGee. "Yer no beauty above the neck, darlin': yer nose is too flat; yer mouth is too big. But those eyes, blue as a Kerry lake." And in my press clippings: *Eyes that mesmerize up to the third balcony . . . not a classic beauty, but Metcalf has presence. Vitality. Brio.*

"Give up," I said, stretching my aching shoulders. "You'll never turn me into a jet-setter. Lewis would hate it. Besides, that fancy plane just saves him time at airports. Safer, too, these days."

"Seems a waste, though, you going around in T-shirts and jeans. Grubbing in the garden. Anything special you want me to do?"

"Just water the plants on the terrace. You've got the number of the company flat in case you have to reach us."

"In my book. See you in the morning."

Late sun filled the neat kitchen; it looked empty and deserted. On the river, an oil barge was heading down to Long Island Sound. Once upon a time Pequot Indians had paddled their canoes on this water, a slow, safe way of getting from place to place, and maybe that wasn't so bad. Those Indian women never had jet lag, no career choices, no empty-nest syndrome.

Suddenly O'Hara sat up, ears pricked forward, nose in the air. After a few seconds I could hear, in the distance, the faint sound of the helicopter coming up the river. Lewis was early; he never got home before seven. Like the Gulfstream jet, the copter he used for commuting was a time-saving necessity, not a status symbol. The first year we were married he had cheerfully driven to work in a car with gaping rust holes in the floor. This was a man of intelligence and vision who hated show and cultivating contacts. A shy man who had needed me then.

"He's early, for once," I said to O'Hara. No time, now, to cut back the geraniums on the terrace or work out on the StairMaster. I went into the pantry and pulled a container of homemade chicken curry from the freezer. There was the usual roar as the copter landed on the pad beyond the apple orchard. Another roar, as Tim, the pilot, took off again.

After a moment, Lewis came across the strip of lawn, carrying his jacket, a tall, dark-haired man with the thin, intense face of a beardless Abe Lincoln. A man driven by the pressures of creating high-tech weapons. Would he notice any change if I found myself a full-time job—or a lover? As always, he stopped to check the temperature on the outdoor thermometer before coming into the kitchen. I reached for the salad spinner; supermarkets had taken to spraying lettuce as if hosing down rugs.

"Hi," I said.

"Hi." He sat down at the huge round kitchen table. For years it had been covered with games, homework, cookie crumbs. Instead of pouring out arias about misplaced faith and greed, I had channeled passion and exuberance into soccer matches, car pools, batches of lasagna. But I knew what my friends were saying: "Terrible about Emma, such a dynamo, stuck in that backwater, married to a workaholic, buried in motherhood slog."

"Good day?" I asked.

"No."

I put down the spinner and looked at him. His face had the set expression of a man holding in anger. "What happened?"

"I may have to stay longer in London. Security problems over there. You may have to come home without me."

"How much longer?"

"Depends on what I find." He was staring at his hands. Mechanically, I blotted the lettuce with paper towels. I had learned, the hard way, not to overdramatize. Many of our friends were divorced, but Lewis and I were good friends in and out of bed. We respected each other's strengths. Like heads of separate departments, I had been the caregiver while Lewis had worked his way to the top of the industrial ladder.

"You'd better go over the schedule with me," I said. "So I know what to pack."

He looked up, frowning. "What's that?"

"The schedule. I have to pack."

"We get to London after nine tomorrow night their time. Wednesday, meetings all day. The International Technology Committee."

I nodded. "I'll spend the day at the new Tate." This committee was a kind of CEO think tank for an exchange of cutting-edge ideas. Lectures. The wives of members were mostly older women with grown children and no careers. Women who went everywhere with their husbands.

"On Wednesday night, Hank and Robina are having a reception. At their house."

"Their house? The wives will love that." Hank Lausch was a close friend from the days when he and Lewis had started out together in New York. Hank was a mediocre engineer but good at public relations. When Lewis was made CEO, he had saved Hank's neck by sending him to be the manager of the token London office. In spite of recent cutting back, there was still a suite of rooms in Berkeley Square. A car and driver and a flat for visiting VIPs and personnel in transit.

". . . Thursday, more lectures. I'll have to work in a meeting with a physicist from Cambridge, a Dr. Estes, top brain in the laser field. Done some of our best projects." Lewis worked closely with a number of Cambridge physicists and had great respect for their intellect and creativity. He often said that without physics the world would be a zero.

"Is he the one who's terrified of computer hackers? The one who carries everything around in a little notebook?"

"When he's working on a concept, he puts his new formulas in that notebook. Keeps it handy in his vest pocket."

"As long as it doesn't get lost at the cleaners. Are we staying at the company flat?"

"No. Hank got us a suite at the Pelham. Remind me to give you the number for Mrs. Gates."

I turned, hand in midair. "A *suite*? At the *Pelham*? That's where movie stars and heads of state hang. Why not the flat?"

"Plumbing problems. High season in London, hotels filled. Best not to argue with him."

"No." If Hank resented Lewis's success it didn't show, but Lewis was careful to keep clear of Hank's small turf—and I never played the role of boss's wife with the imperious Robina. Four years ago, Hank's friends were startled, to say the least, when he married Lady Robina Fyfe, an earl's daughter with money.

O'Hara was dancing around, shaking his toy doll, demanding the nightly tug-of-war. Lewis rubbed his forehead, ignoring the dog.

"Want a drink?" I asked.

"When's dinner?"

"Half an hour, about. You're early." I put the curry into the micro and went back to the sink. "About this security thing. I don't want to put my foot in it."

Silence. I waited. Lewis was staring at his hands. The knuckles were white. Suddenly he looked up and saw me standing there.

"Forget it," he said sharply. "I shouldn't have opened my mouth."

"But—"

"Forget it, Em."

I turned to the counter. "Fine. I will."

He pushed back his chair and got to his feet. "Sorry. Didn't mean to snap. What's for dinner?" My husband was a master at hiding his feelings.

"Chicken curry."

"Sounds good." He went to the pie safe we used as a bar. Poured himself two inches of Scotch malt whiskey and turned.

"Em."

"What?"

"We haven't talked lately. I've been tied up, you had Steve's graduation, getting the boys off to their jobs. I wasn't much help." A rare admission.

"It happens. Not your fault. Goes with the turf." I watched as he went to the refrigerator. Ice cubes rattled into the glass. He stood there, studying the ice.

"It's time you know. About this business of making weapons. It's getting out of hand. We're all—me, the competition—seems as if we're turning into smart-ass kids playing with lethal toys. One of these days we're going to blow ourselves up."

I leaned against the counter. What was he trying to tell me? "That—sounds bad," I said.

"It is. I'm thinking of leaving Galbraith Tech."

My head jerked back. "*Leave?* But *why?* The place would go to pieces without you."

"It may, but I want to help prevent mass destruction, not accelerate it. You can understand why. We've got two sons. Great boys. God knows what they're facing. Turning out new weapons systems isn't going to help them. What goes 'round comes back to hit us in the gut. Always has, always will. Simple as that."

I took a step forward, my mind flapping like a veering sail. "When did you start thinking about leaving Galbraith?"

"A while ago. It won't happen soon, but I wanted to give

you a heads-up. I'll be in the study," and he went through the door and down the hall.

The curry would need rice. I unhooked a copper saucepan from the rack over the stove. Put in a cup of water and shoved it onto a burner, then measured a half cup of rice and put on the cover. At noon, Caroline had told me to get a life. Just now Lewis had slammed the door in my face when I mentioned security in London. Why? Was the talk about leaving Galbraith meant to distract me?

With a need to keep moving, I opened a drawer and took out my favorite place mats, blue and yellow linen from a little shop in Provence. Took down the Sandwich glass goblets, the plates from Pier 1. My crisis rule with the boys was simple: "Don't panic. Take a deep breath and count to ten." O'Hara was shaking his toy again, looking worried.

"Later," I told him, trying not to think worst case like my older sister, Dolly. Poor Dolly couldn't drive from Lake Forest to Chicago without expecting a flat tire or a fatal accident.

The water was almost boiling. If Lewis left his job, it wouldn't be a disaster. We had money. We wouldn't lose the house. The boys could go to graduate school. Lewis would switch his talent for bringing embryo ideas to life to another field. He was a recognized expert at crisis management. Whatever was happening in London, he would find an answer. I knew his views on security:

"It's an ongoing fight, spies wanting to get their hands on weapons projects in the first stages. A good industrial spy can save a company time and money. A spy for a rogue state or a terrorist group can shift the balance of world power. Patents mean nothing to them. The stakes are very high."

O'Hara sat down on my feet, his way of getting attention.

"No," I said, dislodging him. Making time for Lewis had better be one of my new priorities. Tomorrow we could talk on the plane.

"Damn." With a loud hiss, the rice boiled over. I jumped. Burned my hand. Dropped the pan. As water and rice streamed over the tile floor, O'Hara raised his head and began to howl.

"Be quiet," I said sharply, and went to get the mop. There was no way to know that tiny listening devices, not on the market, were busily at work around me. One under a warped board in the broom closet. Another in our bedroom. Another in Lewis's study. Every sound, every word spoken in this house was being transmitted to a satellite thousands of miles away.

two

Tuesday, June 3

London

I love London for the standard American reasons: the dignified buildings, the little streets with a history, the old-fashioned courtesy in the shops.

As usual, Wheeler, the company driver, was waiting when the Gulfstream landed. Wheeler is a solid gray-haired Welshman who loves dog racing. His wife grows African violets. He was fussing like an elderly nanny as Jeff, the flight attendant, took bags out of the plane and put them on the tarmac.

"This all there is, then? They'll fit into the boot. Lovely evening we're having, but traffic's something wicked. Bomb scare in the Underground near Kensington."

I nodded and got into the maroon Jaguar, glad to be on solid ground. Lewis spoke to the head pilot.

"Good flight, Chet. Unless there's a change, we'll leave Thursday morning. Eleven o'clock."

"Right, sir. It's all fixed. Have a good stay."

It took time to get clear of the airport, past the miles of

factories and low-cost housing, but at last we were in central London, entering the whirlpool around Hyde Park Corner. Apsley House, lit with floodlights, loomed ahead. I glanced at Lewis. There had been no talk about the future. He had stayed in the front of the cabin, dictating notes to his assistant in New York. Lorna was a stately, beautiful woman from Kingston, Jamaica. Sharp as a laser beam, getting a law degree from NYU at night. After a year of working for Lewis, she had put her foot down.

"Put all your unreadable notes onto a tape and I'll make them into agendas. It'll save me hours of anguish."

Once during the flight I had walked forward.

"Want a sandwich?" Lewis looked up at me, through me.

"What?"

"Would you like a sandwich?"

"Maybe later."

"A drink?"

"No thanks." After that, I left him alone. Dozed on the pull-out bed, drinking tea and trying to concentrate on a bestselling novel about an anorexic woman of eighty and her teenage lover. Instead, words of Caroline's kept surfacing: "You're forty-seven. You survived losing your singing voice. . . ."

A singer's voice is a genetic gift, but I had worked hard to develop that gift. Learned languages, librettos, scores, stage directions: "Stand still, Miss Metcalf, until Don Carlo swings his cape." When the curtain went up it was *my* passion, *my* discipline, *my* dramatic soprano voice that soared out over the footlights and sent managers rushing to my agent: Was Metcalf available for Verona in three years? Covent Garden? La Fenice?

At age twenty-five, after opening the San Francisco season, I crashed. Hating to disappoint the audience, I sang *Manon Lescaut* with a heavy cold. A week later, I could barely speak.

There were frantic consultations. Tests. A botched operation on two tiny muscles. I can still see the tan venetian blinds in the surgeon's office.

"I'm extremely sorry, Miss Metcalf, I realize this will come as a great blow, but the vocal folds are permanently damaged. You'll be able to speak, but your voice will have no strength."

I flew home to Boston and collapsed. Stayed all day in my room listening to my voice on tapes. My mother talked gently about drawing on spiritual faith; my older sister, Dolly, babbled about support groups. Finally, losing patience, my little brother had dragged me out to a fund-raiser at the Museum of Science. Standing at the wine bar, I met Lewis Streat, a shy, brilliant young engineer who was tone-deaf. There had been highs and lows, as in all marriages, but until now I had never needed to walk on tiptoe around him.

As the car turned into Park Lane, I reached for my handbag, wishing we were at the comfortable, familiar flat a few blocks away. The entrance to the Pelham Hotel was flanked by tubs of flowers; the small parking space was blocked by a stretch limousine attended by men in dark suits. Movie star or head of state?

A few moments later, an assistant manager opened the door to the Wellington Suite on the eighteenth floor. "Delighted to have you with us. Anything we can do—"

As Lewis pressed money into a porter's hand, I studied the sitting room. It was opulent, filled with ornate Louis Quinze furniture. A perfect setting for flaming love affairs and secret meetings, but even the exotic smell was pretentious; it would stay in my clothes for weeks. As the door to the mirrored foyer closed, I kicked off my shoes.

"Do you want to go out or shall I order something?" I asked. "Soup and chicken?"

"Order something. Anything but pasta." Lewis sat down and pulled off his tie. "This place is too damn rich for my blood."

"God, yes. I hope we can open some windows."

The red message light on the white phone was blinking. I picked it up and recognized Robina Lausch's clipped Brit voice.

"Welcome back. Lunch tomorrow, Emma? Ring me in the morning." Then, after a pause, the voice of Lewis's assistant, Lorna.

"Mr. Streat. Please call me as soon as you get in. I'll stay in the office until I hear from you."

I handed the phone to Lewis. "You're to call Lorna at the office. No matter what time."

He frowned, took the phone, and dialed.

"Lorna. Just arrived. You wanted me to call."

A bowl of spring flowers—tulips, iris, daffodils—stood on a nearby table. I took out the card and read it.

Look forward to seeing you both tomorrow.
Hank and Robina

Before Robina, Hank's VIPs used to get tight little pyramids of roses and carnations. This was a lovely, loose arrangement; Robina had trained her favorite florist well. I turned, waiting for Lewis to finish so I could order. He was leaning forward. The expression on his face had changed from tired to grim.

"Let me get this straight, Lorna. He was killed this morning at JFK. The police came to the office at noon. They want to question me." A pause. "I'll have to change plans, do some juggling. You'd better get hold of Chet and alert him to stand by for an earlier flight. You have his sister's number in Surrey, but he may not be there yet. Something else. Don't use my office until security has swept it again." Another pause while Lorna talked and he listened.

"I know they're a good outfit," he said at last, "but I want a double check. There's a reason. Tell the police I'll be back in town Thursday morning. I'll answer their questions then. Thanks, Lorna." He hung up.

I let out my breath. "What was *that* about?"

Lewis hesitated. "It'll be in the papers tomorrow. A Chinese engineer from Hong Kong was killed this morning at JFK. Knifed in the ribs on one of those people movers. Bled to death on the spot."

"Knifed on a *people* mover—you mean, he died moving along on one of those *things?*" Like a scene in a horror film, I could see the man slumped on thick ridges of steel, blood spreading to shoes and bags. People leaning down, helpless, moving along with him.

"According to the police."

"But what's that got to do with *you?*"

Lewis got up. He walked to the carved fireplace and stood looking down at the thick velvety green carpet. "The man came to see me yesterday. The police found my name and the Galbraith company address in his wallet. They're looking for the killer."

"But you weren't anywhere near that airport."

"I'm not a suspect. The police are just doing their job, getting information." He looked at his watch. "I have to call that physicist in Cambridge, meet him tomorrow instead of Thursday. Find time for George Galbraith. I should see him while I'm over."

"Not to worry, he'll be at the Lausches' reception, worse luck." George Galbraith was the pompous eighty-year-old Scot who had founded this cutting-edge high-tech company. He had made his millions and retired, but he was still the major shareholder.

Lewis nodded. "That'll have to do. We'll put in an appearance at the Lausch reception, then fly straight home."

"Fly home? What about that security problem? You said you might have to stay—" I stopped. Sweat was running down Lewis's forehead and Lewis never sweated. In a crisis, he was like a rock. Unbreakable.

"Em. What does it take? You know nothing about a security problem over here." A voice like a whip.

I swallowed. "I hear you."

"We'll need to leave London without causing a stir. Raising questions."

"Fine with me," I said, pushing back my hair. First this mysterious security problem. Now murder on a people mover.

"I'll call Estes from the bedroom. You can go ahead and order."

He started towards the door, wiping sweat from his face. "Jesus Christ," he said under his breath. A low voice I wasn't meant to hear. "Jesus Christ. What next?"

three

Troubled minds produce troubled sleep. I dreamed I was alone on a people mover, alone with a bleeding body. I tried to lift my feet, but they were clamped to the rattling ridges of steel. I struggled, screamed—and woke staring up at swaths of blue silk suspended from a gold crown, the hangings around this claustrophobic bed.

It was seven o'clock. After a moment, I turned my head and looked at Lewis. Sometime after midnight, Lewis had gone into the sitting room. After a while I had called out.

"Is anything wrong?"

"No. Didn't mean to wake you," he said, and came back.

Now he was sleeping, breathing evenly, but his behavior last night had left me feeling as if a mysterious weight had descended on my head. Lewis never sweated and he very seldom swore. Trying not to disturb him, I slid out of bed, pulled on a wrapper, and tiptoed into the sitting room.

It was going to be a lovely day. In Hyde Park, dogs were being walked, deck chairs set out. A faint sound of traffic on Park Lane came drifting up. I pushed back my hair, needing fresh air, and ordered breakfast.

Five minutes later, like a footman approaching a royal presence, the waiter wheeled in a table. Starched pink cloth, red rose in crystal vase. A gleaming silver lid covered my plebian cornflakes.

"Good morning, madam. Lovely weather we're having."

"Yes, lovely." In the company flat, I could pad around in my panties and bra. Make my own coffee.

At a little after eight, Lewis came out of the bedroom, looking white and tired. "It's late. I never heard you get up."

"I didn't want to wake you. You thrashed around most of the night."

"Sorry." He adjusted his tie and sat down on a pink velvet chair.

"Coffee?" I asked.

"Thanks. I miss the flat."

"I know. I feel as if I'm drowning in velvet. Toast?"

"Just coffee. What are you doing today?"

"Lunch with Robina. Visit the Tate." I poured and handed him a fragile cup. "I take it Hank is in the dark about this security thing."

Lewis put the cup down with force. Coffee spilled onto the pink cloth. "Em. How can I get through to you? He sure as hell is in the dark. You'd better cancel lunch."

I let out my breath. "Robina and I always have lunch when I'm over."

"She's too damn sharp. Picks up vibes like a magnet. She may get a sense that something's wrong."

I stared. "Wait a minute. Wait just a minute. Robina may be

sharp as a tack, which she is, but I can't tell her anything *I* don't know." There was no love lost between Lewis and Robina, but I enjoyed her arrogance, her cutting wit, the glimpses of her high-flying English world.

"Call her. Get out of it. You'll see her at the reception tonight."

My neck stiffened. Lewis could be abrupt, but never had he given me an order that made no sense. "In case you've forgotten, I used to make a good living on the stage. I think I can handle Robina."

"This is different."

"What way different?" I paused. Retied the sash of my wrapper. "I'm no good at guessing games, as you very well know. You came home Monday night in a major flap. You said there was a security problem in London. Ever since then you've acted like you were sitting on a—on a keg of dynamite."

Lewis got to his feet as if I had hit him with a cattle prod. "I should never have opened my mouth—"

"But why was that so *bad*? That's what I don't understand. You were alone in your house with a wife who knows how to keep quiet. What's more, if I cancel lunch with Robina, I'll have to pretend I'm sick. Not go to her reception. Then there *will* be questions. From Robina and a lot of people: 'What's wrong with Emma? Where is she?' "

"True." He rubbed his head, a new habit since yesterday. "I guess it's safer not to rock the boat, but watch it, Em."

"Watch *what*? I'm not a mind reader."

He hesitated. "Look. There may be changes over here. I may have to close the office. Hank will be out of a job, such as it is, and Robina is bound to cause trouble. She won't admit it, but she likes the connection to George Galbraith and his millions, his art collecting."

"Oh Lord. She sure does. In spades."

"One other thing. That physicist Dr. Estes. I'm meeting him here. Not at the office."

"Here?" Lewis never held meetings in hotel rooms.

"Hank is too damn careless about security. Always has been. I've had this suite swept for bugs."

"Fine. What time is Dr. Estes coming?"

"At three. Would you mind going out?"

"I can walk in the park. I'll have coffee sent up. How long should I stay away?" Suddenly I was a wife who couldn't be trusted.

"About an hour, I'd say. It's not that you—" He stopped. "The fact is, these geniuses are apt to be paranoid. Estes will do better if he knows we're alone."

I nodded, accepting the weak excuse. "So. Estes at three. The reception at six." No point in saying that I could have stayed in the bedroom. Or reminding him that I hadn't gone beyond Algebra I.

"We'll stay at the reception for an hour and leave. I'm arranging for a special driver to pick up our bags downstairs, then come to Eaton Terrace and take us to the plane."

"Not Wheeler?"

"No, but keep that to yourself."

I nodded. A paranoid physicist and a paranoid husband? "Yes, of course," I said. "I won't breathe a word, but what are you going to tell the committee, why you're leaving a day early?"

"A personnel problem in New York. I'm off. Where did I put my briefcase?"

"Over there. On the table. But you've only had coffee."

"See you later. Be careful." He was walking away. The outer door in the mirrored foyer clicked shut behind him.

I pushed back my chair and went to the window again,

needing to find traction on this slippery slidy road. When I was a child, my temper had been the despair of my mother and teachers. The first singing coach had been stern: "You are far too impetuous and quick off the handle, Mees Metcalf. You are not yet a diva." A moment ago I had come close to having a childish tantrum: "You're pushing me around, Lewis. What in God's name is going on?"

In Hyde Park, beyond the streams of Park Lane traffic, children in navy and white uniforms were playing a circle game, supervised by pretty young teachers. I watched them, thinking about Robina. We had become friends in a guarded way: two tall women who stood very straight and liked classic designer clothes. There were differences: Robina's hair was dark, not auburn, and it was cut close to her head. Her eyes were gray, not bright blue. She had a sharp, penetrating English voice; mine was low and hard to hear. I had children. She had a famous collection of fifteenth-century Italian majolica.

Once, at a benefit dinner for a new wing at the Metropolitan Museum, I had asked a curator about early Italian majolica. He told me that putting together a collection took patience, passion, and money. Lots of money. A twenty-inch plate had recently sold for $90,000 at Sotheby's.

As for Hank, he now wore bespoke Savile Row suits, rubbed shoulders with titles, and managed, somehow, to keep his easy midwestern friendliness. He seemed happy, so I had stopped analyzing this strange marriage that seemed to work.

Turning away from the window, I sat down at the inlaid desk, picked up the phone, and put it down again. Was Lewis right about canceling lunch? I was no good at subtle give-and-take—and Robina had a way of winching out information. She might ask blunt questions and I was a terrible liar, using two nails when one would do the job.

After a moment, I picked up the phone again and dialed. Pretending to be sick would mean spending the day in this suffocating suite; other committee wives might decide to go to the new Tate. Before Hank married Robina there had been a ladies schedule. Harrods, Hampton Court. Robina had put an end to that: "The wrinklies can look after themselves." As Robina came on the line, I took a deep breath.

"Robina? It's Emma."

"I was just going to ring you. The Connaught at one suit you?"

"Why don't we wait until next time? You must be up to your ears with this reception."

"Perfectly manageable. God knows I do little enough for Hank." The clipped, matter-of-fact voice.

"That's not true. You lit a fire under Hank's florist—the flowers here are lovely. You fixed up the company flat. People will love a party at your house, not the usual boring hotel." Whatever her faults, Robina was superb about applying her taste and organizational skills to Hank's lowly job.

"Anything for the Galbraith empire—but never tell me you're looking forward to tonight. You know you hate these ghastly do's."

I laughed. "You have to be a lip-reader to hear Emma in a crowd," my little brother always said. It wasn't easy to communicate with eyes and smiles.

"You're right. I hate them. All the same, let me have a rain check for lunch. No need to have me on your mind today."

"Nonsense. I'm looking forward to it. One, at the Connaught," and she hung up. Robina wasn't one to chat. The phone was ringing. I picked it up.

"Mrs. Streat?" A man's voice.

"Yes?"

"Hotel security here. Your husband asked us to recheck your suite for electronic devices. When would it be convenient to come in? This will only take a few minutes."

"Later this morning, then." I was still in my wrapper with unbrushed hair and teeth.

Robina's flowers needed water; a daffodil with a broken stalk was wilting. I pulled it out, went into the bathroom with faucets shaped like gold swans. Stared at myself in the mirror with no pleasure. My hair was a tangled mop; I needed exercise.

Turning from the mirror, I pulled off the wrapper and threw it on the stool by the shower. Why was Robina always so determined to have her way? I should have stood my ground, not let her call the shots. After all, when push came to shove, I *was* the boss's wife. No excuse was needed, just a firm statement: "Sorry, Robina, but I just can't make lunch today. See you tonight."

At noon, in the black and white marble hotel foyer, English women in large hats and elegant flowered dresses sailed past Americans in designer jeans. This was high season in London, the month for Ascot and grand balls. As I went out, the doorman smiled at me appreciatively.

"Good morning, madam."

"Good morning."

A few hours in the glittering hotel spa had cured the feeling of walking in a minefield. The manicurist had clucked over my gardener's nails. I had brushed my hair into an auburn mass around my face and put on a new white suit with a short skirt. Mrs. Gates would approve: "All you needed was a little change."

In South Audley Street, the windows of Thomas Goode's gleamed with the world's most expensive china and crystal. A clerk wearing a morning coat stood by the open door. Across the street, the Spy Shop was displaying little black devices. I glanced at them, remembering the polite young man who had let himself in and checked the suite for bugs. "Security. Almost done, Mrs. Streat," he had said when I appeared, fresh from the spa.

The Connaught Hotel stood at the corner of Carlos Place, a former town house that still exuded discreet Victorian respectability. I looked at my watch—I was early—and slowed my steps. Paused to study a board with the day's menus. Since Tony, I had been to the Connaught any number of times without a twinge, but today I looked up at a window on the third floor and, like a dog on a choke collar, was jerked back twenty-two years.

Tony Battia was not my first lover, but he taught me how to make love with depth and creativity—an act of total immolation. We met on my last European tour. It opened with *Marriage of Figaro* at the old Royal Opera House in Covent Garden. I was singing Susanna. The conductor was Anthony Battia, a new name in the music world.

Physically, Tony was short, thin, with dark eyes and features drawn at random from a hat. He had the gift of complete concentration on a score—or a woman. On the first night of the performance, I had waited in the wings for my entrance, biting my lips to keep them from drying out. Figaro's voice had been shaky as he measured the marriage bed: "Cinque, dieci, venti . . ."

As Tony conducted, I could see that he was saying the libretto along with me, holding me up, linking me to Mozart.

As the bow lights went on, the polite English audience rose from the sea of red velvet seats, applauding the performance. I accepted flowers, threw kisses. "It doesn't get better than this," the aging Figaro had muttered in my ear.

Back in my dressing room, there were more flowers, messages. People were waiting at the stage door for my autograph. My pretty young dresser helped me take off the itchy wig; for some reason the director had wanted a dark-haired Susanna. Then I went through the old maze of corridors to the Green Room, where singers and their hangers-on were gathered. Tony came straight to me as if no one else existed. For the next five days, we spent every hour of our free time in bed at the Connaught. I learned that he wore silk undershirts and ordered Dom Perignon champagne after performances and before making love. He learned that I wore sports bras and craved mashed potatoes. Exhausted, floating in sensuality, I went on to do *Traviata* in Vienna.

We didn't meet in Rome as planned. Four months later my voice was ruined, my career gone. To give him credit, Tony came to Boston. He held my hand and tried to reach me. We would marry, travel, have children. Build a life on a shared passion for music. In the end, I sent him away. Unbearable, to be one of those hangers-on, to live with singers, unable to sing. He married a volatile Czech contralto and they were divorced a few years later. I wasn't surprised. It would take great self-confidence to compete with Tony's intensity on the podium and in bed. I had been faithful to Lewis, but not from lack of offers.

"My dear Emma. What on *earth* are you staring at?"

I swung around. Robina was walking towards me, hips thrust slightly forward. She was wearing a gray designer suit and a starched white shirt. Antique gold necklaces. I swallowed. "Nothing, really."

She raised her eyebrows. "Are you all right? I watched you as I came down the street. You stood there looking up as if you'd been turned into stone."

"I'm fine. Absolutely fine." Telltale color was flooding my face.

"It must have been riveting." Robina was smiling, delighted to see me flustered and floundering. I dug my nails into my palms and smiled back. It was unnerving to be hit over the head by the past when I was upset and confused. Tony must be locked away again, along with my recordings and clippings, but not until I had used him as a distraction to keep Robina from her usual probing.

As we went into the lobby, once a rich Londoner's front hall, I shrugged my shoulders.

"To be honest, I was having a memory attack," I said. "Ages ago, when I was singing, a conductor and I had a very intense week here. I hadn't thought of him for years."

"Of course. I'd forgotten you were a singer," Robina said as the maître d' led us to a table. We sat down on the velvet banquette.

"It was the old Covent Garden, *Marriage of Figaro.* Strange. If I hadn't lost my voice I might be singing the part of the countess tonight."

Robina gave me a quizzical look. "Is this an 'I'm bored with marriage' attack? Frankly, it wouldn't surprise me to see you break out of your perfect wife and mother mold. Shock us all."

"Shock *you?* Impossible." Parry and thrust.

Robina laughed and shook out the huge napkin. "You're quite right. I'm unshockable. Let's order, then I want to hear more about you and the fascinating maestro."

I nodded and picked up the elaborate menu. "Are you sure? It's a long story."

And with a few additions and subtractions it was going to last us through dessert, coffee, down the hall, and out into the street.

At six twenty I stood on the steps of the Lausches' tall Eaton Terrace house. An elderly maid wearing a black silk dress and white apron opened the door.

"Good evening, Mrs. Streat."

"Good evening." I smiled, trying to remember her name. Something like Peebles or Deebles. A Fyfe family retainer.

The roar of voices drifted down the stairs; these seminars gave committee members a chance to work on their own power agendas. Heavy lifting under bland civility.

The roar grew louder. I went up the carpeted staircase and paused at the door. My old coach had trained me to stand very straight when going onstage.

The drawing room, like Robina, was a beautifully presented work of art. Gold silk upholstery. Chippendale furniture. A large majolica plate, an Annunciation scene in stunning colors took pride of place on the nearest wall.

"There you are." Hank came hurrying forward. He kissed me on both cheeks, a compact, sandy-haired man with a wide smile. A down-to-earth presence in this elegant house, a boy from Grand Rapids who had adjusted very well to his wife's inherited money and titled family.

I put my arms around him and gave him a hug. "Sorry I'm late. The usual hassle to get a taxi."

"I should have sent Wheeler. You look like you're here for a photo shoot. What have you done to yourself?"

I laughed, thinking of Mrs. Gates. "Thanks."

"What's so funny?"

"Nothing, really."

"I wasn't kidding. Boys doing well?" Before Hank left New York to manage the London office, he used to spend weekends with us. He had always wanted children. Once, in confidence, he told me that Robina often spent the day in bed. "You'd never guess it, but she gets nerved up, really stressed out, needs looking after. I'm pretty good at that." Which explained a lot about their marriage.

"The boys are fine, as far as I know. Which isn't much these days."

"You've done a great job with them. Suite at the Pelham okay? Running water, clean sheets?"

I grinned. "You've got a nerve, sending us to that last chance motel, but thanks for the flowers. They're beautiful."

"Grew them myself in a shoe box. Let me get you a drink. You know quite a few people here."

"Don't worry about me; I'll circulate."

In the crowded room, maids were passing silver trays of smoked salmon on toast squares. Lewis was standing against the far wall, talking to a rival for Pentagon contracts. His face looked whiter than his shirt. I had walked in the park, but when I came back he and Dr. Estes had gone. There was a note by the untouched coffee:

Be sure our bags go down to the porter when you leave for the reception.

A hand touched my shoulder.

"Emma, dear." Fat little Marge Peplow was dressed in sequins with a beehive hairdo. She looked like a 1950s housewife in a Las Vegas nightclub, but I had learned, over the years, that Marge was a very kind and generous woman. Her donations to my war orphan funds were large and anonymous. I leaned down and kissed her cheek.

"Marge. I was hoping to see you. Hi, Danny."

"Hi, Emma." Danny Peplow was small and dark, with a permanent cynical half smile. The child of wartime escapees from Poland, he had made his first fortune from junkyard parts and turned it into a communications empire. According to Lewis, Danny was slippery, one jump ahead of the Justice Department. All the same, I liked the way Danny was so fiercely protective of a fat, badly dressed wife. A lot of empire-building husbands would keep Marge out of sight at home. I gave him my widest smile.

"So what's new?" I asked.

He shrugged. "Waste of time, these meetings."

Marge shook her head. "That's not what the man from the Netherlands just told me. He said your speaker from MIT talked about a new kind of bug. Tiny little eavesdroppers in every home. Every room. Kitchens, bathrooms, even closets. We'd have to go outside to say a word. My God, can you imagine, Emma?"

"I can't. What else did he say? Are there any around yet, I mean, on the market?"

Marge looked uncertain. "I'm not sure. We were interrupted, but just the idea gives me the heebie-jeebies. What if—"

Danny raised his hand. "Take it easy, Marge. Forget about that load of crap." I glanced at Danny, surprised at the sharpness in his voice. He caught my look and shrugged again. "Look. The guy's a long-haired professor, earning his fee. He had to give us our money's worth. Right?" The smile was back in place, but it was clear that Danny had let down his guard for a few seconds. Could *his* company be developing these new bugs? I must remember to ask Lewis.

"Hey, Emma, looking good, the belle of the ball." Ed Collins put his hand on my shoulder. At industry dinners it was my knee.

"Ed. How are you? Is Barbara here?"

"Yakking her head off somewhere. You and Lewis free for dinner?"

"I'll find him," I said, sliding away from that stroking hand.

Around me, heads of powerful corporations were talking about the MIT professor's lecture.

". . . . information is the world's biggest weapon. We'd have to change the way we do business. Find new ways to communicate."

". . . . get a handle on it sooner or later, but there'd be a dangerous time lag."

". . . . technology is one big game of leapfrog. You invent, I catch up."

Tough competitors under the friendly surface. Except for a Christmas card or two from the wives, business friendships were apt to wither when husbands died, retired, or were fired.

I looked around and saw that George Galbraith, the founder

of the company, was holding court by the fireplace. A giant of a man with a shock of white hair, pale blue eyes, and a trace of a Scottish accent. To be fair, he had instilled a high level of integrity in his company. And, when he left the helm, he had given Lewis a free hand. That said, Galbraith was a self-made man who had become a crashing snob. Talking with him was an exercise in discomfort.

As he moved in my direction, I braced myself, remembering the years when he had ruled the company with a heavy, old-fashioned hand. Women took dictation in shorthand and brought coffee. Skirts had to cover knees.

"Good evening, Mrs. Streat. You're looking well." The intimidating sideways glance that used to send subordinates scurrying to washrooms.

"Good evening, Mr. Galbraith."

"Your boys are well?"

"Very well, thanks."

Another sidelong glance, calculated to keep people at arm's length. He cleared his throat.

"Fine spell of weather we're having."

"Lovely."

"Let me wish you a pleasant stay."

"Thank you." The ritual was over. I was dismissed.

"Emma." Robina was wearing a deceptively simple green sheath and a necklace of huge Baroque pearls, a shade darker than her pale skin. "What on earth is wrong with Lewis? He looks ghastly. Is he ill?"

I kept smiling. "Lewis? He's fine. Just going flat out."

"Still—rather worrying. I see you've had your dance with Galbraith. He barely speaks to the other wives, but being from Boston makes you acceptable. Thank God he doesn't dare bully *me*."

"Does he ever darken the office these days?"

"Once in a while. Hank says he shuffles a few papers around, but he seems to have lost interest. Not surprising. With Lewis in charge one wonders why he goes to the office at all." A sharp little jab.

"Well, old people hate to lose control," I said quickly. "And being so rich must cut you off from the ordinary world. Does he still live alone at the Savoy?"

"When he's not off fishing or shooting with any title who'll put up with him. Last week he bought a Gainsborough to give to the nation."

"In aid of getting a peerage?"

"What else? He wants me to put in a good word with my father, which I most certainly will never do."

"Sad, really," I said, glancing at my watch. It was almost seven o'clock.

Robina caught the look. "You're not leaving?"

I coughed and touched my throat. "My voice is about to give out. I'd better collect Lewis."

"Deserter. We'll never be rid of the single men and those dreadful Peplows. Hank says he's a crook, clever as a monkey, has a network of informers all over the world. Better than any secret service."

"It wouldn't surprise me."

"What's more, there's talk that he wants to buy into the weapons business. Lewis had better watch his back."

"He will."

"As for that wife—the hair—someone should tell him to send her to one of your marvelous spas."

"Actually, Marge is a dear. Not a mean bone in her body," which couldn't be said of Lady Robina. "Lovely party. Thanks again for lunch." Robina nodded. She never kissed.

"My pleasure, as you people say. And *do* take care of your poor husband. He's looking like the grim reaper."

As Lewis and I emerged from the house, Eaton Terrace was almost deserted. A man with two King Charles spaniels walked by, whistling softly. I took a deep breath.

"That's over, thank God."

As if it had been waiting for us, a black taxi pulled up to the curb. I moved towards the door.

Lewis took my arm. "No," he said, under his breath.

"Why not? It may be ages before we find another." The taxi waited, motor running.

Lewis's hand tightened. "We don't need you," he said to the driver.

After a moment, the taxi went on down the street. I looked around.

"I forgot. You said you had a driver. Where is he?"

"This way."

At the corner, an old Rolls-Royce was parked illegally on a yellow line, engine running. The driver was young, with a square face and burly shoulders. Lewis went up to him.

"Your name?"

"Terence, sir."

"That's right. You have the bags?"

"Yes, sir." He started to get out, but Lewis had the door open.

"Get in, Em."

The car began to move.

For a moment we didn't speak. I stared at the driver's thick neck. Was this burly man a bodyguard? Protecting us from what? Years ago, CEOs were often threatened by kidnapping rings wanting huge ransoms. These days it was terrorists. I began to babble, needing to break the silence. I was going to freeze, flying back in a thin black dress; no, there would be blankets on the plane.

"Ed wanted us to go out to dinner, but I was able to get away. I talked to Marge and Danny. Robina says there's a rumor he wants to go into the weapons business and for you to watch your back. She says he has a huge information network all over the world. Is that true or just Robina making gossip?"

Lewis put his hands on his knees. "I've heard he has a network and the CIA could take lessons from him. The word is, if you want to know something and there's no other way, go to Danny. It'll cost you, but he has his methods." Lewis nodded towards the driver and gave me a warning look. "How was your lunch?"

"Fine. No problem. You and the physicist had left when I got back. You didn't touch the coffee."

"No, we didn't."

He leaned forward and spoke to the driver. "You have directions to get to the plane?"

"Yes, sir. Hotel security gave them to me."

The car was going fast along Cromwell Road, passing seedy little hotels, good hideouts for terrorists and spies. Why in God's name were we slipping out of London like criminals on the run? I reached over and touched Lewis's knee.

"By the way, the man from hotel security came. I assume he didn't find anything."

"Hotel security came to the suite? What time was that?" Under my hand, I could feel Lewis's body tense.

"I was just coming back from the the spa. It must have been around noon. He was there when I came in."

"Did you watch him?"

"Not really. He called ahead, it was just after you left, he said you had asked to have the suite rechecked, wanted to know what time—oh *no.* Are you saying he just broke in?"

"That's right."

"But he acted so official—so businesslike. I never even thought to ask for identification—"

"It wasn't your fault. You couldn't have known." He put his arm around my shoulder. I leaned against him.

"That man—I don't *like* this."

"We'll be home in a few hours."

"Yes." I sat back and closed my eyes. The copter would set down beside the apple orchard. There would be roses on the front hall table. O'Hara would dance around us, accusing us of cruel desertion. I would lean down and rub his ears.

"Enough of that noise. Don't we always come back? Don't we?"

five

Thursday, June 5

Connecticut

The birds in the old maples were exchanging the early morning news, a busy counterpoint to the soft sound of the river. At a little before seven I stood on the terrace, wearing my old blue wrapper, inhaling fresh, clean air, exhaling the poison of the past two days. After a few hours of sleep, jet lag had woken me. I slid out of bed and began to walk around the house, embracing the familiar rooms, the smell of old plaster and wood. This morning all I wanted was to wrap my arms around my home and never leave.

The light on the river grew brighter, catching the top of the swinging buoy. Upstairs the shower was running, a signal to go into the kitchen and start making coffee. As I ground beans from Jamaica, O'Hara began to whine.

"I know, horrible noise. Over in a minute," I told him, then opened a cupboard door and pulled out two Quimper pottery cups. For years, each boy had given me a piece of Quimper for Christmas, a welcome change from gloves and sweaters in the wrong sizes. My boys—Caroline would be glad to know I hadn't given them a thought for days.

The loose floorboard creaked as Lewis came down the hall. He was wearing the blue-and-white-striped shirt I had given him for his birthday, carrying his coat and tie, ready for the ritual morning walk. He looked collected, but the craggy Lincolnesque face showed strain.

"Coffee smells good," he said.

"Almost ready. Raisin bagel? Mrs. Gates must have brought them over."

"Later. I need to walk first, get some air." Lewis loved the woods and the old stone walls, links to the early settlers, reminders of the days when people walked Indian trails to reach the meetinghouse.

"The ghastly smell in that suite. Never again," I said.

"Plane air isn't much better." Leaning down, he began to write on a notepad that lay on the butcher-block counter. O'Hara waited for him, body quivering.

"Don't let O'Hara run off," I said. "Last week he found a nest of baby rabbits and came back with a dead one in his mouth."

"I'll keep an eye on him."

"It was so pitiful, that limp little body." I poured coffee and handed Lewis a cup. We were both making an effort to get back to the old routines.

"Thanks. Haven't had a decent cup of coffee since we left."

"Just one other thing," I went on. "That meeting with the selectmen tonight."

Lewis raised his head. "What meeting?"

"You know, with the selectmen, about giving the point to the Nature Conservancy. You asked me to set it up. It's on your calendar. Seven o'clock."

"Can't do it. You'll have to cancel everything out here."

I put down the coffeepot. "Cancel *everything*. Why?"

"I'll be in town. I've packed a bag."

"For how long?"

"Depends. It'll save time not to commute."

O'Hara was whining, scratching at the screen door. I let him out and turned.

"Oh? Depends on *what?*"

Lewis bent his head and began to write again as if he hadn't heard.

"Lewis." All the uncertainties of the past three days were boiling up like hot steam erupting from a valve. "We barely spoke on the plane or in London. Now you stand there and tell me you've packed a bag and you don't know when you'll be home."

"There's a good reason."

"That's no answer." I took a step towards him. "Listen to me, for once. I've tried to be patient, I've tried very hard, but every time I open my mouth I get slapped down."

"For a valid reason."

"That's not fair and you know it. What's going on? What's been going on for months? Either you're in the office or you're dead tired from running on your high-tech treadmill. Even when we sleep together you're beginning to act like it's something you have to do once in a while. Like cleaning the VCR." I stopped to catch my breath. He put down the pen.

"I'm no good in bed. Is that what you're saying?"

"No, I'm not saying that. I'm simply asking you what's wrong. You look terrible. A man pretending to be security comes in and snoops around our suite. We rush back like gangsters being chased out of town. The police want to ask you questions about a murder at JFK—"

"Hold it, Em."

"No, I will *not* hold it. We've always helped each other. We *talked.* Now you're treating me like a child of five. A *slow* child. You're shutting me out as if I can't be trusted. Why?"

He looked down at the floor, not meeting my eyes. "You're right. It's not fair, but this has nothing to do with trust. It's for your own safety. Until I work this . . . problem out, the less you know the better." He looked at his watch. "Where's O'Hara?"

"He's outside." I pushed back my hair. "All right, I get the message. No more questions, but just don't expect me to sit around chewing my nails. I'll unpack and go up to Manchester today. Ned and Cassia are always after me to come and stay with them."

"Not a bad idea, to visit your brother—"

"For my *safety,* I suppose. Give me a break. Lorna can call Mrs. Gates and let her know your plans, but get this straight. I've had it with all this mystery crap. I'm not coming back until it's over," I said, and headed for the stairs.

Fifteen minutes later, after I hurled some clothes into the laundry hamper, guilt began to neutralize anger. The rare fight had started as a brush fire and now was roaring down the canyon. Lewis was deep in the worst crisis of his career and I was whining, the premier sin in our family: "Whatever you do, guys, no *whining.*"

My raggedy work jeans were back in the closet. I put them on, went to the bed, and pulled up the antique wedding ring quilt, a silent rebuke to knee-jerk temper. Went to the window and straightened the red and yellow glazed chintz curtains. When Lewis came back for his briefcase, no need to apologize, just tell him I'd changed my mind and wouldn't go running off to my brother.

The copter was almost over the house. As I went downstairs there was a final roar and then silence as Tim switched off the rotors.

The kitchen was sunny and peaceful. I gulped down half a cup of coffee and sat down at my desk. Friday was my shoreline soup kitchen day. The fifteenth of June was a goddaughter's birthday. I must get Sophie a present. Clothes? CDs? Maybe just a check. Twelve-year-olds were going on twenty these days. Next week—a line of blank days. No pool parties with music blaring. No kayak races on the river with hot, sweaty boys coming back needing to be watered and fed.

"Mrs. Streat?" Tim, a laconic ex-Marine, was standing by the door. "It's almost eight thirty. Wondered if there'd been a change of plans."

"Don't think so." I glanced at the counter. Lewis's briefcase lay there beside the note he'd been writing. Last night on the plane, he had dictated for hours, but when he was in a hurry he still reverted to notes.

Find a pay phone. Call Estes UK time. Ask him to drop new project. Too dangerous at this time. Insist he have security around the clock.

Dr. Estes, the eccentric physicist who wrote down ideas in a pocket-size notebook. Why in the world would Lewis want to leave the office and call him from a pay phone?

"O'Hara must have run away," I said to Tim. "The usual, punishing us for leaving. I'll send Lewis back, then find him."

"Going to be another great day. Not a cloud in the sky."

"Hot, too." My scuffed sheepskin slippers weren't meant for walking outside, but the ground was dry.

"O'Hara, come," I called as I hurried along the drive; in early spring the holes that terriers dug with such fervor could collapse into deadly mud traps, but there was no danger of that now. A white birch at the bend had lost a branch in the January storm. I must call the tree man. Remember to cancel tonight's meeting with the town selectmen. Tell Lewis there would be strawberry shortcake when he could make it home for dinner. Strawberries from our garden, a good crop this year. Mrs. Gates would make jam for the winter, Jake's favorite.

"Lewis. O'Hara," I called again, needing a whistle; my damaged voice had no carrying power.

At the end of the drive, the dirt road beyond the white gateposts showed a thin cloud of dust. A car had gone by, unusual at this time of year; there were no houses between our place and the point overlooking the river, the point we were giving to the Nature Conservancy. The road was straight and narrow, seldom used except in summer when kids from the village went to sit on the high rocks and drink beer.

I started through the gates, listening for footsteps. If they'd gone back through the woods, I'd have to run at top speed to catch Lewis before he left: "Sorry. I didn't mean to lash out. It's just that I'm so *confused.*"

"Lewis. O'Hara." No answer. I turned away. Stopped in midstep. Stumbled and stared. A man was lying on the grass a few feet away, facedown, his arms above his head like a child asleep in a crib. For a few seconds, I didn't move. A jogger . . . a heart attack . . . I should have kept practicing my CPR . . . no, not a jogger. The man was wearing Lewis's blue and white shirt.

"Lewis. Oh God. Lewis." I leaned down. There was blood under his head. Clear fluid was trickling out of his ear. I straightened, pressing my mouth with both hands. I mustn't faint or be sick or waste time taking his pulse. I must get back to the house, call the Rescue Squad, then Tim. Pilots knew what to do in emergencies.

I ran, racing the stream of blood to the house, my heart trying to pound its way through my chest. I punched out the 911 number. This was a small town, everyone knew where the Streats lived, but calls went first to a central dispatcher.

"Nine one one." A man's voice. "What is the nature of your emergency?"

"I'm Mrs. Lewis Streat. There's been an accident in Hardwick. A man, my husband, is lying by the road. He's bleeding. A car must have hit him."

"Is he breathing?"

"I—I'm not sure."

"Is he conscious?"

"No."

"Where is the bleeding?"

"From his head."

"What's your location?"

"Point Road."

"Can you give me more information?"

"I just told you. Point Road. It's a mile and a half from Route 157. The gates are white. Hurry. Please hurry."

"Ambulance and police personnel are being dispatched to the scene, Mrs. Streat. Do you want me to stay on the line?"

"No. No. I'm going back."

Tim was still at the kitchen door, whistling softly.

"Tim."

He swung around. "What is it?"

"Lewis. A car must have hit him down by the gates. I just called nine one one."

"Is it bad? Is he conscious?"

"He's bleeding."

"I'll get the first-aid kit."

"Hurry. I'm going back."

I ran, my ankles wobbling and twisting in the sheepskin slippers. A green Subaru Outback was parked on the dusty roadside grass by the gates. A woman was leaning over Lewis. She looked up, and I recognized the tall, gray-haired woman who worked in the Town Clerk's office. She was wearing a mask and gloves. Her blue windbreaker had *Hardwick* embroidered on the back in gold.

"Mrs. Streat? I'm Anna Jones, the first responder. The ambulance is on the way."

"I left him. I ran back and called nine one one." I put my hand over my mouth again and went closer. Lewis hadn't moved. His face was resting in a puddle of blood. One leg was flung out at a disjointed angle. Anna Jones stood up. I looked at her.

"Can't you—there must be something you can do."

At the corner, a siren wailed. A red and white ambulance came barreling down the straight stretch of road. Behind the ambulance, a fire engine. Behind the engine, more men were arriving, jumping out of pickup trucks. Volunteers, coming from their jobs in town. I had often seen them on other roads, helping other people. Anna Jones took my arm.

"We'd better move away, give them room."

"What's that coming out of his ear? Is he going to be all right?"

"They'll do their best for him. Did you see the accident?"

"No. No. I came down the drive to find him. He went for a walk with the dog," I said, staring at the red and white ambulance, the fire engine, the trucks. No need for all this equipment.

Half an hour ago, a man had left the house dressed for the office in a blue and white shirt, the trousers to his dark gray suit. In a moment he would open his eyes and ask what had happened.

Two men were placing Lewis on a stretcher. The doors of the ambulance opened. I looked at Anna. "Where are they taking him?"

"To the Newbury Clinic." I nodded. Over the years, there had been a lot of trips to the emergency clinic with the boys and their friends. Gashed heads. Broken bones.

"I'm going with him. Tell the men I'm going with him."

Anna Jones tightened her grip on my arm. "I'll take you. We'll follow them in my car." Like a good emergency room nurse, this woman knew how to deal firmly with frightened people.

A police car was arriving, lights flashing. A trooper got out and spoke into his personal radio.

"Six four eight Troop D. Signal eleven. Evading in Hardwick on Point Road, one and one-half miles from Route 157."

I looked at Anna again. "What's he saying?"

"He's contacting Troop D barracks. He has to speak in code because people listen in. Come to the scene and clog the roads."

"Mrs. Streat?" The young trooper was wearing heavy black shoes.

"Yes."

"I need to ask a few questions."

"Not now. I have to go to the clinic." Those black shoes must be very hot.

"This won't take long. What happened here?"

"My husband went for a walk. He must have been hit by a car. He was late; the helicopter was waiting. I came to find him and he was lying over there."

"What time was that?"

"Oh God, I'm not sure, maybe half an hour ago. The helicopter comes around eight."

"You didn't see a car?"

"I saw dust. As if a car had just gone by. I noticed because there's never any traffic on this road."

"Did you get a license number? We tell people to scratch the number on the ground if they can't write it down."

I clenched my fists. "Don't you understand English? I told you, I didn't *see* the car. What more do I—no, sorry. I'm sorry." In times of crisis, women in my family were considerate of other people's feelings. My sister, Dolly, and I had gone to see the devastated man whose skidding truck killed my father. When Uncle Ted died in a plane crash in Maine, my aunt Laura had been so calm. Laura is wonderful. Aunt Laura would never think of throwing herself on the ground and beating it with her fists. She would never want to scream at the top of her lungs: "Lewis, I'm staying. I love you. I didn't *mean* it."

The Newbury Clinic waiting room was filled with blond wood chairs; the blue upholstery was speckled with gray dots. A pattern designed to hide stains.

As Anna Jones and I came through the automatic sliding doors, a nurse in a short-sleeved flowered shirt with a stethoscope around her neck met us.

"We can use this office," she said, opening a door. "Sit down, Mrs. Streat."

"Where's my husband?" In my mind I could see Lewis and O'Hara coming back from their walk. I was handing Lewis his briefcase, kissing him: "Good luck. See you when I see you."

"Dr. Ingersoll will be in to talk with you."

"When?"

"As soon as possible," she said briskly, and left. As always, the medical world managed to have the last word. I turned to Anna.

"Is he dead? Was he dead when you got there? You should have *told* me."

Anna's expression didn't change. "We do what we can. You've had a terrible shock, Mrs. Streat. You have two boys, isn't that right? Are they here?"

"Not here. They've gone off to summer jobs."

"Is there a friend you can call?"

"Friend—I can't seem to think—there's Mrs. Gates. She lives on our place. She should be there now."

"I know Doris. We went to grade school together. I'll call her."

The office was a small replica of the waiting room. I gripped the arms of the chair, trying to keep my hands still. Lewis wasn't dead. The medics had managed to get his heart going. Right now, the doctor was giving him injections. A transfusion. Lifestar would fly him to Hartford. No one had actually *told* me that he was dead. In a moment Anna was back.

"Doris is on her way. I'll stay with you until she comes."

"Thank you."

"Mrs. Streat?" A young man wearing a white coat and gold-rimmed glasses came in, drew up a chair, and sat down. If he smiled at me that meant there was hope. He didn't smile.

"I'm Dr. Ingersoll. I'm very sorry to give you bad news. I'm afraid there was nothing we could do for your husband."

I let go of the chair. "No. You've made a mistake. There must be *something* you can do. He went out with the dog, he always does. He always walks a mile down the road and back."

"I'm sorry. He never knew what happened, from the look of it."

"In broad daylight. No one uses that road. There was something coming out of his ears."

"The spinal cord was severed when he was hit. It was quick. He wouldn't have known what happened."

"It doesn't make sense. Why didn't the driver see him? The

road is perfectly straight right there. Anyone coming down that road should have seen him."

"Mrs. Streat, I'm afraid decisions need to be made. Do you have family?"

"I'm the only one here, I mean, the only one in Hardwick." Strange, to feel so numb and be able to speak.

"First, you need to understand that a hit-and-run accident is classified as a crime. There are standard procedures to follow. The—er—body must be taken to the Chief Medical Examiner's Office in Farmington. After a postmortem the body may be released to the family."

"*Farmington?* How do I get him back from Farmington?"

Anna leaned forward. "A funeral home will see to that, Mrs. Streat," she said quickly. "All you have to do is let them know."

"I don't know any funeral homes."

"There's McDivitts in New Sutton. They're good people. They've been in business a long time."

"McDivitts. We went to McDivitts for Doris's husband. The night before the funeral."

"Tea, Mrs. Streat." The nurse again, the stethoscope hanging around her neck like a third arm. She handed me a Styrofoam cup filled with black liquid. "Doctor, there's an ambulance coming in."

"Right." He got up. "You should have a sedative, Mrs. Streat. Something to take the edge off. I'll leave a prescription at the desk."

"Thank you."

As he left, the nurse put her hand on my shoulder. "Sorry for your loss, Mrs. Streat."

"Thank you."

"Before you go, the senior detective from Troop D is here. Sergeant Johnson. He wants to talk to you."

"A *detective*? Here?" I put the cup down on the nearest table. "Tell him to go away. I can't talk to him now."

Anna and the nurse exchanged looks. "I know Al Johnson," Anna said. "He's come for a reason."

"What reason?"

"He wants to start looking for the car that hit your husband, not waste valuable time. His own father was killed by a hit-and-run driver. He'll try not to upset you."

The man coming through the door was slight, with a serious, thin face. Brown hair flecked with gray.

"Morning, Anna," he said. "Glad you're here. You're in good hands, Mrs. Streat. I'm sorry for your loss." A deep voice, surprisingly deep for his size. He moved the doctor's chair back a few inches, giving me more space, and sat down.

"You want to get home. This won't take long. First, I need to know if you saw a car."

"I've already told the trooper. No, I didn't see a car. Just dust on the road."

"Heard a car?"

"No."

"Can you tell me more about what you saw?"

"Just my husband lying there. Bleeding. I ran back to the house and called nine one one. Then I ran back to him. He always takes a walk in the morning with our dog. When he's home, that is."

"The pilot told the trooper he didn't see any cars as the copter came down, but the trees blocked his view of the road."

I shook my head. "It doesn't make *sense*. No one uses that road except in summer to get a view of the river from the rocks. That driver should have seen Lewis, I mean, it was broad daylight. I mean, even if he was going fast, even if Lewis didn't have time to jump, the driver could have swerved."

"Hard to say. The helicopter was making a lot of noise. The driver may have been a kid. Racing. Drunk or high on drugs. Too scared to stop." He paused. "Maybe your husband was distracted by the dog. Didn't hear the car until it was too late." I swallowed. Or—maybe a husband distracted by a fight with his wife.

"We'll send out an alert to all police departments. Check body shops in the area for unexplained damage. You'd be surprised how much we can find. Most hit-and-run accidents are not premeditated." Sergeant Johnson got to his feet and picked up his navy nylon jacket. "A bad shock for you. Very bad. I'll go along to your place, no need to disturb you again today."

"Thank you." Everyone was being kind. The ambulance people, the firemen, the doctor. Anna Jones had left her job at the Town Hall to help me.

"Mrs. Streat. Oh my. What a thing to happen. What a thing." Mrs. Gates was standing in the doorway, plump arms outstretched, eyes round.

"O'Hara. Did he come back?"

"He was sitting on the front steps, shaking like he knew something was wrong. I gave him a few treats."

"She's been very brave, Doris," Anna Jones said. "She needs to go home and lie down."

I got to my feet. My head seemed disconnected from a body that wasn't mine. I looked at Anna Jones, trying to memorize her face.

"I don't know how to thank you. Everyone. I never realized about the town—all the volunteers—how much you do."

"Never enough. You take care of yourself."

It was over. As we started through the main sliding door, a nurse handed Mrs. Gates a small plastic bag. "His things," she said.

I looked away. His things. All that was left of Lewis. He wasn't going to come out of the clinic and say, "What the hell's going on?" It was wrong, all wrong, to leave him in the hands of strangers. Medical butchers who would lay him out on a table and cut him up like a side of beef.

Outside the sun was growing hot. The flag drooped on its pole. A boy on crutches was coming towards us on the cement path. His mother was carrying a backpack covered with dangling key chains. Steve used to collect key chains. I moved to let them by, then stood still, breathing hard, holding my stomach.

"Oh my." Mrs. Gates put her arm around my shoulders. "Oh dear. Shall we go back? I put the car way over there under the trees. Can you make it or shall I get the nurse?"

"No, not the nurse. I want to go home." On the morning of 9/11 I had been in my kitchen drinking coffee, composing a fund-raising letter for the soup kitchen, when a broadcaster announced that the World Trade Tower had been hit, possibly by a plane off-course. Then the second plane. I could remember staying in front of the television as the horrors unfolded. My family was safe, but less than a hundred miles away other women were sitting in their kitchens saying, "He can't be dead. He was here an hour ago, having a second cup of coffee."

Mrs. Gates was driving her old Toyota sedan. She opened the doors and put the plastic bag on the backseat. "You get in front. Oh dear, oh dear."

There was a empty Dunkin' Donuts coffee cup on the floor. I stared at the stained cardboard. I must reach the boys. Then Lewis's sister. No, after the boys, Bill Talbot, Lewis's second-in-command. There would be chaos at the office. People would come hurrying to help. There was a protocol for death. Food brought in, flowers arranged. A friend delegated to answer the phone. The kitchen was a mess, but luckily I had made the bed. *In the midst of life we are in death.*

"I'll take the back roads," Mrs. Gates was saying. "You never know, the traffic on the highway."

"No. You never know." Lewis wasn't going to walk away from the copter tonight and stop to check the thermometer. No tug-of-war with O'Hara before dinner. No husband. No father. The waste—the terrible waste—and Lewis didn't have a favorite hymn.

seven

The First Congregational Church of Hardwick was a simple white building with a square bell tower; the town's early settlers had rejected steeples as popish and pretentious.

At eleven o'clock on this hot Tuesday morning, my boys and I walked from a side door and sat down in the front high-sided pew, backs rigid, determined not to show our feelings in public. I stared at the altar with a sense of being in the wrong place. When I came here for funerals, usually for older people, I always sat in the back.

Because Lewis never went to church, we had persuaded the minister to keep the service short, straight from the prayer book. No poems by weeping children, no eulogies about a life cut off in its prime. No singing about saints or protecting sailors from the restless wave. One general-purpose hymn. "For the Beauty of the Earth."

The bearded young minister began to read the Twenty-third Psalm.

"'I will lift up mine eyes unto the hills...'" My lips moved, but my mind drifted. Today I missed my mother with the unreasonable intensity of a three-year-old. Ma, I need you. Why aren't you here when I need you?

"'From whence cometh my help...'" Wonderful, heart-warming help had come from friends and family who had taken over the avalanche of details. "Don't worry about me, I'm fine," I told them as I carried a frying pan upstairs.

My godmother, Caroline, arrived from Newport. Tanning on the world's famous beaches had dried her skin into riverbeds of wrinkles; the bleached mane of blond hair was too long for her face. In the 1940s, Caroline had been my mother's roommate at Wellesley. An odd pair, the flamboyant heiress from Chicago and shy Elizabeth Sage from Boston. Ever since my parents died a few years ago, Pa from a jackknifing truck on I-95, Ma from a misdiagnosed brain tumor, Caroline had been the safety net that never broke—but this time Caroline's astringent approach to loss did not comfort. She and Lewis had never liked each other.

My older sister, Dolly, rushed east from Lake Forest, a woman who needed to be needed. Dolly had made decisions about caterers, florists. Found a printer to do the program for the service. Picked out a dress for me that wasn't black or bright. This morning I had upset her by playing tennis with the boys: "It looks so insensitive." Our kind brother, Ned, had removed Dolly and taken her to the village to pick up ice that the caterers didn't need.

"'May the Lord bless you and keep you...'" The congregation murmured, "Amen." The service was over. Flanked by Jake and Steve, aware of dozens of eyes on me, I walked down the aisle, head high. There was no coffin to be carried out, no trip to the cemetery. Lewis had been cremated. His ashes were buried under an old weeping willow tree, a tall, graceful shape on the path that led down to the shore. Next week I would have to order a stone; my Ordway cousins had buried their mother's ashes in a large pine grove and lost the marker.

By noon the terrace was awash with people drinking champagne and bloody Marys, trying to strike the right note between mourning and socializing. On the grief scale, Lewis's death was midway between aching sorrow for the loss of a child and the celebration of a long, useful life. There was one underlying theme: The waste. The terrible, senseless waste of a valuable man.

Business associates had changed their tight schedules to be here and I was grateful. My large extended family arrived en masse from Boston; our common ancestor had sailed from England in 1680 with the deed to a land grant near Ipswich. Lewis's nice, shy sister flew from Pittsburgh. She taught English in a high school; their grandfather had emigrated from county Cork in 1902 to work in the steel mills.

I moved about with a sense of taking part in a choreographed, well-rehearsed performance. I knew my lines.

"Thank you for coming. So good of you to come."

Marge Peplow, wearing purple chiffon that showed her fat knees, was crying when she kissed me. "London . . . just last week . . . I can't believe it."

"Marge, dear. Thank you for coming."

There was no cynical smile on Danny Peplow's face today. "Lewis thought I was slippery, I thought he was holier-than-thou, but I'll miss him. So will Galbraith Tech. That company will go downhill like a rocket without him."

"Thanks for coming."

"Anything I can do, let me know. You've always been good to

Marge, something I don't forget. Not like some others I could name."

"I'll remember." Did Lewis's death mean a quick Galbraith Tech takeover, a slice of the weapons pie for Danny? It didn't matter. I would never see these people again.

George Galbraith flew over in the Gulfstream with Hank and Robina Lausch. Galbraith looked old and shaken. His lips had a blue tinge.

"A dreadful loss. Your husband and I were to meet before he left London. I planned to tell him how much I valued his excellent work."

"Thank you for coming. He appreciated your faith in him." No point in telling Galbraith that Lewis had been in orbit over a security problem. I had no facts. No evidence.

"A sad time. I plan to endow a chair in his name. The Lewis Streat Chair of Mathematics at Imperial College in London. One of our great centers of learning in the sciences."

"Thank you. Very much." Lewis would have appreciated a gift to MIT in Massachusetts, but that wouldn't have helped with a peerage.

Hank had tears in his eyes when he put his arms around me. "He was a pillar. Indestructible. Anything we can do . . . come over later . . . stay with us in the country."

"I will. Thanks for making things easier today." Hank had come after breakfast and showed Robina the house. Talked to the boys—he had always joked and horsed around with them in a way that Lewis never could. To be with Uncle Hank had helped to give them a sense of continuity.

Today Robina was looking very English in a black and white silk dress and large black hat. She kissed me on both cheeks.

"Frightful. One could understand an accident like that on the streets of New York, not this little road." Robina, in her blunt way, was only voicing what others were thinking. Sergeant Johnson had called yesterday: "Nothing more to tell you, but we're casting a wide net."

Lorna was there, tall and elegant, looking like a model on a runway. "I still can't believe it," she said in a low voice. "Bill Talbot drove me out from the office. He's half-paralyzed at the idea of taking over."

"I told him I'd help any way I can."

"He'll need all the help he can get. Hyenas like Danny Peplow will start gathering. We'll talk soon." I hesitated. Eight days ago Lewis left for the office in his usual collected way. He came home a changed man. Angry. Worried. There *had* to be a reason.

"Lorna, I need to ask you a question." For days this nagging undercurrent of unfinished business had been on hold. The overdone phrase "there's something wrong with this picture" kept circling around in my brain.

"A question?"

"Did something happen—oh damn, here comes one of my cousins. We can't talk now."

"Whenever. Call me. Your husband was a big person. There aren't many these days."

"You did so much for him. Thanks for coming."

Caroline was talking to George Galbraith, a fierce rival in the art world. They had detested each other for years. Her gravelly voice cut through the buzz of conversation. Puncturing holes in pretensions was Caroline's favorite sport. The gold bracelets jangled on her skinny arm.

"Nonsense. I wouldn't *dream* of parting with that Matisse, George. Your problem. You should have told your agent to bid higher at the auction." I turned away. Another two hours and I could escape to my room with O'Hara.

A long buffet table was set up at one end of the terrace. People were helping themselves, finding seats. Dolly was herding Metcalf relatives towards the small tables with striped umbrellas, pausing to speak to the caterer. Now she came hurrying towards me.

"I hope you don't mind, but I told that man the mayonnaise sauce for the salmon has been out far too long. He'd better take it away, I said, or we'll all end up in the hospital with food poisoning."

eight

New widows, like new mothers, are forced to reinvent their lives. Adjust to new schedules, learn a new vocabulary: "Spouse deceased." "Single." "Widow"—a word that resonated of veils and black crepe.

After a week at home, the boys went back to their jobs. It took all my strength to let them go. Jake the overachiever and worrier, Steve the laid-back extrovert. "They're men . . . let them go." Blunt words from Caroline on the day the trouble started. It had hurt, but she was right. For years I had been the on-site caregiver, a hands-on mother. Now, in their new, larger world, they could have used Lewis's help.

A new avalanche of details came hurtling down. Letters came in a flood: "A fine man . . . a great loss . . . thinking of you . . . all our sympathy." As always, the dead were without fault. No one ever mentioned the fact that Lewis had been ruthless with fuzzy thinking and self-promotion.

There were lawyers to see. Papers to sign. Bills to pay. I

missed Lewis in bed. I missed his solid judgment. His companionship at the beginning and end of the day. I found myself telling O'Hara how two women in the A & P had yelled at each other, dumped their groceries on the floor, and marched out. Without Lewis, the strong structure of my life was crumbling.

Worst of all, at two o'clock every morning the nightmare would pounce. I was kneeling beside Lewis. Fluid was pouring out of his ear. He was trying to tell me something and I was screaming the same words over and over: "Lewis, what *is* it? I can't *hear* you. You should have *told* me what was wrong." I would turn on the light, take another knockout sleeping pill, and wake up feeling drugged and guilty. If money was short and I had children to support, I would have to be back at work. Instead, I was spending the days in bed, playing my old voice tapes: Elisabeth in *Don Carlo*. Violetta in *Traviata* at the old La Fenice in Venice—not a triumph. My voice hadn't darkened enough in the last act. The director had been a terror: "*Basta*, Mees Metcalf. Do not wave your hands unless they have something to say."

Mrs. Gates came twice a day to bring food I didn't eat, run the washing machine, and water the plants. Mrs. Gates was a widow, a member of that dismal club, but her husband had died slowly from progressive kidney failure.

This morning I woke to the sound of the telephone ringing. The answering machine chanted: "Please leave your number after the beep."

"Emma. I know you're there." My sister Dolly's accusing voice.

I groaned, rolled over, and picked up the phone. "Dolly. Hi."

"Why don't you answer your messages? I called Mrs. Gates yesterday, but she's hiding something from me. I can tell."

"There's nothing to hide." Dolly had been good at algebra,

she never lost her temper, but she had always been a whiner: "Mother, it's not fair, you sent me to bed at *eight* when I was Emma's age."

"I don't believe you." Dolly sniffed. "I remember what happened after you lost your voice. You shut yourself up in your room for months and listened to your tapes. Mother almost went crazy. If you hadn't met Lewis, you'd have had a complete nervous breakdown and been sent to McLean."

I picked up a corner of the sheet and wound it around my hand. "That was a long time ago. Look. We're having this heat wave, a record for the East. It's boiling hot and I'm working flat out going through Lewis's things."

"Your voice sounds funny. Slurred."

"You woke me up."

"At this hour?"

"It's only eight thirty, for God's sake. How's Ted?"

"The same. Grumpy. We were going to Alaska next week, one of those alumni cruises, but maybe we'd better come to Hardwick instead."

I sat up and pushed back my tangled hair. "Give up your cruise? Ted would have a fit. I'm fine; I swear it."

"You're not. I can tell. You're blocking out again like last time. Stuck in denial. Don't forget, grieving is a developmental process. What you need is a therapist to help you through the different stages."

"Crap. Pyschobabble crap. No one grieves by the book, chapter by chapter."

"Please don't swear at me. If you're having a nervous breakdown, the boys should be told. They would want to know—"

"Dolly, if you call the boys I'll never speak to you again. I mean it. Never again."

"See? You *do* need help. You need to get closure before you have to cope with lawyers and a court case."

"What court case?"

"That hit-and-run driver. One of these days the police will find him. Put him on trial. You'll have to stand up in court and testify. Make sure he goes to prison."

"What the hell are you talking about?"

"You heard me. It shouldn't have taken your police this long, but I suppose they've got other things to do. Maybe you should hire a private detective agency."

O'Hara was pawing his way up from under the crumpled sheet. I put my legs over the side of the bed and counted to ten. For once, Dolly was right. Why *hadn't* the police found evidence? But losing control would prove Dolly's point about the therapist.

"I'm fine. I'm in touch with the police and they're working hard. Listen, I've got to run. There's a man at the door; he's . . . here about the leak in the pool; I've been after him for days."

"Did I upset you? I'm sorry. It's just that we all love you."

"Love you too. Talk to you later," I said, and hung up. Gently. After a moment, I stood up and went to the mirror. The weight I'd lost showed in my face. My eyes looked drugged, The wrinkled T-shirt I'd worn for two days and two nights had a cranberry juice stain down the front. My mother had believed, deeply, in the everlasting arms that never let one down. My faith was still a work in progress. Somehow it seemed unfair to call on God and expect him to help. Like skipping practice and asking the coach to put you in the game.

O'Hara was scratching at the door. He looked at me and gave a sharp bark: "Snap out of it, lady. I'm tired of living under a sheet." Even O'Hara was losing patience.

"All *right,* I'm coming," I said, and opened the door.

The thermometer on the terrace had reached the seventy-degree mark. After letting O'Hara out, I made iced coffee and spread half a bagel with cream cheese. Last night's dinner had been cereal and a banana. I looked around, seeing the room through Dolly's eyes: Unwashed dishes in the sink. Piles of unopened mail on the table. Mrs. Gates had been away yesterday.

In a moment, O'Hara was whining at the door. Ever since Lewis's death, he stayed close to the house, as if a primal instinct was telling him to avoid the road. He drank noisily, slopping water out of his bowl. Then he picked up his toy doll, inviting me to join his favorite game.

"Later."

The untouched bagel lay on a Quimper plate. I picked it up. The plate slipped out of my shaking hand.

"Oh *Christ.*" Too late. The bright blue and yellow pottery hit the red tiled floor and broke into a dozen pieces.

Lewis's small study was one of four original rooms built around a central fireplace. No one had been in there for weeks; the air was humid and musty, but Lewis's presence was still strong. His favorite Peter Corbin watercolor, a man fishing in a trout stream, hung over the mantel. There were fishing rods in a corner. Boxes of papers and tapes that Lorna had sent from the office were stacked out of sight behind a wing chair.

Our wedding picture stood on the desk. It was taken on a hot July day at my grandmother's summer place in New Hampshire. I had worn a pleated white cotton dress from Mexico, not heirloom satin with a train. Lewis had bought himself a new blazer and done his best to make small talk at the reception.

We had escaped in a Model T Ford and spent the night in a Portsmouth motel.

I picked up the photo and studied Lewis's face. The intelligence. The caring behind the shyness. There had been so many good times before he became a stressed-out CEO. Fishing and camping with the boys. In the bad times—the loss of a newborn daughter, my parents' deaths—Lewis was always *there*. The rock that never crumbled.

"If you hadn't met Lewis you'd have had a complete nervous breakdown," Dolly had said. True back then, but motherhood has a way of stiffening the spine. When little Jake came downstairs in the morning with a suspicious stomachache, I had a stock answer: "Get ready for school. Half the work in the world is done by people who don't feel well." If I had been killed in an unlikely accident, Lewis wouldn't be living in a daze of tapes and pills. He would ask hard questions. Demand action. Get results.

I put the picture down and took a deep breath. It was time to exorcise self-pity. Trace the path of Lewis's out-of-character angst. Collect more facts about his death. Questions *must* be asked—and I was the only person who could ask them.

Back in the kitchen, I cleared the round table of bills and letters. Sat down and dialed a familiar number. A stream of assistants had come and gone in the New York office; Lewis had no patience for mistakes, women's lib pretensions, trophy wife hopes. For five years, Lorna and I had worked in tandem, smoothing the two sides of Lewis's life. I trusted her loyalty and her brains.

"Lorna, it's Emma. I need your help." No need to beat around the bush with Lorna.

"Of course. If I can."

"The night before we left for London, Lewis came home in a state. I mean, a *state*. It was worse in London. Every time I tried to find out what was wrong, he'd snap my head off."

"Not his style. When things went wrong he'd suck it in."

"He hated to show his feelings. Look. Did anything unusual happen at the office the day before we left? A reason for him to go off the wall?"

"Let me think."

I waited, seeing Lewis's big corner office on the fortieth floor in Rockefeller Center. The view of the Hudson River. The Hudson River Valley School paintings hanging on the walls. I could sense Lorna's laser brain sorting, discarding. At last, her voice again: "Nelson Bin."

"Who?"

"Nelson Bin. A young Chinese engineer. He came to the office that afternoon, said he was here with a trade mission from Hong Kong. No appointment, but he was so polite, so anxious to see your husband—anyhow, I gave him a few minutes."

"Bin. Wasn't he killed on the people mover at JFK? You called Lewis in London and told him. He was upset about *that,* I can tell you. What else do you know about this Bin?"

"Not much. He was well dressed, quite tall for a Chinese. In his thirties, maybe. I made sure he went through the new security door. He had a big manila envelope in his hand. It was checked downstairs."

"What did he want?"

"All I know is, when he left your husband had that clamped-down look on his face."

"Angry?"

"Very. I asked him what was wrong. He said Bin wanted a visa and a job in this country."

"That doesn't sound so bad."

"I have to admit I was surprised. I thought your husband was overreacting. It didn't seem like a big deal to me."

"Have the police any idea who killed Bin?"

"There's been nothing in the papers, but I can always call my contact at the DA's office and do a little probing. My contact told me it's not easy to run investigations on the Chinese, but Bin seemed to be a bona fide engineer on a trade mission. His colleagues were grilled, kept for two days, then they took Bin home in a box. He had your husband's name in his wallet, that's why the police came here. What are you getting at?"

"Just trying to sort it all out. A Chinese engineer named Bin comes to see Lewis at the office on a Monday. Tells him something that upsets him. Bin is murdered the next day. No arrests."

"Right."

"Lewis comes home that night muttering about a security problem in London. Serious. We go to London. You call and tell him about Bin. Lewis starts to sweat. He sees a physicist in the hotel, not the office. He gets a bodyguard type to take us to the plane."

"Not Wheeler?"

"No. The morning Lewis died, he said he was going to stay in town, he didn't know for how long. Then he went on his walk and was run down by a hit-and-run driver. No suspects. Doesn't this ring bells?"

"Hold on. Are you trying to connect these deaths?" Lorna never threw punches.

"All I know is, it's never made sense to me, Lewis's accident. The *way* it happened. Lewis wasn't deaf or blind."

"There's probably an explanation. Don't your police have any evidence?"

"Nothing they've told me about, but I'm beginning to

think they need to do more than find a dented car." I pushed back my hair. "By the way, are you sure it's safe for us to talk like this? Lewis had bugging on the brain. I heard him ask you to have the office rechecked."

"The checks were done. Nothing turned up."

"Which doesn't mean the office is safe. There are fancy new devices around, not on the market."

"How would you know that?"

"An MIT professor gave a lecture to the technology committee in London. It had all the CEOs on their ears."

"Interesting. Frankly, my guess is that a lot of these big security firms rely too much on routine checks. Just go through the motions."

"Like airports."

"Well, here's a thought. I have a friend in electronics who's independent. Innovative. I could talk to him. See if he has any ideas. Would that relieve your mind?"

"It would tell us if Lewis had a reason to be worried. Back to Bin. You know, his asking for a job and visa shouldn't have upset Lewis. You said so yourself." I hesitated, feeling my way. "Lorna, what if it was something *far* worse? I mean, really bad? You know the high-tech business inside out. What could Bin have told Lewis that would shake him up?"

"Um. That's hard. I guess worst case for any CEO these days is to hear that a spy has infiltrated his company. Stolen a project."

"Yes, but why would Bin come and tell him?"

"Easy. No-brainer. If Bin wanted to get into this country, that was his weapon: 'You help me and I give you the name of the spy in your company.'"

"Which brings us back to the London office. Did they have anything that was worth stealing?"

"Not much, but Galbraith insists on getting blueprints of

our new projects. He's entitled, even if he never looks at them and sticks them away in a drawer."

"Which he probably does. Lewis always said the security system there was terrible, that Galbraith didn't want to install any newfangled security systems. Makes you wonder, a man who founded this high-tech company. Now he'd go back to hand-cranked phones if he could."

"That geriatric itch to revert to the old days. It may not be Galbraith Technologies much longer. The place is falling apart. Bill Talbot just can't cope."

"So soon? Bill's a nice person."

"Nice, but not a fighter. We're heading for a takeover. There are several interested parties, but Danny Peplow is the chief suspect and he takes no prisoners. We're all touching up our CVs."

"Danny again. Do you think he could have bugged the office to get an inside track? Does his company make electronic devices?"

"They do, very cutting-edge. As my toothless old granny in Jamaica used to say, 'Things are never so bad they can't be worse.' I'll talk to my friend the electronics expert and get back to you."

"You're an angel. I can't thank you enough."

"Haven't done anything yet. Now listen, Emma. All this looking under stones—stay cool, and I don't mean the weather."

After shifting through piles of paper, I found Sergeant Johnson's number at the State Police Barracks. A nice man whose wife was a teller in my bank. His boys played soccer for the New Sutton high school.

For a moment, I sat still, fighting the temptation to crawl back into bed. My call to Lorna had broken the mental logjam, but talking with Sergeant Johnson would be much harder. Lorna was a friend who wanted to help. Sergeant Johnson was a detached professional. I wiped my hot face and picked up the cell phone.

"Sergeant Johnson." The surprisingly deep voice.

"Hi. It's Emma Streat."

"Morning, Mrs. Streat. What can I do for you?"

"We haven't talked for a while. I was wondering, is there anything new?"

"If there was, you'd have heard from me. How are you getting on?"

"All right. Hot, like everyone else." Thank God he couldn't see this stained T-shirt. "So there's *nothing* new?"

"I've been going over the photo and lab reports with a fine-tooth comb. Broken glass or paint chips would indicate the make of the vehicle, but there were none at the scene."

"But can't something still turn up? A damaged car or truck?"

"It's possible. I'll keep checking."

My hand tightened on the cell phone. Sweat was running down my face. "Sergeant, I called because I think we need to talk. Meet. I—I can come to the barracks."

"There's something on your mind?"

"Yes. There is."

"Well, no need to drag you out in this heat. I have to be in court in New London at eleven thirty. If I leave early, I could be with you at ten."

I looked around. "At ten? I don't think I—no, yes, that's fine. See you then." I put down the phone and bent down to pick up the broken Quimper plate; half of the peasant woman's smiling face lay under the table, the other half by the sink. Fifteen minutes to clean the kitchen. Twenty minutes to take a shower, put on clean clothes.

In the distance, a siren sounded. I began to count. One long sound meant trouble at the nuclear plant ten miles down the shore. People had been advised to pack bags and be ready to evacuate to New Haven. Seven seconds, eight. At last, the familiar dying wail. No terrorist attack today.

nine

It was too hot to sit on the terrace. I led the sergeant to a screened side porch where there was always a breeze.

"Take off your jacket, why don't you? Coffee? Iced tea?"

"Nothing, thanks. I had a couple of last-minute phone calls, why I'm running late."

"That's all right." I put my hands on the arms of the wicker chair. A nice man, but right now I must put his feet to the fire. "The thing is, everything happened so fast the day Lewis was killed, but now I've had time to think."

"And?"

"You talked about a kid, drunk or on drugs. I still think anyone should have seen a man standing in an empty road in broad daylight. Maybe it sounds crazy, but I'm beginning to wonder if that driver *meant* to hit Lewis." I swallowed. My throat was very dry.

The sergeant gave me a quick look. "Any particular reason for you to think that?"

"Several. First of all, my husband was worried about something. Really worried. I'm trying to find out what it was. Before I called you I talked to Lorna, Lewis's assistant at Galbraith Tech. On Monday the second of June, a Chinese engineer went to the Galbraith office. This engineer—a Nelson Bin—said something to Lewis that upset him. He came home acting . . . not himself. The man was knifed to death on a people mover at JFK the next morning. He was carrying a card with Lewis's name and company address, so the New York DA's office asked Lorna a lot of questions."

"Go on."

"I can't stop wondering. Two men, Nelson Bin and my husband, were killed within one week of meeting each other. No leads. No arrests. What does that say to you?"

Sergeant Johnson put his hands on his knees. "It says a homicide at JFK, then a hit-and-run in Hardwick, two unsolved crimes. About your husband. We can't rule out homicide, but to make a case we need valid evidence. Your husband didn't give you a hint of what was on his mind?"

"It had something to do with security in the London office. It got worse while we were there. Just before he died, I lost my temper. I told him I was tired of being shut out. He told me to leave him alone. For my safety. Then he went for his walk."

"He was worried about your safety?"

"His words. His last words. Then he went for that . . . that walk." My throat tightened, holding back tears.

Sergeant Johnson shifted in his chair. "I'm glad you told me. I'll work this information over, but we still need more evidence."

I sat straight. "But what if you *never* find anything? I want to *know* who killed Lewis, if the man was young or old. Black or white. I want to see a *face.*"

A boat hooted from the river. The sergeant held up his hand.

"Which is a normal reaction. The need to find a missing perp is as basic as the need to find a missing victim." He cleared his throat. "Tell you this, Mrs. Streat. I've had this job for fourteen years. If there's one thing I don't like, it's unsolved crimes on my patch. Right now I'm saying to myself, 'Something doesn't add up, Al. What is it that you're missing?'"

"I don't understand."

"Here's what I mean. Rolls of film were taken at the scene. There should have been brake marks, but no brake marks showed on those films. After looking at them, I drove back and had another look around. You said you saw dust. No horn, no squeal of brakes."

"No. Nothing but dust."

"Studies show that a driver, even one who's under the influence, will slam on the brakes when he sees a large object in the road. An instinctive reflex. Studies also show that no brake marks can be a sign of deliberate intent to run over an object."

"So it *could* have been deliberate?"

"Not saying that. The postmortem report on your husband showed no marks other than those consistent with being struck down by a moving vehicle. He was cremated, so there's no way of getting more evidence there." He glanced at his watch. In a moment he would leave for court in New London.

I leaned forward. "Wait. *If* you thought this was a homicide, what would you do?"

He frowned. "Well, in a routine case, we look for motives. Greed. Love interest. Jealousy. Revenge. We talk to the people closest to the victim. The saddest two words in a detective's vocabulary are 'I assumed,' but for the moment I'm assuming that you're not a perp."

"A what?"

"Perpetrator. It might be helpful to know if your husband had any enemies. A threatening note. An employee who was fired. A rival."

"Some people didn't like Lewis, he didn't have a lot of patience, but I don't think he had *that* kind of enemy. No one out here was fired. I don't know about the office."

White pleasure boats were zigzagging up the river, vying for space. Sergeant Johnson got to his feet, went to the screen, and looked out.

"Mrs. Streat. If—and I say if—this should turn out to be a case of deliberate intent, someone made very careful plans. Knew when your husband took his walk. Figured out when he would be alone, the most vulnerable time in his day."

"His early morning walk."

"Exactly. It might have taken one man to drive the vehicle, another to distract or position the victim."

I winced and stared at the hanging plants, seeing Lewis held by the arms, flung down in front of the racing car. Sergeant Johnson turned.

"You wouldn't know, but my father was killed in a hit-and-run accident. He was crossing Main Street in New Sutton on the way from his shoe store to the post office. It's the reason I went into the criminal justice field."

"Anna Jones told me at the clinic. She said you would understand."

"In his case the drunk driver was found three hours later. In a local bar."

"I'm sorry."

"It gives me a special interest." He paused and wiped his face. "Like I said, I'll think about what you've told me. We'll keep working on your husband's case, but remember this: One month is a very short time in police work. It tends to be a day-in, day-out slog where nothing fits. Then, out of the blue, one little lead can get the case rolling. People remember something that didn't seem right, but wasn't important at the time."

"You mean, one little thing can be key."

"One random observation. You might keep that in mind."

"I will." We left the porch and started down the hall.

As we reached the door, I stopped and shook my head. "The trouble is, you're trained to pick up on small details. Whatever. One might just slide by *me.*"

"True, but you come at this situation with different eyes. You knew your husband. You know the people around him. Keep thinking back. Something might click into place. If that happens, call me."

"Yes. I will."

The heat on the front steps was blinding. He started down the front steps, then turned and gave me a quick look.

"Take care of yourself, Mrs. Streat. Eat. Try not to worry."

"I'll . . . try. Thanks for coming," I said, and shut the door.

The thermometer was reaching eighty and rising. I turned up the air conditioner, called O'Hara, and went upstairs, feeling drained. "Perp." "Brake marks." "Position the victim"—police jargon.

A wedding picture of my parents stood on the bureau. Pa in his Navy uniform, Ma wearing white satin and pearls, her dark hair done in a long page boy. Strong people who came from strong stock and had done their best to raise strong children.

As I lay down on the bed, the telephone began to shrill. Caroline's tuba voice filled the room.

"I hate these machines. Talk to me, Emma."

"I'm here," I said, holding the receiver away from my ear.

"Dolly says you're sleeping all day. Having a nervous breakdown."

"You know Dolly. Always worrying."

"Not just Dolly. I hear you're not answering any calls."

"It's hot. I'm busy."

"Listen to me, darling girl. Did you think I'd let you sink without a trace? Get out of that house and come to Newport. Today."

"Not Newport. I hate Newport."

"I have a man for you. Just getting over a bad divorce. Not old and not gay."

"For God's sake, Caroline. It hasn't been a month."

"Yes, but you won't be celibate for long. Not your nature. What was the name of the conductor you almost married?"

"Tony Battia. I haven't seen him for years."

"Too bad. Just remember to throw out all your old nightgowns when you get a lover."

"I don't want a lover. I don't wear nightgowns."

"You will. Cellulose, or do I mean cellulite? Just don't wait too long. With your looks and money you can afford to be choosy. Men love that husky voice."

"Pushing it, Caroline," I said, trying not to laugh. "I could share a bed, maybe, but not a bathroom."

"Then go to Ned and Cassia. Go fishing in Canada. Dolly is talking about something called intervention, the family sitting around in a circle, taking over your life. For your own good, of course."

"I told her if she calls the boys I'll never speak to her again. I mean it. Never in this world will I speak to her again."

"No dramatics, please. For your mother's sake I won't let you cut each other's throats. Darling girl, take the high road with Dolly. Give her some rope. *You* had the panache. The looks and talent. She didn't. That can hurt."

"She's on my back every morning, treating me like a mental case."

"Then take the wind out of her sails. Tell her you're planning to give a big party over Labor Day. Tables on the terrace and a band. Or—here's a thought—come with me to Cambridge. The English Cambridge. I'm doing a course there in the middle of July."

"You? A *study* course? In *Cambridge?*"

"Not so much shock, if you don't mind. I *am* a Wellesley graduate. I read Jane Austen straight through every year."

"Sorry. What's this course?"

"The Girard Museum in Chicago sponsors a two-week seminar during the summer when the scholars are off on vacation. I'm on the museum board, making sure they don't sell off my grandfather's Italian Renaissance collection. This is my second year as a representative for the board. Besides, it gives my darling maids a two-week vacation. Have you ever been to Cambridge?"

"No. Never." Suddenly wheels began to turn in my sluggish brain. The last thing Lewis had done was write a note to Dr. Estes, the eccentric Cambridge physicist, asking him to stop a dangerous new project. He had wanted Estes to have security around the clock. He was going to call him from a pay phone, not the office. Caroline was still talking.

". . . your father adored Cambridge."

"I know. He was always talking about it." What had Sergeant Johnson just told me? "One little lead can get the case rolling. People remember something that didn't seem right, but wasn't important at the time."

". . . if Cambridge doesn't work, then it has to be Newport. No more spending the day on your back. Alone."

I took a deep breath. "What are the dates of that seminar?"

"Why? You mean you might come?"

"There's a physicist in Cambridge I should see. A loose end to tie up for Lewis." No need to tell Caroline more than that.

"Wait, wait, I've found the brochure: Sunday July 12 to Saturday July 25. A joint program of the University of Cambridge and the Girard Museum of Chicago will be held at St. Paul's College, founded in 1478. Classes limited to fifteen persons. Applications must be received by June 11."

"I'm too late."

"Not if I call the museum office and tell them to put you on the list. It's expensive, the Rolls-Royce of all the Oxford and Cambridge seminars, but a lot of younger people go. Not just the wrinklies in nylon windbreakers."

"What course are you taking?"

"Interiors of Famous Houses. Field trips and private lunches at gorgeous places. You'd love it."

"I'm not sure—I'll have to think about it, call you back. I've got so much to do here. Letters. Lawyers."

"Excuses. Don't tell me you're afraid to travel."

"Of course not. One place is as safe as another these days."

"Then jump in feetfirst. Call Dolly and tell her. Then find yourself a therapist and get a quick fix."

I sat up, knocking over a glass of water. "You're as bad as Dolly. I don't need a therapist. They'll want to lay blame on my parents, pull my marriage apart. It'll take years."

"Not a psychiatrist. I'm talking about a practical kind of therapist; there's a name for them. Darling girl, you've got to get yourself back in shape. Now. I can't cope if you go to pieces over there and lock yourself in a room."

"Don't rush me; I'm thinking. There's the Metcalf family picnic on the ninth; that's up in Manchester. I wasn't going, but I could stay with Ned, then get a night flight from Logan Airport that Saturday night. In fact, we could fly together. Boston's no distance from Newport."

"We could, but I refuse to fly at night. So uncivilized, to be stretched out next to a snoring stranger. I'm booked from JFK that Saturday morning. I'll spend the night at the Heathrow Horizon Hotel, near the airport. Hire a car and meet you in Cambridge."

"So I'd better make my own plans."

"Better yet, why don't you ask Lewis's company to send their plane? That would solve everything."

"I can't do that, but I *could* call Hank Lausch and see if the company driver can meet me."

"Lausch—the forgettable man with the very grand English wife. Rather a mismatch. We met at Lewis's service. Can he afford her clothes?"

"She has the money."

"I thought so. That's settled, then. I'll get onto the museum office and call you back. By the way, St. Paul's is lovely, but I'd better warn you about the rooms. Little cells, one bathroom down the hall. Gridlock after breakfast."

I laughed. "You're seventy-four. I'm forty-seven. If you can stand it, I can."

ten

Hank was as eager as a puppy to help. "A seminar in Cambridge with your godmother? Great idea, gives you a change. Hold on; I'm looking at the schedule for the Gulfstream—no, sorry, that won't work. Galbraith's taking it to Scotland. He's buying land, getting ready to be a laird in case the peerage ever comes through."

"I wouldn't dream of asking. I have to get used to the real world."

"Would you like Wheeler to meet you? It's always good to see a familiar face waiting behind the barrier."

"*That* I'd love."

"Done. What time does your flight get in?"

"Sunday morning, eight thirty your time."

"Will your godmother be with you?"

"No, she's made her own plans. She's flying from JFK. She's seventy-four and only takes day flights. Refuses to lie anywhere near snoring strangers."

Hank laughed. "A character, your godmother."

"She is. In spades. I don't think she knows there are day flights from Logan now, but best not to make any changes."

Dolly saw trouble ahead: "You're still very fragile. Don't forget, there's nothing worse than getting sick in a foreign country." But there was no more talk of calling the boys.

Suddenly my life turned a sharp corner. I went out to buy casual new clothes—my closet had nothing but worn jeans and corporate wife outfits. There were appointments with a Dr. Agnes Simmons in New Haven, a practical therapist who had sensible ways to cope with stress and laid no blame on siblings and parents.

But none of Dr. Simmons's methods worked on my last morning at home. After a restless night, I woke up bombarded by inner signals telling me not to leave. For hours I wavered, mentally standing on first one foot and then the other. There was still too much to do here. I was too shaky to travel. But then the other foot would rush forward: Unforgivable to let Caroline down at the last moment. And, after all, I was simply going to attend a seminar and make a phone call, not fight in a war zone. In the end, the thought of facing Dolly tipped the balance: "I told you, Emma. I knew you were much too shaky to travel."

At noon on Thursday, July 9, I waved good-bye to Mrs. Gates and O'Hara and set off for Manchester-by-the-Sea, the famous old resort on Boston's North Shore.

My brother, Ned, is a laid-back stockbroker with a great sense of humor, married to a volatile Chilean beauty who is also a marvelous cook. Their rambling shingled house smells of sun and seaweed and I was welcomed with open arms: "Emma, you're wonderful. Everyone's so glad you're here."

For me, the annual Metcalf picnic was a booster shot for old-fashioned values, a yearly injection of manners and integrity that never quite left the bloodstream. The setting hadn't changed in fifty years. Generations of adult Metcalfs ate lobster and steamed clams. Children smeared themselves with buttery corn on the cob. After eating, there were songs like "Jolly Boating Weather" and "Sidewalks of New York."

This year I was conscious of deep, intense gratitude for the comfort of big families. I caught up with young second cousins changing from gawky teenagers into sleek adults. I burped new babies, ran after toddlers with adorable sun hats and fat brown legs. A happy time. I had been right to ignore those negative voices.

The next day, as I stood in Ned's big kitchen shelling peas for lunch, the phone rang. My sister-in-law answered it.

"Caroline. How are you?" A long pause. Cassia held the phone away from her ear. "She's right here. I'll put her on."

I took the phone. "Are you in New York? Is everything all right?" I asked.

"Getting old is sheer hell, all the parts wearing out. Now it's a pinched nerve in my neck. The doctor says I can't lift anything heavier than my handbag, not even a carry-on."

"Oh no. Does this mean we can't go?"

"Not that, but I need an enormous favor."

"Of course. What?"

"I need you to cancel your Saturday night flight from Logan. Get yourself to JFK and come with me. Be my pack mule."

"Wait. Today is Friday the tenth. Tomorrow is the eleventh. I can take an early shuttle from Logan, that's no problem, but I may not get a seat on your flight."

"I have one for you. I'll meet you in the First Class lounge. We'll spend the night at the Heathrow Horizon Hotel." A pause.

"Good. Fine. Take care of yourself." I put down the phone and groaned.

Cassia rolled her eyes. "What happened?"

"She's got a pinched nerve in her neck. She wants me to go with her on a day flight from New York, the least I can do, but now I've got to undo all *my* plans."

"What a nuisance."

"It is." For years, the office had made my travel arrangements. I began to make a list. First, cancel night flight from Logan to Heathrow. Then reach Hank and change the time and place for Wheeler to meet me. By now it was afternoon in London. The office would be closed for the weekend. Hank would be at his place in Hampshire.

"Back in a moment," I said to Cassia, and went upstairs to get my cell phone.

Neatness was never my strong point. As usual, my clothes were flung on a chair; a suitcase lay open on the floor. I opened my black woven leather handbag and reached for the cell phone. Felt around, then dumped the contents on the bed.

"Oh no, oh *hell,* I don't believe this," I said loudly. In the last-minute rush, I had forgotten to transfer the phone from the battered canvas bag I carried around at home. I would have to use Ned's fax machine—if he had one.

Ned's cluttered study had a sweeping view of the Manchester harbor. At ten o'clock the tide was going out, leaving ugly patches of rock and seaweed close to the shore. An old computer and a fax machine stood in a corner.

"Cassia," I called. "Be an angel and help me with Ned's machine. I don't want to push the wrong button." Forgetfulness was part of loss, my therapist had said. I must be patient and understand that the healing process took time.

"Better you than me," Cassia muttered, but within minutes a fax was on the way to Hampshire:

Important!! Change of plans! Have Wheeler meet me at Heathrow Horizon Hotel, not terminal!! If ten o'clock Sunday morning inconvenient, you can reach me tonight at this number. Sorry. Love.

As the machine clicked, I realized that I hadn't told him that Caroline would be with me—but it didn't matter. There was plenty of room for us both in the company Jaguar.

"Thanks, you're a genius," I said to Cassia. "And don't even think about driving me into Logan for the shuttle flight. The local taxi will be fine."

"Poor you. Logan is like an armed fortress these days."

"I have to admit, the Gulfstream spoiled me rotten. No waiting, no lost bags. No terrorist lighting his shoes on fire. Don't forget one thing, though."

"What's that?"

I gave her a big smile. "If we get highjacked and blow up, you and Ned inherit the boys."

part two

eleven

Sunday, July 12

London

There were no explosions, no delays, not even a lost bag. At ten
thirty on Sunday morning, I stood near the front desk in the
Heathrow Horizon Hotel, waiting for Wheeler. Caroline had
worn her wristful of gold bracelets and a pink Chanel suit, the
uniform of her generation, but the pain in her neck had kept
her quiet during the flight. There were no loud comments about
shorts and bare legs in First Class. She liked my longer hair and
tight black pants, part of my funky new wardrobe: "Very dashing. The man across the aisle can't keep his eyes off you."

The lobby had the sterile look of a processing area for people
in transit; a garish green palm tree covered a great expanse of
icy white wall. Men with briefcases hurried back and forth
through the wide entrance to the ramp, faces tight with airport
strain. I watched each face with growing concern. Wheeler was
never late.

A group of travelers from India—the women in thin saris—
came through the door looking cold and dazed. I kept my eye

on the street and took several deep breaths, one of my therapist's ways to manage stress. Another dazed tour group arrived. No Wheeler. Oh God, there had been a mix-up. My fault. I should have used my brother's phone and *called* Hank. Kept calling until I reached him. Made *sure* Wheeler knew about the change.

More men with briefcases walked by. I looked at my watch. If I contacted British Airways, Wheeler could be paged. By the time he got here, Caroline would have finished applying her makeup and icing the pinched nerve.

As I turned towards the desk, a black Peugeot sedan pulled up in front of the hotel doors. The driver got out and walked to the desk. An olive-skinned man with a black mustache. He was wearing a gray twill chauffeur's uniform and cap.

"I wish to send a message to Mrs. Streat's room," he said in careful English. "I wish to inform that her driver is here."

I stepped forward. "I'm Mrs. Streat, but I think there's a mistake. I'm expecting another driver."

"Mrs. Streat. For St. Paul's College, Cambridge. You have bags?" He touched his cap, then glanced around, as if in a hurry.

"Wait," I said. "Cambridge is right, but we can't leave yet. The person with me isn't ready."

The man paused, hand in midair. "You have person with you?"

"Yes. Two of us." I glanced at his face. Spanish? Italian? Middle East?

"No one tell me two person."

"That's all right. We don't have a lot of bags."

He shook his head. "One person only."

"No, two. There are *two* of us."

"They tell me one person."

"They? Who sent you? Was it a Mr. Lausch?" The man looked at his shoes. I tried again. "Are you from an agency? Did a Mr. Lausch send you?"

"Mr. Lausch. Agency."

"You'd better call them. The phones are over there. I'll speak to them, if you like." If the man spoke good English I would be losing patience. He was still looking at his shoes.

"One person only. I go for bigger car." Keeping his head down, he hurried to the door. Jumped into the black sedan and pulled away from the curb.

I watched him go, willing myself to be calm, telling myself that this was *not* a valid reason to panic. The concierge could hire a car and a far more competent driver, but Hank must be told: "The most peculiar thing happened at Heathrow. That agency you use sent a very unreliable driver; he barely spoke English. I guess I should have let you know that Caroline was with me. Anyhow, he knew my name, that I was going to Cambridge, but when I told him there were two passengers, not one, he went ballistic. He literally turned and ran."

In the end, for a staggering price, a silent young man in a stretch limousine drove us to Cambridge. Caroline was received with the deference due a museum board member and retired to her room. I had a quick lunch, then went out into the narrow streets, drawn back in time. Scholars studying for the church had walked here long before Harvard was founded—and I was beginning to understand why my father had loved the English Cambridge so much: "Think of a charming old actress, living in the past, surrounded by her treasures."

The college seemed deserted; my fellow students must be in their rooms, resting and unpacking after a long night on the plane. As a church bell rang the hour of four, I began to walk towards the river.

According to my new guidebook, the two connecting courts at St. Paul's were made of medieval brick refaced with stone in the eighteenth century. Long herbaceous borders glowed against a background of gray stone—the unstudied English look I was trying so hard to achieve in mine. Pebbled paths circled lawns of flawless grass and led down to a terrace at the edge of the river Cam, a stretch of water marked as The Backs in my book.

For a few moments I stood there, watching green water move sluggishly past a row of weeping willows. A punt slid under an arched stone bridge; the woman passenger was wearing a large white hat; she lay back, languidly trailing her fingers in the water like a character in a 1920s novel—the essence of tranquillity in a place where life moved in slow, serene measure.

Mallards were diving for their evening meal. I looked at my watch and turned. At four thirty, the civilized interlude between Sunday afternoon naps and tea, I must call the eccentric Dr. Estes. He might have nothing to tell me:

"That meeting in June? I remember it very well. Your husband and I discussed a few minor changes for a project. May I say how sorry I was to hear of his death?"

There was no telephone in my small white room. Earlier, I bought a green Telecom card at the Porter's Lodge, situated just inside the door to Trinity Lane. The busy porter was helpful: "The nearest telephone is inside the door marked Enquiries. Go into the first court and turn left." I had nodded, telling myself that tomorrow I would hurry out and buy a new cell phone.

The door marked Enquiries led to a long, dark hall. The

phone booth smelled of stale cigarette smoke; the wavy opaque glass door didn't quite close. I put the Telecom card in the slot and pressed the number I had found in the phone book.

Two rings. Three. Five. No answer. Dr. Estes wasn't there. He had gone to Provence, to Cornwall, wherever distinguished physicists went for the four-month vacation. I should have written or called ahead.

"Hello?" At last, a woman's voice. I let out my breath.

"May I speak to Dr. Estes? It's Emma Streat, Mrs. Lewis Streat. He doesn't know me, but he knew my husband."

"If you don't mind waiting—"

"No, not at all."

I waited. My mouth was very dry. The numbers in the slot were ticking away, but a Telecom card that cost ten pounds would last a long time.

"Mrs. Streat?" A man's deep voice.

"Yes. Emma Streat. I . . . don't think we've ever met."

"Let me say how distressed I was to hear of your husband's death. A sad loss. He was a man of great integrity as well as vision, a rare combination these days, I'm afraid. Are you, ah, in Cambridge?"

"With the Girard Museum seminar, one of the American study groups. We're staying at St. Paul's College."

"My college, as it happens."

"Oh." I must get to the point, not waste his time. "Dr. Estes, I'd like to ask you a question, but it's too complicated to do it over the phone. Is there a place we could meet? Whatever is most convenient for you."

"I'm afraid I don't understand. A question for me? What might that be?" A guarded voice. I sensed that he wasn't going to make this easy. I might have to pretend I knew more than I did.

"Actually, it's about the meeting you and my husband had in June, at the Pelham Hotel in London. To discuss your new project." A long pause.

"Er . . . yes." Another pause. "Mrs. Streat, I fear I'm rather pressed for time this week. Very pressed. When I'm free of my—er—obligations, I will leave a message with the porter."

"I see." I shifted the receiver, sticky from other people's hands. Somehow I must keep him on the line. "What about next week? I'll be here until Saturday."

"Next week I shall be at a scientific conference in, ah, in Geneva."

I closed my eyes and leaned against the wall. A child of three would know the man was lying—and not very well. For some reason he didn't want to see me. I would have to hold his feet to the fire.

"Dr. Estes, I'd better tell you *why* I'm asking for your help. The day after your meeting, my husband was hit by a car near our house in Connecticut."

"So I heard. Most distressing."

"It was. The thing is, Lewis was worried before he died. Extremely worried. The last thing he did was write himself a note to call you. Ask you to drop your new project and get round-the-clock security."

"Would you repeat that?"

"He was going to call you from a pay phone, not the office. Ask you to drop your dangerous new project. Get round-the-clock security. A few minutes after writing that note he was killed."

Silence. The acrid smell of cigarette ashes on the floor was making my eyes sting. Dr. Estes cleared his throat.

"Mrs. Streat. I fear I'm at a loss. Exactly what is it you want of me?"

"I want to know why my husband felt he had to call you from a pay phone. I want—I *need* to know if that project could have had anything to do with his death."

"His death? Surely not. Now, if you will forgive me, I must go."

"Dr. Estes." I hesitated, then took a desperate leap. "There's something else I should tell you. My husband's death may not have been an accident. It may have been carefully planned. In other words, someone may have *wanted* to kill my husband."

"Ah." A sharp gasp as if I had hit him in the windpipe, cutting off air. I jumped.

"Dr. Estes? Are you all right?"

"I shall be dining at St. Paul's tonight with the Master. I will leave a message for you with the porter." There was a sharp click as he hung up. The line went dead.

twelve

The opening night dinner was under way in an impressive fourteenth-century hall. Small vases of fresh flowers stood on long polished tables. There were menu cards engraved with the college crest and three wineglasses at every place. Caroline motioned me to sit down beside her on a hard wood bench.

"I'm starving," I said. "What are we waiting for?"

"For the High Table people to march in. Instructors and college bigwigs have padded chairs up on the dais. Students get the benches."

I nodded and looked up at the high hammerbeams, arched like the prow of a ship. My call to Dr. Estes had hit a raw nerve, but to cut me off was sheer rudeness.

"Emma?"

"Those beams. What's the food like?"

Caroline was too sharp. "Heavy. Delicious. Filled with fat and salt. I told you, this is the Rolls-Royce of all the seminars, but's it's a mixed bag. Quite a few come from Chicago."

"I like mixed bags." Tonight we were all strangers setting out on an academic journey. No one except Caroline knew I was a widow with two grown sons.

"Be careful. You're apt to be much too nice to misfits. Remember, the first people who come up to you are the ones you have to avoid. There'll be a few older men looking for a purse or a nurse. The younger ones will take a look at your dress and want to jump into bed."

"Oh God, don't tell me it's *that* bad. Our local stores had nothing but these tight black slips. The teenagers have taken over the world."

"Darling girl, you can get away with tight black slips; no one would believe those hunks of boys. There's the bell. Stand up and shove the bench back or it'll bite the backs of your knees."

Suddenly the hall was silent, standing in tribute to scholarship as the line of black-gowned academics walked to the raised dais. Here, it seemed, gowns were worn like shoes and socks. One man sneezed violently and pulled a handkerchief from his sleeve. My father's academic gown had lived a neglected life in the back of the hall coat closet, but after every commencement his family had learned to search the sleeves for missing eyeglasses and notes.

A tall, white-haired man pronounced a Latin grace in a resonating Oxbridge accent.

"—benedicat, benedicamus. Amen."

A young waiter brought a plate of curried prawn bisque. Voices rose as social antennas went up, assessing, sorting. A woman with wild snakes of black hair was talking about bicycles: "One missed me by a hair on Trinity Street. Then a bunch of Italian students almost knocked me off the sidewalk." The chronic complainer, one in every group.

I turned to the man beside me. The large cast on his right arm reached the tips of his fingers. "I'm Emma Streat," I said.

"Tom Myers. Would you mind cutting up my meat? A shame to waste roast beef."

"Glad to. Slide your plate over. What course are you?"

"Interiors of Famous Houses. What are you?"

"Same." Tom's face was tanned, as if he spent a lot of time outdoors. A pleasant face, not handsome. His khakis were rumpled; his blazer was frayed at the cuffs. He didn't have the air of an interior designer, but over the years I had learned, the hard way, not to typecast.

"Are you an architect?" I asked, playing safe.

"More of a builder. Concrete houses in Africa."

"Where in Africa?"

"Zambia. I work for a small foundation. We stick to basics like trucks and housing, hen projects for the local women. There's an institute near Cambridge that experiments with grains. I'll check them out while I'm here."

Beside me, Caroline was jingling her bracelets, a signal that she needed attention.

"So," I said, turning back to her.

"So. Are you missing your television and your Jacuzzi?"

"I *love* my little white cell with orange muslin curtains. I love Cambridge. It's like being set down in a time warp for two weeks."

"Why? You grew up in an old college."

"Yes, but Harvard is bare-bones colonial, the kid cousin—" I stopped. The man across the table was leaning forward, studying my cleavage. A large, high-gloss man with fleshy jowls and a sloping forehead. Sleek black hair carefully brushed to hide the bald spot. Yellow hankie carefully arranged in the crested pocket. Caroline's bracelets jangled. She gave him a sharp look.

"Never say I didn't warn you."

"Hush. Not so *loud.*"

A bell rang. Heads turned towards the dais as the man who had said grace rose to his feet. Like George Galbraith, he had the look of a superior Great Dane.

"I am Jeremy Haverford and I welcome you all to Cambridge University and to St. Paul's College. In fact, for the next two weeks, you *are* the College. You set the tone."

With pomp and circumstance, Dr. Haverford exhorted us to strive for academic excellence and to keep off the grass. He introduced the coordinator from the Girard Museum, a Mrs. Pat Dickinson, and her two young assistants, Christopher and Sarah, second-year Cambridge students with the temporary titles of Resident Tutors.

"Nice job, fella," Tom muttered, as Dr. Haverford sat down. "Borrow our brains and we keep the dollars. Want to check out the college bar? It's around the corner by the classrooms. I can drink with one hand."

"Thanks, but I'm still unpacking."

"Okay. Another night." He smiled, accepting the excuse.

The crowd was moving towards the doors. I followed Caroline down the aisle, glancing up at the portraits on the walls. One dignitary was wearing a long white wig; his lip curled in disdain, as if resenting the invasion from the colonies.

"Hey there." The high-gloss eavesdropper was beside me, grinning down. "Name's Bob. Bob Wininger. Say, there's a place called Sweeney's coupla minutes' walk from here. A lot classier than the college bar. What say we try it out?"

"Sorry. I'm with my godmother." I tried to walk faster, but the narrow aisle was filled with people.

"The one with the bracelets? Tough old bird. Tell her to cut you some slack."

I didn't answer. Oh God, where was Caroline when I needed her? Far ahead, propelled along by the crowd. The eavesdropper was keeping pace.

"Hey. Know something? The savvy people here don't live in cells, one scummy shower down the hall. They stay at the good hotels, have fun and games. Just turn up for classes and a few meals. What say to *that,* doll? My treat."

Hotels. Fun and games. It took me a few seconds to understand that this repulsive man was asking me to go to a hotel and *sleep* with him, a total stranger. For over twenty years I had been protected from this kind of pervert.

"I'm not interested."

He took my arm. His face was so close I could smell his cologne. Polo. Every nerve in my body tightened.

"Hey, loosen up, doll. Got me a Roller. Latest model. Show you a good time."

"I *said* I'm not interested. Please take your hand off my arm."

He laughed. "Oh ho. Playing hard to get?"

"No. Leave me alone or I'll—I'll make a complaint."

"Hey, that's not friendly."

"It's not. I'm not."

"Feisty—I like that."

I wrenched away. "Get lost," I said wildly. "Get housebroken. Believe me, I wouldn't sleep with you if you were the last man on earth—"

"Hey, Emma. Lost you in the crush." Suddenly Tom was beside us. He leaned across me and spoke in a loud voice: "Emma and I are meeting people in the bar. Care to come along?" No answer. The people behind us protested as the big man swung around and pushed his way through. Tom gave me a wary look.

"Hope it was all right I barged in."

"God, yes. I was about to make a scene. It was like being

run over by a bulldozer. He called me *doll.* Asked me to go to a hotel and *sleep* with him. Just turn up for classes."

Tom laughed. "The old first-night technique. He had his sights on you at dinner. Hard to miss the body language."

"Technique? That was *technique?*"

"Barge in and stake a claim. It can work."

"Not with me. My husband died—not long ago."

"Sorry about that. I guess you didn't need a hassle."

"I didn't. I don't. I wasn't expecting it. Not here."

"Well, whatever you said, you sure punched his ego. I saw his face when he turned. If looks could kill, we'd both be dead."

"I lost it. I was trying not to make a scene, but I lost it. I told him he wasn't housebroken, that I wouldn't sleep with him if he was the last man on earth. With hindsight, maybe I should have laughed at him. Treated him like a joke."

"Still, he came on pretty strong. More than the usual kind of pass."

"Why do you say that?"

"That look he gave you. If he bothers you again, we'll circle the wagons. Keep the psycho out."

"If he comes near me again, I'll look through him. Ignore him. But thanks anyhow."

We were reaching the door. "There's your friend with the bracelets," Tom said. "I'm off to the bar. See you tomorrow. Take care."

An open passage divided the kitchens from the hall and served as a connecting link between the two courts. The hardcore smokers were gathering with their coffee cups. Caroline opened her Hermès bag and took out a pack of filter cigarettes.

"Don't bother to preach. I'm cutting down," she said.

"Why didn't you wait for me? The ghastly man across the table—first he wanted to take me to a pub tonight. Then he invited me to go live in a hotel with him, just appear for a few classes. He says all the savvy people here do it."

Caroline's eyebrows went up. "But that's outrageous. I'll speak to Pat Dickinson. The museum should be more careful who they take."

"No, don't, no need for a fuss. In fact, it's quite funny. I suppose I'll have to get used to being single. Fair game."

"That dress. I warned you. How did you get rid of him?"

"The man with the cast came to the rescue. He pretended we were together."

"I can see the line is forming."

"Don't worry, Tom's not my type, but he's nice. Laid-back. Anyhow, that cast keeps him harmless. He says he'll circle the wagons." And as soon as I got back to my room, I would throw this dress into the wastebasket—no, it could go to the next church rummage sale. Some teenage nymphet would love it.

Caroline coughed. "If that boor bothers you again, I'll reduce him to tears. It's my greatest talent. What are you going to do now?"

"Finish unpacking and take a walk. My body thinks it's midafternoon; it's screaming for exercise. I just wish my entry was closer to yours. Does your neck hurt?"

"Not much. The pills are working. By the way, it's called a staircase here, not an entry. Remember, the porter pulls all the levers. Takes messages, answers questions, calls taxis. Another thing. Don't forget to take the key if you go down the hall to the loo at night. The door can shut behind you and it's out to the Porter's Lodge in your nightgown."

I laughed. "I'll be careful. See you at breakfast?"

"Not at that hour. I'll be icing, stretching, painting, flossing. The price you pay for getting old."

"No breakfast? You'll starve by noon."

"There'll be biscuits and coffee during the morning break. At Wellesley your mother and I used to brush our teeth and dress in five minutes. Shetland sweaters and tweed skirts. I miss her."

"I know. Were you always great friends?"

"After the first week. My mother sent me east with a trunk full of expensive silks and cashmere. *Your* Boston grandmother didn't believe in college for women. She said it made them introspective. Now known as finding yourself."

I laughed. "Granny's favorite saying was that courage has to be exercised like muscles. Straight spine, no tears. She and her friends supported charities and wore brown cotton stockings to Friday afternoon symphony. They were wonderful."

"I couldn't stand her and she couldn't stand me. With good reason, as it turns out. I wanted to be a writer and I ended up writing checks, alimony to all those rotten men."

I shook my head. "Don't say that. You're a safety net for me. For a lot of people."

"A net full of holes. I'm off to bed."

"Sleep well," I said.

"Darling girl, only babies sleep well. You'll find that out."

In the court, early evening shadows had dulled the herbaceous borders. The brilliant grass was paling to a soft pastel.

"I'll leave you here," I said to Caroline. "Have a good sleepless night. I take it the streets are safe for walking after dark."

"Safe? Of course they're safe. Safe as churches. Darling girl, this is *Cambridge.*"

thirteen

At nine o'clock I picked up my guidebook and my key and left my little room. The long hall was divided by checkered glass doors, standard fire prevention in England, but it was a stretch to believe that these doors could hold back a wall of flames.

The three flights of stairs were narrow and circular, with hollows in the middle of the stones, worn down by generations of student feet. I went carefully, holding on to the iron rail. A fall on these stairs might end in a broken neck.

In the court, dull circles of light shone down from iron lamps set in the walls. A small passage connected the first court to Trinity Lane; there seemed to be a lot of these small stone passages at St. Paul's. Two porters were standing in the Lodge. One was thin and wore gold-rimmed glasses. The other had heavy shoulders and thick eyebrows that met in the middle of his forehead.

"I'm so sorry, I seem to have left my key in my room," a woman was wailing. I went to the alphabetically compartmented wooden box that held mail and looked under the letter *S*. No message from Dr. Estes.

Outside in Trinity Lane, I studied my guidebook again. The buildings of Old Schools were on my left, facing Clare College Chapel. At the end of the lane, the lit pinnacles of King's College Chapel rose high into the sky like a line of carved pagodas. Later this week I must go to Evensong and hear the boys choir. For years, my tapes of those pure soaring voices had lifted the Christmas spirit above last-minute lists and crowded malls.

The narrow Senate Passage led to a large central square called King's Parade. At this hour, the small shops were closed and dark, but people were emerging from a large church on the corner. I began to walk, staying away from the shadowy side streets, wanting to relive those peaceful moments by the river. Instead my mind kept going back to the peculiar driver at the Heathrow Horizon. "One person only." One thing was clear: The man hadn't been randomly cruising the hotel lobby. Hank must have given him my name, told him I'd be going to St. Paul's College.

I walked faster, swinging my arms, hearing Dr. Estes' voice: "I will leave a message for you with the porter." If there was no message tonight, I would call him tomorrow. All he could do was hang up on me again.

Another turn around the square, and I started back along the Senate Passage, stopping to study the stone medallions set in old brick walls. A man passed me, his black academic gown slung over his shoulder. A car inched by and he waved to the driver.

"Talk to you tomorrow, Giles, about that meeting."

"Right. We'll need to get a quorum."

"Shouldn't be a problem unless the Master has some objection."

Official Cambridge going about its business. Tomorrow I would be immersed in the academic world—and Tom had said he would protect me from the pushy boor. Thank God he had come along just then. If not, I might have lost my head in a very public way.

The booming Great Saint Mary's bell was striking ten o'clock as I reached Trinity Lane. A few yards away, a group of people had gathered near the Old Schools gate. They were standing in a circle looking down.

"I'll fetch a doctor," a man said.

"No time for that. Go to the Lodge and have the porter ring for an ambulance." A woman's voice, shrill with crisis.

"Right you are." The bearded young man sprinted past me towards the Lodge. Through a gap in the circle I could see a man lying on the cobblestones. A tall man with a fringe of white hair and closed eyes. One trouser leg was pulled up, exposing a bony white ankle. There was a dark blur on the stones under his head.

A tiny, elderly woman was on her knees beside the man. She looked up and spoke to a young girl with pink and purple spiked hair.

"You were here first. What happened?"

The girl shrugged her shoulders. "He was going into Old Schools, see, like he left a car in the court. This bloke on a bicycle comes from the gates at the end of the lane, see? Runs straight into him and knocks him flat. We yell and the bloke scarpers off."

"Disgraceful. Did you see his face?"

"Nah. He was wearing a helmet." The girl pulled at the stiff spikes of hair and backed away.

More people were gathering. "Why is that old man lying there, Mummy?" a child asked. "Why is he asleep in his clothes?"

The heavyset porter was making his way through the crowd. He leaned down, then straightened and ran a hand over his forehead.

"Dear me. It's Dr. Estes. All right, ladies and gentlemen, the ambulance is on the way. Nothing you can do to help. Stand back, please, and make room. It'll be a tight squeeze for them, this lane."

I stumbled to the high wall and dug my nails into the rough stone. Two hit-and-run accidents—but Lewis had been knocked down by a car on a dirt road.

The tiny woman was still on her knees, holding the man's hand. A few feet away from me, huddled against the wall, the sulky girl was arguing with a skinny boy wearing jeans and a Bruce Springsteen T-shirt.

"I shouldn't never have listened to the old bag. Told her we seen him knocked down. Don't want any trouble. If my dad gets to hear we wasn't at Heather's he'll kill me straight."

"Ought to tell the police what we seen."

"Police don't come, not for every bicycle accident. Besides, nothing they can do. No one but us was here, and we never seen a face under that helmet."

"We seen him get off the bike, didn't we? Lean over the old man."

"Trying to help, he might have been."

"Don't be thick. More like scooping his wallet, the way he took off when I yelled. Here comes the ambulance."

I moved towards the teenagers. Another accident—and these two seemed to be the only witnesses. A hand touched my arm.

"Aren't you in our seminar? What happened?" It was the wild-haired woman who had complained at dinner about the bicycles.

"A man was knocked down by a bicycle. Sorry, I have to speak to someone." I turned. In those few seconds, the young couple had disappeared into the darkness.

A white ambulance with a wide green stripe was turning the blind corner. The crowd moved back, silent and respectful, as two attendants leaned over the motionless figure. In a moment, the ambulance was backing down the lane. The siren shrieked its ominous message. The child screamed. People began to walk away.

I stood by the wall, struggling to clear my head. Dr. Estes wasn't my responsibility. This wasn't my country. On the other hand, the police should *be* here. They should be putting up yellow tape. Asking for witnesses. Looking for a bicycle.

At the entrance to St. Paul's, the porter was talking to the bearded man who had sprinted for help.

"Estes is the name, sir," the porter said. "Dr. Samuel Estes. He's a Fellow here. He went by just now, coming from the Master's House."

"Bad luck. You'd better have this." The bearded man handed the porter a crumpled black silk gown. "He must have been carrying it when he was hit."

"Very kind of you, sir. I'll see it gets back to him. Is that all? I'm needed in the Lodge. It's the first night for the Americans."

Several people from the seminar had gathered just outside the Porter's Lodge. The chronic complainer was in full cry.

"I was talking about those bicycles at dinner and then this happens."

"The fellow who was hit, I sure hope he isn't one of us," a man said. "Wait, here comes Sarah, the girl who was introduced at dinner. Fancy title like Resident Tutor. Maybe she knows. Sarah, listen, the fellow that went off in the ambulance. Was he one of us?"

Sarah was small and blond, with peaked eyebrows that gave her a look of permanent surprise.

"No. Good heavens, no," she said, alert to troubled waters. "He lives in Cambridge. Pity, but one does have to pay attention. Look both ways. Accidents involving bicycles are far too common."

Nods and murmurs from the group. "Dangerous, these bicycles . . . have to watch both sides of the street."

In the Lodge, the porter was standing behind the varnished counter, talking on the telephone.

"Yes, sir, it happened by Old Schools gate. He must have been coming from your dinner. A bicycle, one of those non-stops, a nasty head wound. Yes, unconscious. The ambulance left here about five minutes ago. He should be in hospital by now."

I stared at a dented bicycle basket filled with an assortment of packages wrapped in crumpled brown paper. The porter must be talking to the Master of the college.

". . . right, sir. I thought you might want to be in touch with Mrs. Estes."

I winced. Before Lewis's accident I had walked down the driveway in my sheepskin slippers, calling O'Hara. Right now, the woman who had answered my call this afternoon might be sitting in bed, reading the paper, wondering what the Master had served for dinner. *In the midst of life we are in death.*

"Yes, madam?"

I jumped. The porter was looking at me.

"I'm Mrs. Streat. I'm at the seminar. I was in the lane just after the accident happened. Dr. Estes and my husband—that is, they worked together. In fact, I talked to Dr. Estes just this afternoon."

"Ah. Very rare, these accidents, though the students do

cause a bit of trouble. Older tourists, too. Park in the lane, get a handful of tickets, and then leave the country."

I nodded. Not what Sarah just told us, but the man's first duty was to soothe a panicky visitor. Prevent tales of mayhem in the lane.

"The thing is, I heard two teenagers say the man may have taken Dr. Estes' wallet before they frightened him away. I don't know your laws, but it must be a crime to knock a man down, then take his wallet and go off. Will the police be coming to investigate?"

The black eyebrows came together in a straight line. "I can assure you, the police are very good about these things. No need to concern yourself, madam."

I leaned forward and looked the porter in the eye. Ma's bright blue glare, my boys called it. As a child, I had rushed into confrontations with sound and fury. I had learned to count to ten, but right now frustration was stomping on calm reason.

"But I *am* concerned," I said sharply. "For a very good reason. Dr. Estes was badly hurt. His wallet may have been taken. Those teenagers may be the only witnesses. Now they've disappeared. The police should *be* here getting evidence."

"Madam, I can only tell you that the police are very thorough. They'll do whatever is needed." He picked up a paper on the counter, dismissing me. I could read his mind. A troublemaker, one in every group.

I straightened. "Just a moment. What's the name of that hospital? I need to call and find out how Dr. Estes is."

"Ring Addenbrooke's? I shouldn't do that, madam. They're always very pressed."

"Addenbrooke's. The number must be in the phone book."

The porter frowned. He folded the black gown carefully and put it on a chair. "You'll get nothing out of them tonight, madam. They won't give you information, not being a relative." A pause. "If you'll stop by tomorrow morning I'll ring the hospital for you. I know someone who can get a firsthand report."

"Thank you."

The gown was sliding off the chair. The porter turned and picked it up. Then he placed his hands on the varnished counter. "Too bad to have this happen your first night here. Bit of a shock for you, Dr. Estes being a friend, but doctors do wonderful things these days. I was in the Army. I saw head wounds far worse and no harm done."

"Yes. Of course." I took a deep breath. After all, Dr. Estes was unconscious, not dead. By morning, he might be sitting up in bed, talking to a nurse: "The wretched chap had the nerve to knock me down and then take my wallet."

"Best to put it right out of your mind, Mrs. Streat. Nothing like a good night's sleep, I always say, to set you right. Before you leave, a gentleman rang a few minutes ago. I put the message in your box."

"Thank you." I pulled the piece of paper from the slot and unfolded it.

Call me at this number tonight. Urgent. Hank.

I refolded the paper, wishing I had never seen it. By now I was exhausted, wanting my bed. Not like Hank to call so late, but best to find out what was so urgent.

The court was deserted; only a few lights shone from windows. I walked quickly past the looming walls to the arch marked Enquiries, thinking that someone should give the college a grant for better lighting—while they were at it, a few more phones wouldn't hurt.

All the doors in the dark hall were closed; English children must be taught at birth to close doors. As I reached the telephone booth, I could hear a woman's voice. She was saying that England was incredibly expensive, she needed money transferred to her checking account.

I leaned against the wall, feeling drained. An endless day, starting with the driver at Heathrow. The wrestling with Wininger. Finding Dr. Estes lying in the lane. My feet were icy. I would never get to sleep without a heating pad. Now the woman was babbling about a theater weekend in London.

At last, the door was opening. It was the flaky complainer with the wild snakes of hair.

"Oh, sorry," she said. "I didn't know anyone was waiting."

"That's all right." If this woman hadn't distracted me I could have talked to the two teenagers. Tried to find out out exactly what had happened.

"It's so weird to see money ticking away. What do you do when it runs out? Can you put in more or do you have to get another card?"

"Haven't a clue." I closed the opaque glass door, tried not to breathe in the stale smell from the cigarette butts on the floor, and dialed the number Hank had given me.

"Pronto." Italian for "hello."

"I—is Mr. Lausch there?"

"Non capisco." Shouts for Dominic. A man came on the line.

"You wish to speak who?"

"I'd like to speak to Mr. Lausch."

"No here."

"Is this the right number?"

"Not right. No person that name here."

"Sorry." At least I had tried. I hung up and saw, out of the corner of my eye, the outline of a figure standing just outside the booth. A tall shape, distorted by the wavy glass. The handle of the door began to turn.

For a few heart-shrinking seconds I stood as if my feet were bolted to the floor, staring at the shadow. Then a primal reflex jolted my brain out of paralytic fright. I put the receiver under my chin and pressed random numbers on the call box.

"Porter? It's Mrs. Streat," I said loudly. "I was just talking to you. Yes, that's right. Look. I'm sorry to bother you again, but I'm in the phone booth, the one in the hall beyond Enquiries. There's a man standing here. He's trying to get in. I need help. Please come as quickly as you can." The handle stopped turning. The shadow disappeared.

I waited, heart pounding wildly, lungs struggling to take in air. Then, swinging my handbag around my head like a club, I ran down the hall braced to hear footsteps coming up behind me.

No hand seized my shoulder as I flew through the court. Now only a few more steps to the arch and finally the dark winding stairs. My knees were buckling; my hands slipped on the railing as I climbed.

Two people were coming down. I jumped out of their way and clung to the iron railing.

"Hey, take it easy," the man said. "Where's the fire?"

As they went on down, I could hear the woman talking: ". . . wonder if they have sprinklers in these old walls . . . can't imagine fire doors would be any earthly use. . . ."

I climbed again, scrabbling to safety. At last, my room. The key turned; the door opened. I slammed it shut and collapsed onto the floor.

When the wheezing finally stopped, I stood up and walked to the cupboard. Put on my coat and my warmest sweater.

Crawled into the narrow bed and curled myself into a tight ball. Years ago, panicky with homesickness, I had called my mother from a sleepover: "Ma, come and get me." Now I was the mother. The strong, capable adult.

For what seemed like hours I lay there, clutching the thin covers, forcing myself to go over what had happened in a rational way. I had been trapped in the aisle with Wininger. He had grinned down at me: "Show you a good time. . . . Playing hard to get? . . . Feisty—I like that."

I had lashed out at him: "Get housebroken. . . . I wouldn't sleep with you if you were the last man on earth."

Tom had come to the rescue, then warned me: ". . . punched his ego. . . . If looks could kill, we'd both be dead." Like a fool, I had tramped with both feet on a sick ego. I had to be punished—but it was all so incredibly *unfair.* The museum should have done a better job of vetting the applicants, weeding out psychos. There were plenty of younger, good-looking women in the seminar. Women who might be impressed by a new Roller and the caveman approach. Why *me?*

fourteen

Small children discover that night terrors have a wondrous way of disappearing when darkness turns to light. The monster shadow with strangling fingers becomes the branch of a tree silhouetted against the wall. No hungry gorilla is hiding under the bed.

At seven thirty, sunlight shining through the thin orange curtains woke me. Two sleeping pills had stopped the spasms of shivering. I had woken once, afraid to go down the hall to the loo, then slept again.

The long window had a broken sash cord. I pulled myself off the bed and went to look out. The lane below was peaceful; an uneven line of massive chimneys showed against the bright morning sky. Across the lane, a pigeon was preening himself on a slate roof, twisting his head and making raucous noises.

I watched, considering my options. Go to the museum coordinator? There would be a major fuss. Lock myself into this little room and prove Dolly right? "I knew you weren't fit to travel." Pretend I had received an urgent message and was needed at home? Too complicated. Caroline would be quick to spot any trumped-up lie.

The pigeon gave a final cry, then flew off to a tree in the garden across the lane. I pulled off the heavy sweater I had slept in and looked for my white cotton shirt. What, in fact, had actually happened last night? A pushy man had made a crude pass, nothing worse. The shadow by the booth could have been just that—a shadow. I *had* been worried about Dr. Estes and the accident—and worry had a strange way of distorting reality. The solution was simple: Never be alone. Keep close to other people.

The mood in the hall was subdued: "Please pass the juice. . . . May I have the butter?" Young student waiters in blue jackets were bringing fresh pots of coffee, refilling the silver racks of toast on the long tables. I paused at the door and looked up and down the tables. No sign of Wininger.

Like schoolchildren, people had returned to last night's places. Tom Myers was there, trying to butter his toast with one hand. I put my book bag with the Girard Museum logo on the floor and climbed over the bench.

"Can I do that?" I asked. "I owe you."

"Thanks. Damn nuisance, this cast."

"It's so big. What happened?"

"Car accident in Zambia. Arm broken in three places. I went to a clinic in Lusaka, but they didn't set it right. Had to be rebroken in London. Coffee?"

"For sure." I filled my cup.

Tom took the toast. "No sign of your good buddy," he said. "There's a cold going round, probably the bad air on the plane. If you're lucky, he's sick in bed."

"With a high fever. Thanks again for stepping in." I buttered a fresh piece of toast for Tom and decided not to tell him about the dubious shadow.

"Anytime. We had a guy like that in my company in Vietnam. Classic bully, couldn't take rejection. Don't forget, we'll circle the wagons if he steps out of line again. You ready to hit the books?"

"Ready, but it's lucky we don't have exams. How will you take notes?"

"I'll tape. Besides, there are sure to be slides of those houses."

"Ersatz academia, my father would say. Where did you get that banana?"

"At a table near the kitchen, next to the oatmeal and eggs."

The coffee was strong and hot. I drank a second cup and decided against the banana. There was just time to go to the Porter's Lodge and ask about Dr. Estes.

"See you later," I said, and climbed back over the bench.

In the Lodge, people were buying postcards and checking the mailbox. The porter, Mr. Bennett, was summoning a taxi, recommending a dentist. Finally he was free.

"Good morning, Mrs. Streat." A wary look.

"Good morning. How is Dr. Estes?"

"I—er—haven't had a spare moment. I'll ring the hospital now," he said, and picked up the telephone. "Connect me to Mr. Jerrold, please. . . . Morning to you, Matt, Jim Bennett here. I'd like the latest report on a Dr. Estes. . . . Yes, I'll hold."

I stood against the dingy cream-painted wall. Tomorrow I would call Mrs. Estes. Ask how her husband was getting on. Maybe send flowers. Try to see him before I left.

"Yes, Matt." A long pause. "No, I hadn't heard. Early this morning. Never regained consciousness. Dear me. A sad loss. Ta, Matt." He hung up the receiver and turned, not meeting my eyes. "Bad news, I'm afraid. A blood clot, it was. A massive hematoma. The surgeons operated, but there was no way in the world they could save him."

I put my hand on the counter for support. "He's *dead?*"

"So I was told."

"Are you sure?"

The porter's lips tightened. "I'm sure, madam. The obituary will be in the papers. Dr. Estes was very well-known." He turned and spoke to the thin porter. "That message goes in Mrs. Dickinson's box, Fred."

In the stone passage, a bulletin board was covered with notices. I stood in front of it, staring at the black printed letters. Last night that damn porter had been so convincing: "Doctors do wonderful things these days." And: "Nothing like a good night's sleep, I always say, to set you right." Like a fool, I had chosen to believe him. Bury my head in the sand.

Around me, people went in and out of the Lodge. Tourists with cameras were strolling into the college; two small boys ran onto the smooth grass and began to wrestle, digging their heels into the sacred turf. I looked at them, through them. A *second* fatal hit-and-run accident. Two men dead. Three, if you counted the man from Hong Kong.

"Watch it." A man spoke in my ear. I jumped, my hand at my throat.

"What?"

"Sorry." Tom was standing there. "Didn't mean to scare you. Those kids. Roadkill when the porter sees them."

"Oh. The kids." Dr. Estes' project had barely started when Lewis had written that note to him. I knew it by heart: *Find a pay phone. Call Estes UK time. Ask him to drop new project. Too dangerous at this time. Insist he have security around the clock.* Oh God, why had Lewis decided to keep me in the dark? Did anyone

else know that these two men had been working on a dangerous new project? What kind of project?

"Went out to get the *Herald Trib*," Tom said, "but it's not in
yet. Ten of nine, we'd better move. Our class is in the Music
Room; that's above the Junior Combination Room—hey, what's
wrong?" A perceptive man, Tom Myers. I pushed back my hair
and picked up my book bag.

"Look. I have to do an errand. Be an angel, will you, and tell
the instructor I'll be late."

The King's Parade was filled with strolling tourists. A row of
German students wearing red and white Kampus knapsacks sat
on the wall in front of King's College, staring as a man held up
a battered bicycle. "I was like this bicycle until God made me
straight," he shouted.

I hurried towards the traffic warden on the corner, a young
woman wearing a smart navy uniform and dark tights. My
sense of direction was a family joke: "If Ma says go left, go
right."

"How do I get to the nearest police station?" I asked.

The woman pointed to the map in my guidebook. "You
want to go to Parker's Piece. From here, it's about a twenty-
minute walk."

"Thanks. Thanks very much."

Walking fast, I passed several colleges. Peterhouse, Corpus
Christi, the great gray Fitzwilliam Museum; later in the
week there would be time to see the exhibits. Now a neighborhood of chemist shops, news agents, small houses with bicycles propped against walls. Unless the attacker had been
arrested, it would be impossible to find the bicycle that had hit
Dr. Estes.

Parker's Piece was an open field where a few kids in T-shirts twirled on skateboards, babies lay in prams, and old people sat quietly in the sun. A large printed sign stood in front of the concrete and glass police station:

KNIVES. HAND THEM IN HERE.

A stooped elderly man wearing a battered tweed hat went by. He stopped to read the sign, his back to me. Inside the station, behind a high grill, a policewoman was talking on the telephone:

"You say the garage door was open when you came home. I suggest you look around, see if anything is missing." I waited, seeing myself through the woman's eyes. Why would an American tourist involve herself with a local death?

"Ring back when you're done." She hung up. "May I help you?"

"I—my name is Emma Streat. I'm at a seminar at St. Paul's. Last night a Dr. Estes was killed in a hit-and-run bicycle accident in Trinity Lane."

She nodded.

I pressed on. "The thing is, I was there just after it happened. Two teenagers *did* see the accident. I heard them talking about it."

The policewoman frowned. "Yes?"

"The boy said the man on the bicycle got off and leaned down. It looked as if he was reaching for Dr. Estes' wallet. When the boy yelled, the man took off." I paused. "Dr. Estes was a . . . a family friend. You may have found the man who hit him by now, but I thought I should come in, I mean, in case you're still looking for witnesses."

"Right." A long pause. "I see." The policewoman was too well trained to give out information, but the hesitation was a giveaway. As I described the funky striped hair, the Bruce Springsteen T-shirt, she took it down. Took my name and thanked me. A polite, low-ranking policewoman going by the rules.

Outside, two buses were parked across the street: *Go Whippet to London. Summer and Daily Tours.* Two middle-aged women passed me. One was wiping tears from her eyes. The other was trying to comfort her: "It isn't as if he robbed a bank. You never had a day's trouble with him until now." The old man in the tweed hat was still reading the sign. Knives. Shoplifting. Petty crimes.

I stared at the empty buses. Suddenly the bar had been raised. I must go higher than the Cambridge police, but where? Lewis had always said, "If it's important, ignore the small fry. Go straight to the top." Advice I seldom took, but a dangerous laser project was bigger than a mistake on my bank statement. I began to walk. Like O'Hara with his rag doll, I must shake, tug, not let go.

The Riverbank Hotel was tucked into a cul-de-sac between a fen and the river.

"Good morning," I said briskly to the uniformed doorman. My sense of direction never wavered when it came to finding ladies' rooms and telephones.

"Good morning, madam," he said, recognizing distinction.

Settling myself in a comfortable booth with a chair, I dialed the U.S. Embassy in London.

"Mr. Yates, please. Nicholas Yates." Nick Yates was my nephew Davy's best friend. The two had lived in Lake Forest, outside of Chicago, and had come east to the boarding school near us. I used to pick them up and bring them home to eat nonstop meals and drink cases of Pepsi. My much younger boys had trailed after them, wide-eyed, absorbing every word. At fourteen Nick had been high-strung, a bit twitchy, but bright. Now he was in the State Department, doing something in culture over here.

"Mrs. Streat." Nick was on the line. "Great to hear from you, really great. Where are you?"

"I'm in Cambridge, actually, at the Girard Museum seminar. You lived in Lake Forest, you must have been to the Girard Museum."

"Seventh-grade field trips to see the Italian Renaissance paintings. How's Davy?"

"Still in love with the actress, still commuting back and forth to the West Coast. Not as settled as you are." I paused. "Nick, I'd like you to do something for me. Professionally."

A barely perceptible hesitation. "Of course. If I can."

"It's a bit complicated. Last night a Dr. Estes was killed outside St. Paul's College. A hit-and-run bicycle accident. Dr. Estes is—was—a well-known physicist."

"I don't know the name, but Cambridge is full of physicists."

"The thing is, you may not have heard, but my husband was killed in a hit-and-run accident a few weeks ago."

"I read about it. I was going to write. I never saw much of him, those visits. He was quite a man, but you kept the wheels turning. All those movies and meals."

"It was fun. I miss it. Nick, the person who killed Lewis hasn't been found. Neither has the one who killed Dr. Estes, as far as I know. It would take too long to give you all the details, but there could be a connection between these two accidents. I need to talk to a top person in the British police."

"What about the Cambridge police?"

"I went to the station a few minutes ago, but I'm just a visitor, a tourist with no clout. I've got to go higher. I thought of you because you know me. Plus, you understand how the system works over here."

A long pause. "You want to talk to someone who will listen to you, then push the right buttons, if necessary. The ambassador would be your best bet. Do you know him?"

"He and Lewis used to meet at Senate hearings, but I gather he's just taken over this post and these buttons need to be pushed right away."

"I'm getting the picture. Your boys used to say, 'When Ma's voice gets really low, watch out.' Now that I think of it, there've been some mysterious accidents to British scientists. This might—well, let me see what I can do. Where can I reach you?"

"Not easy. No telephones in the rooms and I didn't bring my cell phone. Nick, I know this sounds dramatic, but I'd like to come down to London. Right away. Spend the night, if I have to."

"Today? That's pushing it."

"I know, but there's no time to waste."

"In that case, I'll lean on our legal boy. He has a lot of contacts at New Scotland Yard. About tonight. I'm afraid I'm on duty. There's a reception at the Residency for big patrons of the arts. Culture hacks like me have to be front and center."

"Of course. I understand."

"But here's a thought. Why not come to the reception? The ambassador would be happy to have you. Then, if my legal colleague does manage to nail down an official, we could take it from there. If not, I'll arrange something for tomorrow."

I hesitated, but only for a second. "That might work."

"Only problem is where you can stay. Our flat is tiny and the baby is teething, howling his head off. Marnie's losing her mind. Shall I pull strings and get you a hotel room?"

"First I'll call my friend Hank Lausch at Galbraith Tech. In fact, I have to call him anyhow. If the company flat is free, I can stay there. What time is the reception?"

"Six. At the Residency. Regent's Park. By the way, your friend Lausch is on the invitation list. His wife is a big mover and shaker in the arts circles."

"I know. Nick, this all sounds very far-fetched, but do your best, will you?"

"I'll build a fire under my colleague. I'll never forget the time Davy and I were asked to a formal dance and you spent the afternoon driving us around, looking for rented tuxedos that didn't make us look like clowns."

"I always went to bed praying you weren't smoking pot in the bathroom. Until tonight, then." I hung up and sat back. At last, wheels were turning. Nick, at least, knew that there might be a significant connection between the two deaths. Now to reach Hank.

Mrs. Dean, the elderly secretary at the Galbraith Tech office, was a dedicated talker. "Such a loss, to lose Mr. Streat. So unexpected." Finally she put Hank on the line.

"Emma. Good trip over? How's it going?"

"Fine, so far. Cambridge is gorgeous. Look. I'm sorry I didn't reach you last night. I hope it didn't matter."

"It didn't. I never called."

"But there was a message from you. The porter took it."

"Must have been a mistake."

"I don't see how—" I stopped. Another mystery, but it would have to wait. "Brace yourself," I said. "I need a favor."

"Try me."

"I'm coming down to London tonight, to a reception at our Residency."

"The big arts do. Robina signed us up. Where are you staying?"

"That's why I'm calling. I need a room in town."

"No problem. Let me see if the company flat is free. If not, you can stay with us."

I waited. In a moment Hank was back.

"It's free. How are you planning to get yourself down?"

"Train. Bus. Maybe hire a car."

"Got a better idea. Wheeler will come and pick you up. What time is the reception? Robina keeps track of these things."

"Six."

"Wheeler will be there at four. That should work. St. Paul's College, right?"

"Trinity Lane, tell him. I'll be at the door. You really are a saint."

"First to be fired when they make the cut up above. See you later."

At the Silver Street bridge, young people were standing outside a pub, laughing, waving plastic glasses. Foreign students working hard on their English—or so their families were told. A boy called out, inviting me to join them. I smiled and went on. It was too late to join my class, but I could meet Caroline for lunch. She would grill me about missing the first class and I would have to tell her about London: "Such a nuisance, I know it's very sudden, but the ambassador and Lewis were great friends. Besides, I'll only miss one class tomorrow."

In the center of the old market, an ancient cross stood above the rows of booths with faded striped awnings. I bought postcards for the boys and Mrs. Gates. A pot of pink geraniums for my desk. Then I started back towards St. Paul's.

Trinity Street was once a main thoroughfare for horses and carts; today the narrow sidewalk overflowed with tourists carrying cameras, shoppers with bags. Across the street, a large red and white sale sign hung in Liberty's window. Everything was cheaper at home, but Liberty scarves made good presents, easy to pack.

"Pardon me, miss." A woman with a pram was trying to get by. I stepped to the edge of the shallow curb. With bicycles in mind, I looked to the right and then to the left.

A double-decker Cambridge Tour bus inched towards me, moving slowly over the cobblestones, a huge green and gold bus that almost filled the street. I waited, thinking that some afternoon I must take this tour, see the parameters of the town.

The blow on my shoulder was quick and hard. I fell forward, dropping the pot of geraniums. The round headlights were level with my eyes; the wheels loomed in my face. I was falling, falling under those monster wheels.

The sudden pull nearly wrenched my arm from its socket. Hands grabbed my waist, held me up, then lowered me to the pavement. I lay there, seeing feet around me, hearing voices: "Tripped . . . taken ill . . . not paying attention."

"Are you all right?" A girl leaned down.

I lifted my head. "I didn't trip. Someone pushed me."

"*Pushed* you?"

"Didn't you see?"

"I saw you start to fall—I had to close my eyes. Shall I call an ambulance?" The girl was wearing a Berkeley is Cool T-shirt.

"No." I took several deep breaths and sat up. Young people in bright shirts were gathering around, talking loudly in Italian. The boy who had saved me handed me my bag.

"Lady, lady, just in time I catch you."

"Thank you. Grazie. Did *you* see who pushed me?"

He turned to the others. Much head shaking. A torrent of Italian. He picked up the envelope holding postcards and gave it to me with a flourish, ignoring the broken pot of geraniums. The white roots, showing through the dirt, looked like splintered bones.

"Just in time I catch you, lady. Watch where you going," and he swaggered away, an arm around the waist of a large-breasted girl with long black hair. I stood up, crossed the pavement, and leaned against the window of a print shop.

"You're sure you're not hurt?" The American girl was still hovering.

"Just my arm. Not bad, but someone *did* push me."

"In front of all these people? There was a woman with a baby carriage taking up most of the sidewalk. An old man was walking behind you, but I sure didn't see him push you."

"Was he wearing a tweed hat?" At the Parker's Piece station, a man in a tweed hat had been reading the sign about knives. I hadn't seen a face; his stooped shoulders had made him look old. Standing straight, he could be the same size as Wininger.

"I didn't notice the hat. If you're okay, I've got to meet someone for coffee."

"I'm okay. Thanks. Thanks so much."

"No problem. Take care," and she disappeared behind a gray-haired couple wearing white nylon parkas.

I pressed my back against the glass window and rubbed my arm. The bright sunlight looked amber, as if filtered through gauze. If the Italian boy hadn't had such quick reflexes, by now the street would be filled with police cars. A white and green ambulance. Yellow tape to keep the crowd from seeing the smashed body under the bus. Poor Caroline would have had to call Jake and Steve. Take what was left of me home.

My feet seemed disconnected from my brain as I ran through the King's Parade, past Auntie's Tea Shop, past a vendor selling New England ice cream.

In Trinity Lane, tourists were taking pictures at the Old Schools gate. In the first court at St. Paul's, a woman smiled at me. I hurried by, seeing myself in her eyes: The mass of nearly shoulder-length auburn hair. The bright blue eyes. The straight, self-confident posture. Not the look of a woman in the grip of full-blown terror, heart thudding, sweat running down her back.

In the safety of my small room, I sat down on the bed. Put my head in my hands and began to rock back and forth. Sounds drifted up through the open window, the hammering of workmen repairing an old brick wall across the way. A group came down the lane singing Verdi's "Va Pensiero." Maybe the same Italian students.

I rocked, remembering the lump in my breast that turned out to be benign. The plane losing altitude over the roofs of Geneva, sinking so low I could people's faces on the streets. Lately I had worried about global war, jihads, the threat of a terrorist attack on the nearby nuclear plant. Never, never the possibility that someone wanted to kill *me. In the midst of life we are in death*—but not *my* death.

After a while I got up, went to the fixed basin in the corner, and washed my face in cold water. With a need to keep moving, I opened the cupboard door. No nymphet sheath for tonight. Luckily I had brought a favorite dress, a dark blue silk with a subtle pattern of green and gold. "With your hair and eyes you can carry it off," the designer had said. The wrinkles would steam out while I washed my hair. At this time of day, no one would be using the showers down the hall.

Reaching under the nightshirts, I took out my velvet jewelry case. The necklace that went with the dress was made of semi-precious stones from Brazil set in chunky gold. A present from Lewis on our twentieth anniversary.

Stockings. Shoes. Toothbrush. If I decided to leave Cambridge and go home, I would need my passport and credit cards. I pulled them from a drawer and began to throw more clothes into the bag. Finally I sat down and ripped a piece of lined paper from my notebook.

Surprise surprise. Off to London, a last-minute invitation to a fancy do at the Residency. Knew you'd approve. Hank Lausch is sending a car. I'll be staying at the company flat; you can reach me at this number. . . .

Inadequate. Caroline would be furious—but it was the best I could do.

"One step at a time" was one of my therapist's ten commandments. At exactly four o'clock I would walk across the court to the Porter's Lodge. Put the note for Caroline in her little mail slot. Wheeler would be waiting in the lane. I would jump into the maroon Jaguar. Keep my head down as we went through the King's Parade. Wininger had followed me around Cambridge, but he would need a helicopter to find me in the traffic on the M11.

fifteen

The evening rush was peaking in London, the proud center of British power. High-sprung black cabs darted past lumbering red buses, speeding the public to dinner, the theater. I took out my little travel brush and began to work on my hair. Wheeler's calm, solid presence had neutralized the panic. After an hour on the road, the choking lump of fear in my throat had started to shrink to a manageable size. The girl in the Berkeley is Cool T-shirt hadn't *seen* anyone push me. I *had* been so close to the curb that a clumsy passerby could have knocked me forward.

As the car stopped for a light at Prince Albert Road, Wheeler shook his head.

"Don't remember when I've been this late. It was that accident at Bishop's Stortford held us up."

"The mess at the roundabout didn't help." Wheeler took great pride in his work. My story about the Heathrow driver had shocked him to the core.

"I can't understand it. Last week Mr. Lausch's secretary told me to be at the terminal Sunday morning. The terminal, mind you, not the Heathrow Horizon Hotel. She gave me your flight number. Then on Saturday there was a message on my machine saying I wouldn't be needed at all. I figured Mr. Lausch must be meeting you himself."

"Does he often use a rental service?"

"Never. There's just me and sometimes Ron as backup."

"I know Ron. Did Mrs. Dean send you the message, I mean, was it her voice?"

"That I can't say. My wife takes all the messages off the machine and gives them to me. I don't understand it at all. Mr. Lausch will be very upset."

"Don't worry. I'll ask him about it tonight."

In Regent's Park, the gold dome of the Central Mosque glinted in the early evening sun. Wheeler spoke over his shoulder.

"I'm to drop you off, take your bags to the flat. Be back here at seven thirty sharp. I believe Lady Robina has made reservations for dinner."

"Oh." I studied the subtle pattern on my dress. *Another* complication if Robina was expecting me to join them for dinner.

At the gates of the Residency, a man in uniform came forward. He looked at my invitation and motioned Wheeler down the short driveway. After World War II, heiress Barbara Hutton had given this handsome but far from stately brick house to the U.S. government.

The pillared reception hall was crowded. The new ambassador and his wife were receiving in front of a huge Coromandel screen near the stairs, smiling and shaking hands. No sign of Nick.

The line moved. My name was announced.

"Emma dear." The ambassador's wife pressed my hand. Lips brushed cheeks. We hadn't met for several years. "You look marvelous, as always, but what a sad, sad time. Such a wonderful man. Such a loss."

The ambassador leaned forward and spoke under his breath. "Young Yates has been busy. Wheels are turning, rather big wheels. As soon as I can get free we'll talk."

In the beautiful green chinoiserie drawing room, the big reception was in full cry, voices rising, the men better dressed than the women. Needing something to steady my twanging nerves, I took a glass of champagne from a passing tray. In a moment the juggling act would begin. A woman in a green flowered dress stepped on my foot.

"I beg your pardon."

"It's all right," I said, and saw that Nick was making his way towards me.

"Mrs. S. There you are. Sorry, I must have missed you at the door."

I reached up and kissed him on the cheek. "Nick. I am *so* glad to see you. Really glad." In the last ten—no, twelve— years the tall, gangly boy had turned into a tall, thin man with horn-rimmed glasses. Diplomatic life hadn't done much for his clothes. His coat hung open; his tie was crooked.

"How are the boys?" he asked.

"Jake's a sophomore at Brown. Steve will be a freshman at Harvard."

"Hard to believe."

"I know. And even taller than you."

"Those little *kids,* always following us around." He pulled at his tie. "We need to talk. It'll be quieter out on the terrace."

"Lead the way." I must remember that Nick was now an adult, calling the shots, but the old mind-set still persisted. In their wrestling matches, my nephew, Davy, had tied Nick in knots.

A green and white marquee covered one end of the long terrace. Rabbits nibbled peacefully at the bottom of the sloping lawn. Nick walked to a deserted corner. He took off his glasses, blinked, and put them on again.

"First of all, you seem to have hit a nerve with the Brits, Mrs. S."

"Why do you say that?"

"After your call, I went to my legal colleague. He has ties with the FBI."

"FBI?"

"They do security over here. The CIA gathers information. As I told you on the phone, there've been some strange accidents to English scientists in the last few years. My colleague thinks losing Dr. Estes may have been a real blow."

"So I'll be talking to a top Brit police person."

"Not police, but someone with influence. As you know, a lot of work is done behind the scenes."

I put my hand on the stone balustrade. "I know about the old boy network. Nick, I need to talk to a police official. High up."

"I hear you, but put yourself in their shoes. Lewis Streat's widow has to be given red-carpet treatment; she can't be taken down to the Vine Street station and put in an interview room. My guess is, some government official picked up the phone—"

"And called his old school chum: 'Have no idea what this American wants, but do me a favor, old chap, and give her half an hour.'"

Nick laughed. "Got it, but you don't have much choice. Also, the old boy in this case happens to be a big player."

"What's his name?"

"Andrew Rodale. Lord Rodale. He consults for a Ministry.

My colleague can't be sure, but he thinks that may be a cover for one of the secret services. He says the man has clout. You'll be getting a chance to tell your story to someone who can push buttons. If he wants to."

"I see. What happens now?" No Scotland Yard commissioner, but Nick was right. I didn't have a choice.

"We get out of here pronto. We're already late. Do you have a coat?"

"No, but Hank Lausch and his wife are expecting me for dinner."

"We'd better find them."

As we began to push through the crowded green chinoiserie room, a man spoke to Nick.

"Where's your charming wife?"

"Couldn't make it tonight, sir."

At the edge of the room with pillars, Hank and Robina were standing in a small group. Hank looked happy and well fed; even the bespoke suit couldn't hide a little paunch. He turned and saw me.

"Emma. There you are. We'd about given you up."

"The traffic was awful. Thanks for sending Wheeler. A dear man."

"You're welcome. We had to come in a cab."

"My heart bleeds. Nick, this is Hank Lausch. He's with Galbraith Tech over here. Hank, Nick is with the embassy, spreading culture. I've known him since he was fifteen; his thing then was pop and pot."

Hank laughed. "How long have you been in London, Nick?"

"A little over a year, sir."

"Best place in the world to live. Robina, here's Emma."

"Emma. At last." Robina was wearing a short black and gold sari skirt and an expression of barely contained annoyance on her face. "Frightful crush. Was Wheeler late? We couldn't imagine what had happened to you. I've got a table at the Connaught."

"Robina, this is Nick Yates, an old friend, he's with the embassy here. Look, I couldn't be sorrier, but I promised ages ago to have dinner with Nick and his wife. See my new godchild—"

"And George Galbraith is joining us. I'm sure Mr. Yates will understand."

I gave her a quick look. Even for Robina, this was high-handed.

Hank, sensing trouble, took her arm. "Relax, Bina; it can't be helped. Emma decided to come down from Cambridge at the last minute."

Robina raised her eyebrows. "Indeed. But she planned ages ago to see her godchild."

I opened my mouth, then closed it. Oh God, Robina would never give up till she found out why I had lied to her. She glanced at me as if she had more to say, then shrugged her shoulders.

"I rather wish I'd known. I'll give you a ring at the flat tomorrow, Emma. Will you be going straight back to Cambridge?"

"I've got classes." True. I smiled. "Thanks, Hank, for Wheeler and the flat. I'm afraid we have to run. I want to see the baby before he goes down for the night." At least Robina wouldn't know that small babies have no schedules.

Hank put his arm around my shoulders as Nick and I moved away. "Sorry about that. Robina's in a flap tonight," he said in my ear. "The rumors about Danny Peplow and a takeover have finally reached Galbraith. He's in a royal rage. Not good for Robina's nerves. She wanted you for a buffer zone."

"You'll manage. Give him my best." No chance, now, to tell Hank about the driver at Heathrow. As we reached the front door, I looked at Nick.

"I hope you didn't mind me making myself a godmother."

"Honored. I have to say, that woman acted like losing you tonight was a major disaster. Is she always like that?"

"Not always, but she hates to be crossed and I'm a terrible liar. What now?"

"Wait for me on the steps. I told security to have the car handy."

"I won't move."

The air was blessedly quiet after the barrage of voices. An endless day, beginning with the the porter's grim words: "Never regained consciousness." Tonight's meeting meant yet another plunge into uncharted waters. For the next few hours I must concentrate on telling my story. Fall back on the old disciplines. Whatever the crisis—the wrong costume, a cast with stomach flu staggering around the stage—principal singers had to keep their concentration.

"All set, Mrs. S.?" Nick opened the passenger door of a small Ford Escort. I got in, fitting my long legs under the dashboard.

"All set. Where are we meeting this peer?"

"At the House of Lords. He's a member; he's giving us dinner there."

I turned my head. "The House of Lords? *Dinner?*"

"He's fitting us in between meetings. It seemed to work out best for him."

"For him maybe, but I thought we'd be going to an office. A *private* place where we could talk."

Nick stopped for a light. His hand drummed on the steering

wheel. "Look, Mrs. S. You called and asked me to get you together with a top person. Right?"

"Right."

"The head honchos are doing their best. They have no idea what you want, but you're the ambassador's friend and Galbraith Technologies carries heavy weight."

"Yes, but I can see exactly what's coming. I've met a few of these old boys. They think American women have awful manners. Ghastly voices."

"Aren't you being a little hard on them? Besides, you're not wearing long mink and diamonds in July. You never speak much louder than a whisper."

"All the same, he'll think my necklace is much too showy. Not that it matters if he has an open mind."

"Open to what? You haven't given anyone much to go on."

"I know. To be honest, I'm jumping in way over my head, why I'm so touchy."

"Well, at least you won't be on your own. My orders are to stick with you at dinner. Officially, as well as a friend."

"You mean, to protect a U.S. citizen? What from?"

"All we know is, there must be a reason for the big guns to go into action so soon after your call to me. Bring in this man."

"You think so?"

"I know so. Even the ambassador was surprised. Wants to be kept informed."

The traffic was still heavy as we turned away from the Thames River. Parliament Square loomed ahead. We passed Westminster Hall, the seat of ancient kings, then the Houses of Parliament, that collection of tortured Gothic Revival pinnacles, towers, flying buttresses. As we reached the massive Peer's Entrance, a helmeted policeman nodded us through a gate.

Nick slowed and pulled a large green card out of his pocket. "Your invitation. You'd better go ahead and charm His Lordship while I park."

I unwound my legs and picked up my bag. "Do my best. I just hope he isn't deaf."

"Why is that?"

"My voice. It's so low. Old people have a really hard time with my voice."

sixteen

The lobby was surprisingly small. A cozy gas fire burned in a grate. As I came in, an elderly man with medals across his chest appeared from behind a line of coatracks. I smiled and handed him my card.

"Good evening, Lord Rodale," I said.

The man gave a slight bow. "I'll let Lord Rodale know—ah, here he is," he added as a tall man in a dark pinstripe suit came forward.

"Mrs. Streat?" He held out his hand. "I'm Andrew Rodale. Very good of you to come on such short notice."

I kept the smile on my face. "I—good evening." Not doddering. Not deaf.

He glanced around. "I understood a Mr. Yates was coming with you."

"He's parking the car. The traffic from Regent's Park was terrible."

"Can be a slog, this time of night." He paused as Nick came through the door.

"Lord Rodale? I'm Nick Yates. Sorry we're late."

"Not at all. We'll go right down," and Lord Rodale led us across a blue carpet with gold stars and down a small winding staircase. I followed, giving myself a mental kick. *Why* had I assumed that Lord Rodale was old and shaky? This was a confident man with great physical presence. I must feel my way inch by inch.

The dining room was vaulted with low arches. A maître d' took us to a corner table under a large Turneresque landscape. A TV screen high on a nearby wall was showing the progress of a debate in the House upstairs.

"What will you have to drink, Mrs. Streat?"

"Cinzano, please, with ice."

"Right. Shall we order now? The turbot is rather good." A practiced manner designed to put us at ease, a junior diplomat and an American woman who had some bee in her bonnet.

As Rodale spoke to the waiter, I did a quick inventory. Dark hair, two deep vertical lines in a strong-featured face. Perceptive gray eyes set in a straight horizontal line. A tanned, muscular neck that fitted well-tailored shoulders. A hard dog to keep on the back porch.

As the waiter left us, Rodale turned to me.

"Most unfortunate, Dr. Estes' death. A brilliant man. I gather there's something about the accident you want to pass along."

"Yes, there is, but first I'd like to go back to June when my husband was killed."

"Of course. We can sort out anything that seems irrelevant."

Years of living with Lewis had taught me that men want straight facts with no embellishments. Speaking slowly, I talked about the Chinese engineer who had come to the office and been killed on the people mover. The hotel meeting with Dr. Estes. Lewis's note asking him to drop the project immediately and have security around the clock. The hit-and-run accident on a country road. My call to Dr. Estes yesterday afternoon. His death in the lane.

Andrew Rodale didn't interrupt. He seemed to be concentrating on a distant view, the squire gazing out over his fields, assessing his cattle and the weather.

Soup plates were removed. The waiter brought the turbot. Rodale put his wineglass down on the starched white cloth.

"A question. Why did you feel you had to get in touch with Dr. Estes?"

"A few weeks ago I began to wonder if that project had something to do with my husband's death."

"Was there a particular reason for this feeling?"

"Yes. There was. My husband was extremely worried when he wrote that note to Dr. Estes. I had never seen him so upset."

"Ah."

"It didn't make sense. In fact, I really came to Cambridge to talk to Dr. Estes. Ask questions. This morning, when I heard he was dead, I decided to see someone who could find out if there's a link between these two deaths and the project." I took a sip of water. The turbot was sitting like a stone in my stomach.

"I see. Very good of you to come forward with your story. Most people go out of their way to avoid trouble these days. Will you have pudding? Coffee?" Nick had said Rodale was fitting me in between meetings.

"Coffee, please." I stared at the Turneresque painting on the wall. After coffee, Lord Rodale would lead the way upstairs and leave, congratulating himself on a job well done. Later, he would make a report: "I gave her rather a good dinner and she went away quite happy."

"Lord Rodale."

"Yes?"

"The Cambridge police never came to Trinity Lane. I gather the man who killed Dr. Estes hasn't been found. I'd like to know if there *will* be a serious investigation."

Lord Rodale folded his napkin. "I can tell you that we are taking this death very seriously."

"I see." I twisted my gold wedding ring. Last night the porter had been so quick to reassure me: ". . . the police are very thorough. They'll do whatever is needed."

"Will you be looking into that project? At a very high level?"

"As I say, what you've told me has been very helpful. I'll make sure your story is heard." He raised his hand and signaled to the waiter.

As the waiter handed him a slip to sign, I sat still, clenching my fists. Lord Rodale was dismissing me with vague assurances. The whole matter might fall between official cracks. Before we left I *must* get a real commitment. I touched my necklace and made the leap.

"Just one thing," I said. "A number of Cambridge physicists do important research for Galbraith Tech. When I go back to Cambridge tomorrow, I'm going to meet with them. Find out if they knew about this project. And I mean to talk with Mrs. Estes."

Lord Rodale gave me a quick look. "Go around Cambridge asking questions? Talk to Mrs. Estes? That might not be wise. I gather she's very distraught."

"Which I can understand better than anyone. We've both had the same loss. The same shock. If no one in Cambridge has any answers, I'll go to our ambassador. He's an old friend. He thought a great deal of Lewis."

During dinner, Nick had said very little. Now he began to drum his fingers on the arms of his chair, a bystander caught in a sudden cross fire. Lord Rodale put his hands on the table. Strong, square hands with long fingers.

"Mrs. Streat. I can appreciate your feelings, but the wrong approach might do real harm. Far better to leave the investigating in the hands of trained people. Professionals who know how to make assessments and act on them."

"Oh?" I picked up my coffee cup and put it down. "Lose your temper, lose your soul," my old nurse used to say, but sometimes losing one's temper was entirely justified.

"Lord Rodale. I'm *not* a professional, but my husband and I were married for over twenty years. He had brains and judgment and integrity. I *am* going to find out who killed him. I *am* going to find about this project. No matter how long it takes or whose fingers get burned."

At the next table, a man in a dark suit and bright red socks was talking about reform in the House of Lords. I kept my eyes on the TV screen above us and waited.

After a moment Lord Rodale cleared his throat. "It seems we've reached rather an impasse. I don't want you going around Cambridge asking questions. You want assurances that Dr. Estes' death will be taken seriously, not swept under an official rug. Assurances that this project will be investigated."

"Yes. I do."

"Right." He looked at his watch again. "Tell me. Where do you go from here?"

"From here? To the company flat. The Grosvenor House flats, next to the hotel."

"I know the place. I'll drop you off on the way to my next meeting, save Mr. Yates the trouble. That should give us time to discuss our differences."

Nick blinked. He pulled at his tie. "It's no trouble for me, sir."

"Not at all, glad to do it."

"Very kind of you, but I was planning to take Mrs. Streat—"

"That's settled, then. If you're quite ready," Lord Rodale said, and stood up.

As we reached the lobby, an elderly man in evening clothes hurried towards us.

"Rodale. I've been trying to reach you all day. My committee needs an agenda for Tuesday." As they talked, Nick motioned me over to the coatracks.

"May I speak my mind, Mrs. S.?"

"Speak. Forget when I was the keeper of the zoo."

"Under the dashing peer image, that's a very tough man. If he's involved in the British scientist disasters, he may be working on the Estes case. Why he doesn't want you going around making waves."

"Then he shouldn't have been so bloody high-handed. He thought he could pump me dry and walk away. Give me nothing."

"Not much he could give you, under the circumstances."

"He didn't have to put me down. Tell me I wasn't qualified to ask questions."

"Be fair. You twisted his arm and he didn't like it. Pretty blunt, though, the way he's trying to cut me out of the loop. I wonder why. When he comes back, you'd better thank him for dinner and leave with me."

"Not hear what I've forced him to say?"

Nick took off his glasses and put them on again. "We're not talking about a tennis match, Mrs. S. You stood up to him just now, but for God's sake don't try to match wits with him again. If the Estes death is a high priority, if Rodale is working with a secret service, he doesn't want you muddying the waters."

"And just how could I muddy the waters?"

"There are ways." Nick had the pained look of a man running the last few feet of a marathon. "For starters, there's the matter of British security. Their services often work with ours, share information, but everyone wants to have the upper hand. Protect his own turf. This may be one of those cases."

"So?"

"Let's assume that Rodale is working the dark side of the street for the Brits. He was asked to see you. Let's say he got more information than he expected. Maybe a lot more. Now he can't let you go off on your own. Maybe cause trouble."

"He can't stop me from asking questions."

"I wouldn't be too sure. Worst case, you might find yourself on a plane going home. For your own protection, of course."

"For God's sake. No way can he order me out of the country. I haven't broken any laws. I'm an American citizen."

"And he's got clout. Look. You have other options. Tomorrow I'll take you to our LegAtt. See what he can do."

"And what do I say to Lord Rodale?"

"Just say you expect him to keep in touch."

"He won't be in touch; you know that. And I really do need answers."

"Which you won't get in the car or anywhere else. If he thinks you're careening around like a loose cannon, he'll stop you. And he knows how to lay on the charm."

I looked around. Lord Rodale was walking towards us, a tall, arrogant man who expected women to jump when he said jump. I squared my shoulders.

"Let him try," I said to Nick. "Just let him try."

seventeen

Across Parliament Square, the illuminated towers of Westminster Abbey rose high into the night sky. At this hour, no tourist lines waited to pass through the iron gates. There were no custodians in traditional robes walking about with watchful eyes. The souvenir shops were closed.

A small black sedan waited at the Peer's Entrance. As I got into the backseat, Lord Rodale paused and spoke in a low voice to the driver.

"Right, then, Jenkins." Lord Rodale sat down beside me and put a shabby leather briefcase on the floor. The car pulled away.

At dinner we had faced each other across a table in a lit room. Now we sat in near darkness, shoulders almost touching, the long line of his leg stretched out beside mine. He turned his head and looked at me.

"Before meeting you tonight, I asked a few questions. I gather you were a singer. Opera."

"A long time ago. I damaged my vocal folds. Why my voice is so low."

"What very bad luck. Perhaps you don't want to talk about it, but which roles did you sing?"

"My first real role was Zerlina. *Don Giovanni.*"

" 'Vedrai, carino.' A lovely aria."

"It is." So he knew his opera. "I should have stayed longer with Mozart, but I was pushed too hard. People kept telling me I had a Verdi voice and I longed for Verdi."

"The great conflicts between church and state as well as the personal tragedies."

"Actually, it was *Manon Lescaut,* not a Verdi, that did me in. I rolled around on the stage singing 'Sola, perduta, abbandonata' with a sore throat. Someone should have told me to go back to the dressing room and wire my jaw together. Today the surgeons would have done better."

"A terrible blow for you."

"It was." I sat back. Charm was being applied with a shovel, but it was no hardship to be driven around London with a man who led a fascinating double life. The title, the seat in the House of Lords—but under the surface of good tailor, good looks, and deep voice, this was a hunter working the dark side of the street. In any case, the playing field was even. He had taken a long look at my legs as I got into the car.

As we waited for a light, I looked out. We had passed Buckingham Palace, but instead of going towards Hyde Park Gate we were doubling back on Piccadilly.

"I don't know London that well," I said, "but aren't we going around in circles?"

He shifted his leg as if it was hurting. I had noticed that he walked with a slight limp.

"Jenkins is just following orders. I needed time to tell you what couldn't be said in front of Mr. Yates."

"I see."

A pause, as if he was searching for words.

"Mrs. Streat. First of all, by giving you this information I'm breaking every security rule in the book. Putting my neck on the block. I'll have to trust you not pass on what I tell you to Yates. These cultural chaps have an interesting way of turning out to be CIA."

I hesitated. "I suppose that depends on the information," I said, trying to picture Nick as an undercover CIA agent. He was intelligent, certainly, and that disheveled appearance could be deceptive.

"Fair enough." Another pause. "Very well. About Dr. Estes. Police pathologists did a postmortem this morning. They say his death was caused by a severe blow to the head."

"I know *that*. I saw him lying on the cobblestones."

"The pathologists say it wasn't the fall that killed him. His attacker struck him on the left temple with great expertise. It could have been done with one quick blow as Dr. Estes lay on the ground. The case is now being treated as a homicide."

Homicide. Murder. The deliberate taking of life. I stared at the wiry cords in the back of the driver's neck. I mustn't think about Lewis until I was alone in the flat. Lord Rodale cleared his throat.

"This is a shock, I'm afraid, even if it doesn't come as a complete surprise."

I didn't answer. It would take time to make sense out of confusion and anger. Who had wanted Lewis dead? Wanted it enough to *kill* him?

"Mrs. Streat?"

"I—it's not a shock. Not really. Until now I was thrashing around in the dark. Suspecting the worst. In a way, it's a relief to know."

"Understandable."

"Do you think—is it possible that the same man killed my husband?"

"Early days for that. So far the killer or killers have managed to cover their tracks extremely well. They may be part of a well-organized group working closely together or they may be a network of isolated cells. We'll be using every resource to find them. Because of your husband, there'll be investigations on both sides of the pond. Your people joining forces with ours. I believe this is what you wanted."

"Yes. It is." I closed my eyes. From now on I could sit back. My part was over. The two deaths were connected and official machinery was in charge.

". . . I should remind you again that this is extremely sensitive information. I'm relying on your discretion."

"You can. Look. I . . . really appreciate your telling me the truth about Dr. Estes. For taking the chance that I could be trusted."

"You seem to be deeply involved in both of these deaths. I felt you had a right to know." A pause. "As well, your instinct to find a link was very perceptive, but to go around asking questions about that project could be counterproductive."

I opened my eyes. "Why is that?"

"To find these bad actors we have to work quickly and quietly. Keep the press off the trail. Crime reporters are like bloodhounds. They hang around police stations and hospitals; they have paid informers. If they hear that Lewis Streat's widow is asking questions about Dr. Estes' work, they'll want to know why."

The car was passing Purdey's. Thomas Goode's. The Spy Shop. Familiar sights in this bewildering night. In a moment we would be at the flats. I leaned forward.

"Before I get out, there's a question I have to ask. Dr. Estes sounded so frightened when I told him my husband's death might not have been an accident. Badly frightened. It was almost as if he himself had been threatened."

"Go on."

"Five hours later he was killed. Now—I have to wonder if my call had anything to do with his death. If his line could have been bugged."

Lord Rodale hesitated. He crossed his arms. "Difficult. Let me say this: You must never blame yourself for making that call. My view is that his days were numbered. His attacker just had to move faster."

"Oh God. You mean the line *was* bugged?"

"This morning Cambridge Force went over the Estes house with a fine-tooth comb. They found state-of-the-art devices. Nothing we've ever seen before. The same type of devices may have been placed in the hotel suite when your husband and Dr. Estes talked in June."

"And they may have been in Lewis's office in New York."

"It's a serious problem. Those damned little devices are what keeps these criminals one jump ahead of us."

We were at the corner of Reeves Mews. Lord Rodale turned towards me. He cleared his throat.

"In the light of what you now know, let's go over this once more. You rang Dr. Estes Sunday afternoon around half past four. You asked him questions about his project. You told him you suspected foul play in the matter of your husband's death. Right?"

"Right."

"I don't want to alarm you, but we must face facts. Because the line was bugged, you are connected to the two deaths and the project. That means that you're at risk."

"But I *don't* know anything about the project. It's *why* I came over and asked questions."

"Granted, but these people may *think* you know too much. See you as a threat." A pause. "I'm afraid there's only one solution. You must go home. Tomorrow. Our security will pick you up at the flat and take you to Heathrow. We'll arrange for you to fly back to New York. With an escort, of course."

There was a small tear in the leather seat beside me. I pressed the edges together. Back to square one. Nick had warned me: "If he thinks you're careening around like a loose cannon, he'll stop you. And he knows how to lay on the charm." Once in the car, opera talk to soften me up. Then the shared information. For a few moments he had seemed sympathetic and concerned. Now the push to hustle me out of the country. I began to swing one foot.

"Please don't go to any trouble," I said evenly. "I'd rather make my own plans."

"You're going back to Cambridge?"

"I may. Or I may stay in London for a few days." Tomorrow, without fail, I must tell Nick and his legal colleague about Wininger.

"I'm afraid that won't do. You may be a target. You must leave the country. As soon as possible."

The car was reaching the cul-de-sac that led to the Grosvenor House hotel and the adjacent flats. Lord Rodale put his hands on his knees.

"Perhaps I haven't made myself clear. These are clever, vicious people playing for high stakes. There are dozens of ways to kill in a crowd. Poison pens. Bullets the size of a fingernail. Two seconds of contact and the attacker walks away. You'd be extremely foolish to put yourself at risk."

"I understand," I said, and touched my sore shoulder. Lord Rodale ought to know that someone had tried to push me under a tour bus on Trinity Street; the wheels had missed me by inches. Instead, my foot swung faster. This high-handed peer of the realm was not going to tank over me. Send me home Air Express.

The car was pulling up to the small Flats Entrance. A few hundred feet away, in front of the hotel, taxis and cars were arriving; the top-hatted doorman was running up and down the steps. I leaned down and picked up my handbag.

"Thank you for dinner. The turbot *was* very good. And thank you again for telling me about Dr. Estes. I won't pass it along to Nick Yates. Anyone."

"Right." The clipped tone of controlled anger. He got out. Jenkins reached in to help me.

"Mind your head, madam."

"I will. Good-bye, Lord Rodale."

"Good-bye, Mrs. Streat."

The concierge nodded as I came into the small lobby. "Good evening, Mrs. Streat. Very nice to see you again. Your bags are in the flat. Dennis will take you up."

"Thanks. It's nice to be back."

An elderly porter came with me to the elevators. As we waited, the floor indicator began to swing wildly. Suddenly the doors opened and two beautiful dark-skinned children came tumbling out, shrieking with laughter.

"An Arab family on the eighth floor," Dennis said in a mournful voice as we went up. "Games in the elevator. Bodyguards. Comings and goings at all hours."

Once in the flat, he shuffled around, pointing out the small kitchen, the drinks cupboard, the button to turn on the gas fire.

"I won't need a fire," I said, giving him a large tip and herding him towards the door.

The flat was designed for convenience, not show. No exotic smell or pink velvet or Louis Quinze gilt chairs; Robina's decorator had settled for sensible repro furniture and neutral upholstery. Flowers from Hank and Robina—an arrangement of daisies, larkspur, and summer stock—stood on the fake Georgian piecrust table.

I went into the bedroom, opened my bag, and pulled out the thin white T-shirt I wore at night. The alarm clock, the picture of Lewis and the boys taken in another carefree, protected world.

The flat smelled strongly of fresh enamel paint. I coughed and went to open a window. A fly was stuck in the new white paint on the sill, moving its legs feebly, beyond help.

Below, in the cul-de-sac, limousines were arriving at the Grosvenor House hotel. There must be a big party under way. I watched, trying to ignore the feeling that I had overreacted in the car. Rodale *had* put his neck on the block by telling me the truth about Dr. Estes' death. The invasive devices *did* have me in their sights. But then he had issued orders like a boot camp sergeant: "There's only one solution. You must go home. Tomorrow." If only he had said, "Look, it's up to you, but it might be safer to go home," I'd be boarding a plane tomorrow. Instead I had dug in my heels like a head-tossing teenager.

The doorman was blowing a whistle, waving for the next

taxi in line. I shut my eyes, thinking. No way in the world was I going back to Cambridge until the killer was found. Tomorrow I must talk to Nick. I could stay here in the flat. Or—I pushed back my hair, testing a new idea. Last week in Manchester, my sister-in-law Cassia had talked about her daughter, my niece, a rising young singer. "I wish you'd go over to Paris and see Vanessa," Cassia had said. "She'd love it. She's singing at the Opera Bastille." And Cassia had given me Vanessa's schedule.

Paris. I hadn't been there for years, but for me Paris meant special light on cream-colored buildings. A city where good food and wine were staples and beautification was a cult. Vanessa would be pleased—and after this terrible day I deserved to *wallow* in pleasure. I crossed the room, picked up the telephone, and dialed the concierge.

"It's Mrs. Streat. I'd like to get a reservation on a Eurostar train tomorrow afternoon."

"For Brussels or Paris? First Class?"

"Paris. First Class." I could hear my sister Dolly's voice: "They say it's safe to go under the channel, but how do they know?"

"I'll take care of it right away, Mrs. Streat."

"Oh, and I'll need a hotel room, I'm not sure for how long. A single will be fine. One of those small hotels, not the Ritz."

"I'll see what I can do."

After a moment, I went back to the window and stood there, rubbing my arm; it was still hurting from the sudden hard pull that had saved me from going under the bus. Lord Rodale would be furious when he heard I had gone off alone. "These are clever, vicious people . . . There are dozens of ways to kill in a crowd. . . ." But even vicious people wouldn't dare try to kill again so soon. I would put on a scarf and dark glasses. Slip out of the flat by the service elevator and walk to South Audley Street. Take a taxi to Waterloo Station.

The line of cars below had slowed. The doorman was standing still, slapping his gloved hands together. In the distance, a siren wailed, a warning of pain and disaster. Below me on the sill, the fly had stopped moving. A sticky, lingering death.

Sheer exhaustion should have knocked me out the moment my head hit the pillow. Instead, I lay awake, leg muscles twitching, having second thoughts about Paris. It was childish to take chances because of a knee-jerk reaction to a man's arrogance. I *would* go home, but my embassy could make the arrangements.

For an endless time I did deep breathing. Added another two feet to my new herbaceous border. Rearranged my bedroom. Thought about Vanessa's opera. I knew *Don Carlo* well. In San Francisco I had struggled with the role of Elisabeth, the star-crossed French queen; I could still feel the weight of the jeweled costumes.

After the performance, the hangers-on and guests would meet in a Green Room and sip champagne from plastic glasses. The principals, makeup removed, would come down from a shared high. Go off to sign autographs at the stage door. Go off to parties, private little suppers. Some would just go to bed, saving their voices for the next performance. This was Vanessa's life, and she might not be all that glad to see me. We were close when she started to make a name for herself. She had wanted my advice then. Not now. And losing one's voice sent a message no young singer wanted to hear.

At one o'clock, I gave up and got out of bed. My eyes felt raw; the ache in my arm had spread to my shoulder. The flat was silent, the street noises faint; no cars and taxis hurried around the cul-de-sac.

I went to the tiny kitchen, pulled out a saucepan, and heated a cup of long-life milk. Drank it and went back to bed, still tense and restless. In my frenzied packing, I had left my sleeping pills in Cambridge. A mistake that saved my life.

Experts on biochemicals estimated that I couldn't have lived until morning. I remember turning over in bed and seeing streaks of brilliant light zigzag through my head, as if my eyes were disconnecting from my brain. I stood up, and the floor tilted like the deck of a boat.

I was barely conscious of staggering towards the foyer door. My numb fingers struggled to turn the knob. I took a few steps into the hall and fell facedown on the red carpet.

I was lucky. Five minutes later a foreign correspondent just back from Pakistan came up in the elevator. He was exhausted from a twenty-four-hour flight and was heading for a bath and a bed. The sight of a woman's body lying in the hall gave him no pleasure, but help was summoned. I was lifted, covered with blankets, given oxygen. Sounds around me faded away, but through the growing paralysis I could hear my sister Dolly's voice:

"She's too young to have a stroke . . . can't trust foreign doctors . . . worse, no decent hospitals over there."

eighteen

Tuesday, July 14

The lake water was brown and murky. I swam towards the surface, away from the soft, leechy bottom. My baby was being born, but something was wrong. A labor nurse was holding my hand.

"You're safe, Mrs. Streat. It's over. You're safe." A woman was standing there. Not the labor nurse. Not a hospital. This woman was holding a flowered china cup.

"Ah, you're awake. Here's coffee. You'll be the better for something hot inside you."

I lay still, then moved my legs. The numbness was gone. I raised my head. The woman moved the cup closer.

"Just a few sips, love. I'll hold you up." An Irish voice with the lilt of my old nurse, sweet Biddy McGee, but this stranger had freckles and frizzy sandy hair.

The coffee was strong and hot. I swallowed and my head began to clear. After a moment, I looked around. The large room was filled with heavy Victorian furniture. The white silk lampshades needed straightening.

"Where?" A ragged little croak of a voice.

"You're in South Kensington, Mrs. Streat. The house belongs to a friend of Lord Rodale's. When she's in Majorca, he has the use of it. I'm Detective Inspector Eileen Grady."

Majorca. Inspector. Police, but not in uniform. She was wearing a saggy beige knit suit. I looked down and saw that I was still in my white T-shirt. My tongue was swollen. My skin was sticky, but my brain was beginning to work.

"Stroke. Fell down."

"Ah, not a stroke, praise God." She took the empty cup and put it on the bedside table. "It's poisoned you were." Poisoned. It took a moment to process the thought.

"Hot milk. Couldn't sleep."

"Not the milk, love. You inhaled poison. There was a time-release chemical in your closet beside the extra pillow. A small can marked Air-freshener. Luckily you got yourself out before any lasting damage was done. You were taken to hospital; then we brought you here."

Extra pillow . . . small can . . . I rolled over on my side, needing to sleep. The woman put her hand on my shoulder.

"Sorry, love, but you have to get up."

"No."

"Cruel, that's what it is. I'd have let you sleep it out, but you're wanted at Lord Rodale's house. He needs a word."

I lay still. "No clothes," I muttered. The concierge must have told Lord Rodale about my plans to go Paris. I was going to be lectured like a teenage runaway.

"Your clothes are here. It's nine o'clock. Lord Rodale's personal assistant has been on the line three times. I told him you couldn't be rushed, not for the Queen of England, but that was two hours ago."

"Need to sleep." I buried my face in the pillows.

She pulled back the covers. "Another physicist was killed last night in Cambridge. There's a flap on, everyone working around the clock. Up with you now, and we'll get you sorted out."

Jenkins and the black sedan waited in the street. Beyond the front door, the square was quiet and peaceful; a leafy central garden was surrounded by identical white Regency houses with small balconies and iron railings. Discreet. Anonymous.

A man went by, pulled along by a large Doberman. I shrank back and gripped the railing. Jenkins gave the man a sharp look and opened the car door. I got in, followed by Eileen Grady, the soft-voiced detective inspector. She had put me back together again with hot showers, massage, and humor. I was weak, aching in every muscle, but functioning. Jenkins started the car.

"Good morning, Mrs. Streat."

"Good morning," I said, and sat back. The black linen trouser suit was a mass of wrinkles; whoever packed my things had rolled it into a tight ball. My hair was washed and clean, but no amount of makeup could camouflage the dark circles under my eyes.

As we left the square, Inspector Grady turned to me. "Lord Rodale asked that you be told about the physicist, Dr. Lineham. It'll save time."

"Tell me," I said, closing my eyes against the bright sun.

"I should warn you, it's not a pretty story. Last night Dr. Estes' widow, Joanna Estes, went to a Dr. Lineham's house on Jesus Green. She was the one who found the body."

I touched my throat. "She didn't need that, not after what she's been through."

"Ah, she didn't. Yesterday after she heard her husband was a homicide victim, she went into high hysterics. A constable told me the screams would have raised the dead. Cambridge Force put minders in the house, but just after eleven last night she slipped out the back door and walked to Jesus Green. Two of the constables on duty followed her in the car. She went into the house. A minute later she came out howling like a banshee. One constable pulled her into the car before the neighbors came running. The other went in. He found Dr. Lineham in bed with his throat cut and . . . there was other mutilation."

Throat cut. Mutilation. Horror was spreading like a malignant virus. I looked out of the window. In Brompton Road, shoppers were streaming into Harrods, normal people going about their business in a normal world.

"Mrs. Estes was sedated and put to bed. A woman detective was called in this morning, an expert at getting frightened people to talk. Mrs. Estes acted as if one word would send her straight to the hangman. Now she's gone silent. Not a word out of her."

I turned my head. "What did they expect? To walk in and find a man dead, it's no wonder she's in shock. Did she know him well?"

"There's talk in Cambridge that they were lovers."

My hands jerked up. "Lovers? He was her *lover?*" Joanna Estes had answered my call, a pleasant voice on the phone. I had thought of her with sympathy while the porter told the Master of St. Paul's about the accident.

"It seems the next-door neighbor can see over the Estes' wall from a bedroom window. The neighbor told Cambridge Force inspectors that Dr. Lineham often went to the house nights when Dr. Estes was away. Slipped through the garden and in through the kitchen door."

"My God."

"The inspectors suspect that Mrs. Estes is holding back information. An unbalanced woman altogether. Much younger than Dr. Estes. This was his third marriage. She was playing viola in a second-rate orchestra in Sheffield when he met her."

"What about family? Friends?"

"No one has come."

"No one at all?"

"So I'm told. Our sources say Dr. Lineham was bisexual, a second-rate scientist. Heavily in debt, therefore a prime target for blackmailers. We need to find out if Dr. Lineham was a middleman passing on information to criminals, or if he had a hand in Dr. Estes' death. Using Mrs. Estes as an accomplice." She paused. "I understand your husband and Dr. Estes worked together. Did you know Mrs. Estes?"

"I talked to her once on the phone, but we never met," I said, trying to put myself in the place of a woman who had lost her husband and maybe her lover in two days. A woman who had no friends and was being grilled by the police. No wonder she was afraid to talk.

We were passing the American Embassy in Grosvenor Square, an unprepossesing building decorated with spread eagles above the entrance. Right now Nick might be sitting in his office, wondering when he'd hear from me. Last night I had flounced off and plummeted straight into trouble.

The car was turning into a side street. As we cut behind a row of narrow town houses, Jenkins spoke over his shoulder.

"We're using the rear entrance today, Inspector. Just a precaution."

A neat flagged walk separated the backs of the houses. Inspector Grady escorted me to a black-painted door. It opened before she could knock.

"Good morning, madam." The elderly butler was wearing a morning coat and gray striped trousers. I followed him into a larger hall; the walls were lined with paintings of racehorses hung on velvet cords. In the distance, a telephone was ringing. A door opened and I had a quick glimpse of men sitting at a long table covered with papers. The butler went to a tall mahogany door across the hall and stood back.

"Lord Rodale will be with you in a moment, madam."

"Thank you." As the butler left, I went to a deep sofa and sat down. My neck was stiff. My legs felt heavy, my head ached, but once the lecture was over I could go back to bed. Block out this new chapter of violence.

After a moment, I looked around. The linings of the faded maroon curtains were torn. The yellow stains on the carpet looked like ancient dog pee. The brass fender needed polishing. A neglected, dreary room with not a flower in sight. Was there a Lady Rodale who never left the country?

"Mrs. Streat." Today Andrew Rodale was wearing a tweed coat with patches at the elbows. Brown suede shoes. Brothel creepers, Robina called that kind of shoe. He drew up a straight chair and sat down. His face was drawn, eyes pulled down at the corners as if he'd had no sleep.

"I'm extremely sorry about last night. A very bad experience for you. I would have come to Kensington this morning, but two deaths in two days means we're stretched very thin." He gave me a quick look. "I'll try not to keep you long. Do you feel able to answer a few questions?"

"Yes."

"Good. First, who knew you were going to the flat?"

"Yesterday morning I called the manager of the London office, Hank Lausch. I asked him if I could have the flat. That's the only—no, I left the flat number in a message for my godmother."

"Left it where?"

"At St. Paul's College, in the Porter's Lodge. I put it in the slots we use for mail."

"Could anyone else have seen it?"

"I—yes. I didn't have an envelope."

"So it's possible that someone in Cambridge read this note and followed you to London. Went to the flat." He rubbed his forehead. "As it turns out, I should have laid on tight security for you."

I concentrated on the brown suede shoes. "With hindsight, I should have told you that someone in Cambridge has been trying to kill me. I thought it was my imagination, but now—"

As I talked, he listened. When I finished he got to his feet, limped across the room, and went to stand under a full-length portrait that hung over the carved mantel. A little slave in livery peered up round eyed at the haughty ancestor wearing white knee breeches, scarlet coat, and sword.

"We'll check out that fellow Wininger," Rodale said. "Now that we know you're at risk you'll be well protected—yes, Ian?"

"Sorry to interrupt, sir." A young man with pink cheeks and a halo of fair curls stood in the doorway. "Sir James is on the scrambler."

"I'll ring him in a moment, tell him."

"Right. Glad you're safe, Mrs. Streat."

"Ian Trefusis, my PA," Lord Rodale said as the young man left. "A computer wizard with the face of a cherub. He's working around the clock with Wiesbaden, Interpol, the Data Centre, tracking down every known high-tech spy, every lead. At thirty you don't need much sleep, harder at forty-nine." He stopped. Men were talking in the hall.

". . . off to Fleet Street . . . if he feels strongly, Sir James could hold the press off with a D notice. A matter of national security."

". . . a top priority, to get our hands on the notebook."

". . . all in agreement. The notebook is key."

The voices faded. I touched my neck and looked at Rodale.

"Are they talking about Dr. Estes' notebook? The one he kept in his vest pocket?"

He frowned. "You know about that notebook?"

"My husband told me it's where Dr. Estes put his latest theories—oh God." I pulled myself up from the cushions. "Those teenagers in Trinity Lane. They saw Dr. Estes being knocked down. They said the man was bending over him, they thought he was looking for a wallet, but it must have been the notebook. We don't know if they actually saw the man take anything. The police never came."

"Mistakes were made, I'm afraid."

"A lot of mistakes. Lewis wanted Dr. Estes to stop the project. He said it was *dangerous*. Now we'll never know *why* it was dangerous. Never." I lay back, feeling exposed and vulnerable, as if layers of my skin had been stripped away.

"Wait." Lord Rodale raised his hand. "That's not quite the case, Mrs. Streat."

"Not the case?"

"Please listen. Part of my job is to smoke out spies who infiltrate this country and steal our research. A month ago I went to Dr. Estes with questions about a former colleague. Fortunately he kept my number. He rang me a few minutes after he talked to you."

I stared. "He called *you*?"

"He suspected someone was getting into his house, looking at his work in progress. Last Saturday he went down to London for a Royal Society meeting. Before he left, he set a trap. When he came back on Sunday the papers in his desk had been moved. Then out of the blue you rang and told him that your husband's death might not have been an accident. By the grace of God he had sense enough not to use his phone. Go to a call box and tell me he had almost finished the first concept of an extremely sensitive project. Ask for protection until he could get it into the right hands. Do you follow?"

"I think so." My head was hurting again.

"Once again I'll have to trust in your absolute discretion. Dr. Estes told me, in layman's terms, that he was working on a revolutionary use of laser. A concept that would make our present weapons systems obsolete. A breakthrough that would turn the world as we know it upside down."

I pressed my hands against my head. "Are you saying *all* our weapons? All? Nuclear?"

"Think of it this way. Historically, guns replaced arrows. Fission replaced guns. Laser could replace fission. In the hands of the wrong people, this project would become a deadly global threat. The stakes are very high. It's why you've been attacked. These people can't afford to leave any loose threads—*Christ.*" I jumped as Rodale hit the palm of his hand with his fist. "Special Branch from London was on the way, but I should have had local constables go straight to the Estes house. Given them orders to keep the bloody fool locked in."

"You didn't know."

"My mistake. He was killed. The notebook has disappeared. Lineham can't be questioned. By tomorrow there may be headlines: 'Police Attempt to Hide Deaths of Brilliant Physicists.' 'Sex Orgy in Academia.' The Prime Minister may be asked some very hard questions about national security. Who is destroying our best brains. Why the police haven't made arrests."

I didn't answer. This was not the arrogant man in the pin-stripe suit whose high-handedness had goaded me into head-strong behavior. This dazed woman in wrinkled clothes wasn't the confident Emma Streat who had tried to level the playing field. He ran his hand over his forehead.

"That's the situation," he said abruptly. "It's not pleasant. Now, before there's another interruption we need to talk about your plans." He shifted his weight to the other foot and looked at me. "My mother tells me I'm high-handed. My colleagues say I have a one-track mind. Last night I behaved like a drill sergeant barking out orders. A bully prefect. I apologize." I hesitated, but only for a second. It was important to meet him halfway.

"*My* mother would have said I overreacted. Don't worry, I'll go home, there's no choice, but first I need to get in touch with my godmother in Cambridge."

"Of course. Inspector Grady will take you back to Kensington. You can sleep while we lay on the details."

I didn't answer. Instead of this dreary London drawing room I could see Lewis sitting alone in the back of the plane. A man who had started a world-altering project and was having second thoughts about its implications. A man agonizing about the danger to his country, the future of our sons. Jake who looked like Lewis. Steve who had my dark red hair. Lewis was dead. He couldn't help them now. I could.

"Lord Rodale."

"Yes?"

"Last night at dinner I told you I wanted to see Mrs. Estes."

"Indeed. You twisted my arm."

"Inspector Grady says Mrs. Estes won't talk to the police."

"True. A serious problem. Our best people can't get a word out of her."

"Not surprising, if they're treating her like a suspect."

"Which may be the case."

"It may, but put yourself in her shoes. Her husband and her lover have been murdered. She's a prisoner in her own house. Terrifying her won't work. She needs sympathy. Kindness."

His lips tightened. "What are you suggesting?"

"Before flying home, I'd like to go back to Cambridge. I think I could get through to her. Ask questions. I know it sounds crazy, but don't forget, Mrs. Estes answered the phone when I called Sunday afternoon. She knows who I am. She doesn't connect me with the police."

"That may be, but seeing her is just not on. Far too complicated."

"Then tell your experts they'd better try a different approach. She needs to understand that she can help herself by telling the truth." I stopped. Ian was back at the door.

"Sorry, sir. Sir James again. Urgent, he says."

"I'll be with him directly."

As Ian left, Lord Rodale went to a long window. Put his hand on a frayed maroon curtain. I waited, aware that I was a very small cog in a large wheel. There was no reason to think I could do better than the experts—but at least I could identify with this woman. Identify with blind, helpless fear. Rodale turned.

"Very well. It's on. Using you is bound to churn up official waters, but at this point we're racing the clock." He paused. "One thing."

"What?"

"You've had a bad shock. There may be delayed reaction from the trauma. Are you sure you can make the effort?"

"A few weeks ago I couldn't have. I'd have jumped into bed and pulled the covers over my head."

"But now?"

"It's something I have to do. For my husband. My boys."

"I'll speak to Inspector Grady."

The worn carpet was moving like waves. The sofa was deep, even for a tall woman. I pulled myself up and stood there, swaying.

"Steady." Rodale crossed the room and put out a hand. Suddenly I wanted to bury my face in the tweed coat with elbow patches. Be held close against his neck. Hear him say: "You've been very brave. Now you need looking after."

Holding my elbow, he led me to the door. As we went into the hall, he hesitated, then looked down at me. The intent, searching look. His hand tightened on my arm.

"You're a remarkable woman, Mrs. Streat. And you have the most beautiful eyes."

nineteen

As Jenkins drove up the M11 towards Cambridge, Inspector Grady outlined the plans: "We don't want you seen in Cambridge, so the sooner we leave the better. We'll be liaising with Cambridge Force. While you're with Mrs. Estes, a policewoman will collect your clothes. The Chief Superintendent will go to St. Paul's College to meet your godmother and the museum coordinator. They'll be told there was a kidnap threat in London and the decision was made to escort you home today."

"That won't play with my godmother, I can tell you that right now. She'll want to hear it from me. See me, or at least find out where I am."

"The Chief can handle that. No one argues with him. The coordinator will be asked to hand over paperwork concerning the seminar. There'll be thorough background checks, starting with Mr. Wininger."

"I'll write a note to my godmother. That might help."

The brave morning sun was retreating behind an overcast of

gray clouds. As we came into the outskirts of Cambridge, I smoothed the wrinkles in the linen trousers. From now on I must keep an open mind. Mrs. Estes, it seemed, had let her husband's colleague into the house at night. The two of them might have made love, gone through desk drawers, copied papers, then passed them on—madness to think I could force facts out of this unstable woman. I turned to Eileen Grady, needing distraction.

"Tell me," I said. "How did you get to be an inspector? It must take a *lot* of training."

She laughed. "I did my share of walking the streets in uniform." She told me that she had been born in Skibbereen, county Cork, and had come to England as a child. Her husband had walked out eight years ago and she had fourteen-year-old twins. "Hellions, they are. Luckily my mum can cope while I'm on duty."

"I don't know what I would have done without you today."

"You'd have managed." She paused. "I have to say, Mrs. Streat, it isn't everyone who could pull themselves together and make this trip. Not after what you've been through."

"To be honest, I'm surprising myself. Six weeks ago I'd have been a basket case. I must be getting used to trouble."

We passed a Pizza Hut, a WH Smith bookseller, a Boots chemist. As we reached a residential neighborhood and started down a quiet street, Jenkins slowed.

"It's the next house, Inspector," he said. "I'll let you off here. Less noticeable, in case anyone's watching the house." Wiry little Jenkins seemed to wear a number of hats.

The Estes house was gray stucco, built in 1920s Georgian style, hidden behind a high concrete wall. The planting near the front steps was sparse and overgrown, exuding a strong feeling of neglect.

A woman in a police uniform opened the door. We stepped into the narrow front hall. I glanced around with a sinking feeling. The wall paper was dingy tan and cream stripes. The house smelled of musty books and—faintly—of cat.

"You made good time, Inspector," the woman said.

"There wasn't much traffic. Does Mrs. Estes know a Mrs. Streat is coming?"

"It seemed best not to tell her. She's down the hall in the Florida room."

"Is she responsive?"

"She's not speaking. Not eating."

As we went down the hall, I looked at Eileen Grady. "Where will you be?"

"Just outside the door. I've been given special permission to tape in case she talks. Good luck."

The misnamed Florida room had sliding glass doors that opened onto a sad little imitation of a Japanese garden. The hanging begonias had gone to rubbery stalks and needed watering. Joanna Estes was sitting inside on a rusty green chair, hugging her chest. All I could see was a thin back, narrow shoulders, long uncombed dark hair. She was wearing a faded pink man's shirt. I swallowed. Whatever she had done, this was a woman in deep distress, receiving no support from family or friends. I must concentrate on getting information, not sit in judgment. Convince her that we were both victims and that I wasn't here to take her away in handcuffs.

"Mrs. Estes?" No answer. After a moment, I sat down on a flaking iron bench and began again. "Mrs. Estes, I'm Emma Streat. I called your husband Sunday afternoon. You answered the phone. We talked." Silence.

"You may not know this," I said, "but our husbands worked together on projects. His name was Lewis Streat. He was killed in June. It looked like a hit-and-run accident, but now there's evidence that he was murdered. Maybe by the same person who killed your husband." The shoulders moved slightly. I folded my hands.

"The same person—or people—tried to kill me last night. Now the police are guarding me around the clock. I hate being watched all the time. I guess you hate it, too, but until the people who killed our husbands are found, you and I are both in danger. Terrible danger."

Suddenly she turned. The face was thin and white, with the blank eyes of a frightened child deep in the grip of a nightmare.

"I didn't kill Samuel." A hoarse whisper. "Neither did Charles. We were at the Cambridge Arts Picture House that night. There were witnesses." She stopped. I let out my breath. Oh God, the woman was *talking*. Actually talking. I must speak slowly, not rush ahead.

"The police know that," I said. "They know very well that you didn't kill him."

She stared at the fan over my head as if she hadn't heard. "Samuel only cared about his work. His friends didn't like me. There were times I hated him—I hate his house—but I never wanted him dead. Never." Another silence. I sat still, beginning to see a picture. A dismal house, an unhappy marriage. It would take great inner resources to be married to a dedicated genius—but now I must focus on stolen papers.

"Mrs. Estes, the police are trying to find this killer. Quickly, before he kills again. They need our help."

She turned her face away. Her shoulders were shaking. "My help? For a moment—but you're from the police. You're trying to trap me." Her voice was rising. A bad sign.

"I'm *not* police. I'm *not* trying to trap you," I said. "I'm

American. I live in Connecticut. My husband was the CEO of Galbraith Technologies. I've told the police all I know about his murder in June. Now they want to talk to you; that's all they—"

"You're lying. I know what you want. A suspect. Someone to blame. Whatever I say, you'll take me to prison."

I closed my eyes. The pain in my head was getting worse. "Believe me, please. I'm *not* police. The police don't want to hurt you. What they want from you is very simple. They've been told that Dr. Lineham came here to see you. They want to know if he ever tried to see your husband's papers."

She gave me a wild look. "Spies. The old cat next door. She liked Alice, his second wife. When I married Samuel she tried to turn everyone against me. I wasn't good enough. Now it's the police—"

"Mrs. Estes, the police don't give a damn if you and Dr. Lineham slept together. That's your business. No one can arrest you for that. They want—they *need* to know if Dr. Lineham ever tried to see your husband's work. His papers. His notebooks."

". . . sitting up in her bedroom night after night, spying on me."

I put my hand to my head. "Listen to me. The police aren't interested in neighborhood gossip. They're trying to find a murderer. Your husband did important work. Someone killed him to get that work."

"Oh God." Joanna Estes bent double, as if I had hit her. "Oh God, Samuel could be so cruel, so cruel. He was always putting Charles down. He kept Charles from being made a member of the Royal Society."

"But did . . . Charles . . . ever have a chance to look at your husband's papers?"

"I should never have married Samuel. After the first month he began to treat me like a char, someone to wait on him hand and foot. I was stupid; I didn't do things *his* way." Tears were seeping through her fingers. My own eyes began to sting.

"Your husband sounds like a difficult man," I said. "Brilliant men often are. But did Charles go through the house the nights he was here? Did he ask to see your husband's work?"

Joanna Estes straightened. She kept her hands over her face, but the words began to pour out.

"We made love. Afterwards he gave me sleeping pills to calm me down. When I woke up he was always gone. It was wrong, what we did, I knew that, but I needed him."

"You were unhappy. Lonely."

"After the police came and told me about Samuel, that he was dead, I tried to reach Charles. He didn't answer his phone. I went to his house. He was wearing his white silk pajamas. He was lying in . . . the smell. The blood. The things they did to him." She began to pound the arms of the chair with her fists, sliding into hysteria. I held my hands tightly in my lap, resisting the instinct to reach out and touch her.

". . . he didn't love me. He was weak; he told lies. He collected early Turner watercolors that cost a fortune. He always needed money."

"He always needed money?" What had Eileen Grady said? "Heavily in debt, therefore a prime target for blackmailers." I grasped the sides of the bench and leaned forward. "Do you think—would Dr. Lineham have copied your husband's work to get money?"

"Oh God, Samuel found out about us. He came back from London that Sunday morning and locked himself in his study. When he came out he was very angry. He told me to start packing my things. That night he had to go to a dinner at his college. The Master rang me and I went to the hospital. I never meant him to die."

"No. You didn't."

"The police came. They turned the house upside down; they even looked in the cat's litter box. They found listener things. They acted as though I was a criminal."

"Asking questions is their job."

"They frightened me. I couldn't tell them about sleeping with Charles. About the sleeping pills. Charles didn't love me. I know that now. He was using me. He was using me to get into the house, *using* me to get to Samuel's work, but who could have killed him—like *that*?" She reached up and pulled her hair over her eyes.

I sat still. It was over. Joanna Estes had talked to me. The investigation could move forward, but it would be cruel to leave this sad woman without a word of comfort. After a moment, I pulled myself to my feet. My head was on fire. The stunted plants in the garden were blurring into strange shapes.

"I'm going now," I said. "Thank you for talking to me. I'll think of you often. I hope—no, I'll *pray* that you can leave this house soon and go back to your music. Find peace."

No answer. I walked to the door and went out.

part three

twenty

I flew home to high summer in New England, nature's generous dividend. A lazy respite between spring's frantic growth
and the cold bite of frost and ice. As Inspector Grady and I
were leaving for the airport, Lord Rodale had called the Kensington house.

"Well done. To be quite frank, I didn't think you'd succeed,
but you must have hit the right note."

"She was terrified of the police. I had to do a little hand-
holding," I said, wondering how he had explained me to the
interrogation experts.

"We'll look into Lineham's contacts. Follow his money trail.
You won't be thanked publicly, but we're very grateful."

"One thing. What will happen to Mrs. Estes? She'll go mad
if she has to stay in that house much longer."

"Now that we know she's not an accomplice, she can go to a
safe place in the country."

"Tomorrow?"

"I'll look into it." A pause. "Again, thank you. Well done. I hope you have a good flight back and a well-deserved rest." Over and out. What had I expected?

After Eileen Grady handed me over to two FBI agents, she and I had hugged.

"Thanks again, we'll keep in touch," I had said, knowing that we wouldn't.

As the plane droned over the endless water, there had been endless time to think. Less than a week ago I had stored my precious tapes on a shelf, packed my clothes, and beetled across the ocean to ask Dr. Estes a question. I had stumbled from disaster to disaster. I was lucky to be alive, but from now on I would be protected around the clock. According to my FBI escorts, there had been discussions in high places about going straight to one of their safe houses or letting me go to Hardwick. Either way, my home would be turned into a high-tech fortress.

"Brass wants these people caught," the older one said. "Top priority. It's possible that you may be followed. You may want to go to the safe house."

"I'm going home," I had told them.

This morning I slept until ten, then put on the old jeans and sheepskin slippers I had worn the day Lewis died and went downstairs. The kitchen was warm and sunny. Unchanged. I took down three mugs and began to make coffee for the two resident FBI agents. O'Hara lay on my feet, not letting me out of his sight.

"Relax; these people like dogs," I told him. O'Hara would have to get used to having agents around, like workmen who didn't quit at four. For more than two hundred years my house had survived fires, floods, and hurricanes. It could survive an FBI invasion. So could O'Hara.

"Got a moment, Mrs. Streat?" The agent named Bill appeared from the mudroom, a former catchall for coats, tennis racquets, and general clobber. Now it was filled with electronic equipment and looked like an intensive care unit.

"Sit down. Coffee's almost ready."

"You'll spoil us." He pulled a chair up to the kitchen table. Bill had brown eyes, thinning hair, and the serious expression of a grade school math teacher. He was wearing a Red Sox cap back to front. His partner, Janet, was a young blond woman with a ponytail. The FBI agents on the plane had worn dark suits and had forgettable faces.

"Sugar for you? Milk?" I asked, refilling the sugar bowl.

"Both, thanks. About the telephones. I've put in a couple of safe lines. The devices we found have gone to a lab to be analyzed." He gave me a wary look. A few hours before I got back, he had found a tiny chip under a shelf in the broom closet. Another in Lewis's study. A third in the bedroom. Last night Bill had been patient while I exploded.

"Not *again*, not in *my house,* for God's sake. Who could have put them there?"

"Child's play for any so-called repairman. Why the perps were able to follow you to Cambridge. You feel like your privacy's been invaded. It has, but it could have been worse. Someone could have planted a chip under your skin."

"Stop right there. I'm going to bed."

The coffee was ready. I handed him the mug. "So. Tell me. What horrors have you found this morning?"

"No more horrors. Say an intruder comes onto your property. I've put a microwave barrier around the perimeters. He'd have to break this barrier. The intrusion would be picked up by one of the pan and zoom cameras on your house. Every move he makes would be recorded. We'll be monitoring the place around the clock. These honchos may come here or they may give up on you. No way to read minds. Simple as that."

I put down my mug. I was well protected, but the incarceration might go on for a long time. "You'd better tell me what you want me to do," I said.

Bill pulled at his cap. "Okay. Keeping you safe is our top priority. Stay close to the house. No wandering down to the river or out to the vegetable garden. Don't let the dog run off. You may have to keep him on a leash."

"Not go to my garden? Even with Janet?"

"Someone could be watching. Better to play it safe."

"All right." I must learn to think of my house as a cage, separated from the rest of the world. "By the way, people may start calling, wondering why I'm back. What should I tell them?"

"Whatever will keep them away."

"Let me think. There were lethal stairs at my college in Cambridge. I can say I fell down those stairs and dislocated my shoulder. I'm in a lot of pain. I won't be able to drive a car for a while."

"Sounds good. By the way, I'm your new landscape gardener. Doing a big job, takes me all around the place. The van in front has a Shoreline Gardens logo."

"What about Janet?"

"Personal trainer . . . no, make that therapist. I've talked to Mrs. Gates. She'll take care of the marketing. Do errands. Nice woman."

"She is. Very."

"That's it for now. Thanks for the coffee," he said, and went back to his toys.

With O'Hara at my heels, I walked around the house, looking at the Willard clock above the lowboy. The Grandma Moses painting in the hall. Finally I went into Lewis's study.

Nothing had been touched. The dust was thick on the desk. I stared at the wedding picture, remembering what Sergeant Johnson had said on that blistering hot day a few weeks ago: "One month is a very short time in police work. It tends to be a day-in, day-out slog where nothing fits. Then, out of the blue, one little lead can get the case rolling." By going to Cambridge and calling Dr. Estes I had helped start an international hunt for a stolen notebook and a gang of killers. A hunt that might go on for years.

O'Hara began to whine. I leaned down and scratched his neck. There were still boxes of papers behind the wing chair. A desk that hadn't been emptied. The sins of omission.

After a moment, I straightened. There was one thing I *could* do while I was locked in my cage. I could find the tapes that Lewis had made on the plane coming back from London. All those hours of dictating—he *must* have been sorting and analyzing critical information: what the engineer Bin had told him in the New York office, why we had to leave London with a bodyguard.

In the kitchen, the telephone was ringing. After a moment Bill came to the door.

"It's a man called Don. He's heard there were cars turning into your driveway. Wants to know if you're back. You know him?"

"I know him." Don was one of my lawyers. An old friend whose wife had left him last winter and had gone to Santa Fe to paint. It was clear by now that Don had more than probate on his mind.

"You want to speak to him?"

"I'll have to put him off. Jet lag. That bad shoulder. Come," I said to O'Hara, and went out. Lewis's tapes had been lying there for weeks. They would be safe for one more day.

By early evening, the weather had changed. Damp air lay like a soft blanket on the river. In the apple orchard, the cicada chorus was in full cry.

After dinner, Janet helped me carry the glasses and bright pottery plates from the round table to the sink.

"I'd put them in the dishwasher for you, but everyone has a system. Anything else I can do? If not, I'd better call my daughter before she goes to bed." Janet was married to a real estate agent in New Haven. She had the bouncy look of a high school cheerleader and was a graduate of the FBI Academy.

"Go ahead," I said, scraping at a patch of meat sauce that had stuck to the pan. Making lasagna from scratch was more trouble than it was worth, but the tense atmosphere was easing. "Call me Emma," I told them. "I'm not *that* much older."

This afternoon, staying close, Janet had helped me cut back the geraniums. "I love this house. It sort of puts its arms around you. A lot of work for one person, though."

"The boys will be coming home soon with friends—no, I forgot, they can't. That's going to be a problem, what to tell them."

"Orders have gone out to put watchers on them. Just a temporary precaution."

"Watchers—you mean bodyguards? Good Lord. Won't my boys know?"

"They won't know."

"I hope not." It was a relief to know they were protected, but what would happen in a few weeks when their jobs were over?

At last the pan was clean enough to go into the dishwasher. My body was still recovering from jet lag and accumulated stress, but going to bed early meant waking at five in the morning. I was picking up a pile of mail when the door to the control room opened.

"There's ice cream in the freezer if you're still hungry," I said over my shoulder. "Mrs. Gates left blueberries from our bushes on the counter." No answer. Bill crossed the room and took my arm.

"Keep quiet," he said in my ear. "Pick O'Hara up. Come."

"What—"

"*Quiet.*" Holding my arm, he hurried me along the hall and down the front steps. As we reached the far side of the circle he stopped.

"Okay. The monitor is showing a blip."

"What does that mean?"

"A moving object near the river. May be nothing, but I'm not taking any chances. Go to the barn. Go up to Mrs. Gates' apartment. Lock the door behind you and keep O'Hara quiet. I'm getting backup from New London." My heart did a high jump.

"What if he comes to the barn?"

"The monitor will show it long before he gets there. I'll send someone to you as soon as I can. Go on; you don't want to be seen from the river."

The barn was fifty yards away; the distance meant shoveling a long path in winter, but it gave Mrs. Gates privacy and a good view of the driveway and front door. Clutching O'Hara, I ran.

As I came up the stairs, Mrs. Gates was in the small kitchen, wearing a big apron. She was pouring a batch of jam into jars, and the smell of sugar filled the small apartment.

"I thought I heard someone." She lowered a heavy pot into the sink and turned. "Mercy. You're all out of breath. What's wrong?"

"There's a blip on Bill's fancy equipment. There's someone down by the river. Bill's sending for backup." My heart was pounding in wild staccato beats.

"Gracious heavens." Mrs. Gates leaned against the counter. The flushed color in her round face deepened. "Well, you can't make an omelet without breaking eggs, is what I say. The sooner they lay hands on that man the better." She took off her glasses, wiped them, and put them on again. "Might as well finish the jam. Nice crop this year, what the birds don't get." A calm voice, hiding fear.

"Might as well," I said, trying to match her calm. "I locked the door. Bill's sending someone to be with us."

"I should hope so. Least he can do."

Still holding O'Hara, I went into the small, cluttered sitting room, turned off the lights, and walked to the window. In the dusk, the old carriage lamps at the front door shone out on the steps and driveway, welcoming guests. In the distance, a horn sounded on the river. I waited, eyes probing the darkness. When the telephone in the kitchen rang, Mrs. Gates answered.

"It's Janet," she called to me. "Sergeant Johnson is on his way. On foot. We're to watch for him. He'll knock three times. Good thing she called first or we'd have died of fright."

"I'll go down and let him in."

For an endless five minutes, I waited by the door, remembering a game my cousins and I used to play on hot summer nights. I would stand against the large oak tree, my face pressed against the bark, ears straining to hear footsteps creeping through the grass. Then, after unbearable suspense, the gotcha blow between the shoulders. I never screamed, my grandmother had no patience with nerves, but the fear of standing still and waiting went deep.

At last, three quick knocks.

"Who is it?"

"Sergeant Johnson. Al."

"One second," and I slid back the bolt.

"Thanks." He wore a navy jacket and carried a radio attached to his belt. "I was less than a mile away, Meecham Road, when I got the call. I parked in the woods up by the point. You okay?"

"So far. What's happening?"

"Last I heard, the intruder was down in the laurel bushes by the shore. Must have come in by water. You go on up while I check the locks."

"All right."

A few minutes later he was standing with me at the sitting room window. In the dimness, I could see the outline of a holster by his waist.

"I'm glad you're here," I said. "Who else has Bill called?"

"A SWAT team is on the way from New London. My guess is, the intruder will take his time, try to figure out how the place is monitored. I gather you just got back from England."

"Last night. I don't know how much you've heard. Lewis's death *wasn't* an accident. The same people killed two British physicists. Tried to kill me."

"I was going to come by tomorrow, get the inside story."

"It's a long one. You won't believe how much has happened since we talked." I swallowed. "About tonight. To be honest, I never dreamed that anyone would come after me so soon."

"It happens."

"But the thing is, if the man who killed Lewis is down there, he knows the place like the back of his hand. He's much too smart to walk into a trap."

"He's smart, that's for sure, but don't forget, even the smart ones make mistakes. After a while they begin to think they're above the law and no one can touch them." I shook my head.

"Maybe, but I'm the one he can't seem to get. This time he'll make sure he finishes the job. He's not going to do something stupid."

"Like I say, there's always the first mistake. The plan is for Janet to move around the kitchen in plain sight. Do what you might do, put things away, turn off the lights downstairs as if you were going up to bed. Then she'll leave the house. He may decide the coast is clear and make a move."

"They forgot one thing. I always let O'Hara out."

"Too late to worry about that. The SWATs will have thermal imaging equipment to pick up body heat. If the guy gets too close, shows any sign of aggression, they'll move in. Cuff him. Collar him."

"Collar him?"

"Keep him from popping a cyanide pill. The FBI wants to know who gives him orders. Dead, he can't talk."

"True." I pressed O'Hara against my hip. "Even so, I just can't believe he'll stick his neck out and step into a trap. He must know the place is full of security."

"Can't read his mind, but like I say, the SWATs will keep him in their sights. Keep him from doing any harm."

"I want to believe you, but I've learned what he can do."

A dog barked in the distance. In the orchard, the cicadas were still singing. Beside them, hidden in the grass, armed men were playing a deadly game of cat and mouse. I looked at Sergeant Johnson.

"When we talked in July I told you I wanted to see a face. I still do. Whatever happens, I want to see this man's face."

"Like I said then, it's a very normal feeling. A kind of closure."

O'Hara began to pant, wanting water. "He's getting heavy;

I've got to put him down," I said. "I suppose this could take hours."

"Could be all night."

"I'd better tell Mrs. Gates."

In the kitchen, jam was cooling in little jars on the windowsill. Mrs. Gates was lying down in the bedroom, watching a police chase on television, lights flashing, sirens screaming. She turned it off.

"My ankles swelled up from standing. What does Al Johnson have to say?"

"It may be hours."

"You want me to take O'Hara in here?"

"If you don't mind. He's getting restless; I'll give him some water. Just don't let him bark," I said, noticing the cracks in the plaster ceiling. The painter must fix them when he came to redo the guest room. There would be new curtains. Off-white walls with no holes from pop concert posters. Two antique sleigh beds instead of bunks. When I went back to the sitting room, Sergeant Johnson was pulling out a pack of cigarettes.

"Do you mind? I'm down to two a day, don't want my boys to get the habit."

"Go ahead." I sat down in the overstuffed armchair covered with a pink crochet throw and lay back, breathing deeply. After a while, I began to drift. I thought about Rodale—not old or deaf, a man at the height of his physical powers. That dreary London house—no sign of a wife *there*. He'd been overbearing and arrogant Monday night. Exhausted and human on Tuesday. "You're a remarkable woman, Mrs. Streat. And you have the most beautiful eyes." Tomorrow, with luck, the intruder would be in custody behind bars. Rodale would call:

"Well done over there. This gives us another step up the ladder. A lead to follow."

As for Caroline—my trip to Cambridge had been sheer disaster. I hadn't been to a single class, never made it to Evensong in King's College Chapel. Never listened to the boys choir or recited the litany in the Book of Common Prayer: *Lighten our darkness, we beseech thee, O Lord. And in thy great mercy defend us from the perils of this night* . . . a strange word, "beseech." I clutched a corner of the pink throw in my hand and closed my eyes.

The explosion catapulted me out of the chair. I landed facedown on the floor. The frame of the old barn shook. Windows rattled in their frames as glass broke and shattered. Through the roar I could hear Sergeant Johnson shouting, "Keep down. Cover your face."

Glass crunched under my feet as I stood up and flung myself towards the window. Flames were rising with unleashed fury, turning the sky red. Fire, an uncaged beast leaping onto the back of its helpless prey. My *house*—but my house was two hundred years old. The old boards, the old plaster, had lasted for two hundred years. I turned and started for the stairs. Sergeant Johnson held me back.

"Get down on the floor. That was a bomb. There may be another. Get down. Nothing you can do."

The radio on his belt began to crackle. A man's voice cut through the static: "Five to all posts. Stand by. Five to all posts. Stand by."

I pulled away and ran back to the window. The monster leaped higher. Little stick men were running around in the driveway. Behind me, O'Hara was howling. Mrs. Gates was standing in the doorway, screaming, "You might have been in the house; you might have been burned alive—"

Sergeant Johnson turned on her. "Get ready to leave. It may spread."

In the distance, sirens shrieked; then the first engine swung into the circle. Men climbed down, the same volunteer firemen who had come racing down the road when Lewis died. They were here again, leaving their televisions, jumping into the pickup trucks that were always parked heading out.

Vehicles began to clog the lawn. A helmeted fireman began to direct traffic, shouting orders to let the engines through. Others began to pull out hoses. I could hear a few words over the roar.

"Get down to the river . . . need to set up a holding tank . . . use the pool." Useless. Against that solid sheet of fire, human hands were useless. Sergeant Johnson put his arm around my shoulders. I pulled free and hit him on the chest.

"I *told* you he was too smart. I *told* you. He got away. He got away. He set *fire* to my *house*."

Two hours later, the relentless flames were still out of control, feeding on the carcass of old beams and floorboards. Fire and water, two primal forces of nature, wrestled for a toehold. Red and yellow colors filled the sky, my favorite colors, the colors in my bedroom. Sergeant Johnson did his best to distract me.

"They're not just running in circles down there. Each fire is different; the chief has to decide how to contain it. A lot of engines are from Mutual Aid; they take turns filling the holding tank. New Sutton is getting in line. Warwick's right behind. Good thing the wind is blowing upriver. At least the garage won't go."

By midnight the flames began to die down. The beast was slinking back to its cage, leaving the stripped carcass. In *Rebecca,* when Manderley burned, the servants managed to take out pictures and furniture. I had nothing. For some reason, God was punishing me again. Stripping me bare. Racheting up the thumbscrews to see how much pain I could take.

As Sergeant Johnson and I left the garage, dampness had turned to light fog. The heavy smoke was thinning, but the air was dense and foul. In an open space behind the trucks, the Hardwick Fire Company's Ladies Auxiliary was serving sandwiches and coffee. Anna Jones was there with women from the town and the church, the stalwart pillars of the community.

"Thank you," I said. "All of you."

"Terrible for you, Mrs. Streat. Just terrible."

A young fireman came up. His face was streaked with sweat and black smoke; his boots were wet and filthy. I had last seen him in a spotless blue uniform, marching in the Fourth of July parade. After Lewis's death, I had given the fire department a machine called the jaws of life, designed to pull victims out of cars. The EMTs had received a new fibrillator.

"Jim Peters, assistant chief," the fireman said to me. "We did what we could, Mrs. Streat, but we didn't have a chance. My grandfather was a mason; he used to work on these chimneys. Great old house, don't make them like that anymore." He turned to Sergeant Johnson. "A network news van is here, looking for a story. How much do I tell them?"

"Tell them it's a historic house. Owner away, no one killed."

As Jim Peters left, I turned and faced Sergeant Johnson.

"Where is he?" No answer. I reached for his arm and shook it. "You've been talking to people. Did he get away?"

"Seems he was lying low in the bushes just above the shore, taking his time. Had a good view of the house. He may have seen Janet walking around, thought you had gone upstairs—"

"Never mind Janet. What happened to *him*?"

"I'm trying to tell you. The SWATs figured they'd waited long enough. They started to move in. He got to his feet and fired off an explosive."

"What do you mean, fired off?"

"It was a kind of slingshot contraption. Big target, couldn't miss. The substance exploded on contact. It'll be analyzed—"

"I don't care what it was. Where is he?"

"The SWATs nearest him were knocked down by the blast, maybe what he was counting on. He was heading for the river. A SWAT standing on the shore took him down."

"Killed him?"

"One shot. In the back."

I let go of the sergeant's arm. "You told me the SWATs would put a collar on him. Get names."

"That was the plan. Didn't work out."

Around me men were dragging hoses back into a truck. Another truck began to make its way down the driveway towards the road, leaving. I looked at Sergeant Johnson.

"I want to see his face."

"Sorry about that. They're taking him to a police morgue. Start trying to get identification."

"I have to see him. Here or at the morgue."

"Can't be done. I'll take you back to the garage."

I took a step forward. "Don't you dare; don't you *dare* try to stop me. That man killed my husband. He almost killed me. Now he's blown up my house. You owe me for this. You *all* owe me."

Sergeant Johnson hesitated. Then he hitched up his belt. "Wait here." He turned and began to make his way through the tangled hoses. A group of men were standing near the holding tank. Bill was there, his clothes covered with black soot. Mistakes had been made, but I was past laying blame.

"Mrs. Streat." Sergeant Johnson was back. "It's fixed. I said you might be able to identify him, best way to cut through red tape."

A small overgrown path led past the terrace, through the bank of mountain laurel, and down to the shore where the boys kept a scull. Lights and yellow tape had been set up around a small clearing in the crushed and trampled bushes. Two men were standing near a dark shape covered with a blanket. Sergeant Johnson went forward.

"Detective Sergeant Johnson, Troop D. This is Mrs. Streat, the owner. She may be able to identify the perp."

"Have to get clearance, Sergeant."

"Done that. Any flak, not your problem." The two men exchanged looks.

"As long as that's clear. Nothing much to see, ma'am. Shouldn't upset you. Okay, Ron, just the face."

One of the men pulled the blanket down to shoulder height. I stepped forward. There were no burns. No blood. The face had been carefully blacked with camouflage. The eyes were closed. After a few seconds, I leaned closer and studied the features. The set of the mouth and eyebrows. The way the hair grew back from the forehead.

The man holding the blanket cleared his throat. "That do it for you, ma'am?"

I straightened, my hands at my sides. Not an unknown terrorist. Not a stranger. This man had a pleasant face, not handsome. I had cut up his meat. Buttered his toast.

"I . . . he—" The words wouldn't come.

Sergeant Johnson took my arm. "Lost her husband last month, now this. We'll go back."

I tried again. "I know him."

"You know this guy?" The man dropped the blanket. He gave me a sharp look. "What's his name?"

"I tell you, I *know* him. He was in Cambridge with me. His name is Tom Myers."

twenty-one

Thursday, July 16

Before dawn, the far-reaching global investigation was gathering fresh momentum. Because a Mrs. Lewis Streat in Connecticut, USA, had given a name to the bomber, coded messages flowed through Internet holding tanks. Experts rushed to verify identification.

Early in the morning, O'Hara and I took refuge in the brown-shingled rustic pool house, built ten years ago with a small bathroom, a kitchen, and pullout sofas for an overflow of boys. Their CDs were piled on tables. A poster of the Guns N' Roses rock group hung on one wall. A place designed for good times.

I must have slept. When O'Hara woke me with his whining I lay still, knowing that the pain, when it came, would be overwhelming.

O'Hara's whining escalated into frantic scratching. I pulled myself up and saw that I was wearing blue jeans and a T-shirt, last night's clothes. A man from Hardwick had given me his sweater; it was dark brown and smelled of tobacco. I let O'Hara out, then stood at the door, hearing the sonic boom of my house exploding, seeing Tom's face under the camouflage. "We'll circle the wagons," he had said at the opening night dinner. Until now my nemesis had been a stranger. An enemy I had never met. My faith in my ability to judge people was crumbling.

People hurried to help. By noon, chicken casseroles filled Mrs. Gates's freezer. A woman from New Sutton arrived with a carload of size 4 clothes. A neighbor, my size, brought sweat suits and shoes. Friends were told that I was resting in the pool house.

"She can't stay there," they said to Mrs. Gates. "We've got a guest house. She can be perfectly independent." But today a new security team was operating out of a camper by the helipad. Until the mastermind in this operation was found, I had to be guarded.

I talked to Jake in San Francisco, Steve in Montana. Gone, all their treasures: the trophies, the stamp and baseball card collections, the collection of *Playboy* magazines I had found in the closet when they left for camp years ago. A door had slammed shut on their childhood. Their base. They did their best to hide the loss.

"Look, Ma, all that matters is that you're all right. We'll come back and give you a hand."

"Later, when things get sorted out." It was the right thing to do, but I wanted desperately to see them, touch them. I wanted to tell them the truth, not keep them at a distance.

Mrs. Gates went out to buy me a toothbrush. Bras and panties. By late afternoon I was beginning to realize what it was like to be stripped to the bone. When Lewis died, I still had my singing tapes, the safe haven of my four-poster bed. Gone, the special bed pillow, the prescription shampoo. Pictures of

Lewis and the boys. The wedding photograph of my mother and father. And—the tapes Lewis had made on the plane. Tapes that might have named names. By dragging my feet yesterday, I had missed a chance to find the desperately needed evidence. An irreversible sin of omission.

Dolly called. "I can't believe it, but this time you've only lost *things*. We all need less as we get older."

"I've heard that."

"Ted and I were going up to the lake, but I'd better come east. You'll need help. There must be insurance, but I suppose all your papers are gone."

"Some are in the bank. You go on up to the lake. I'll call you when I need help; I promise. Talk to you soon."

"You can't just stay in that damp little pool house. Go straight to Ned and Cassia in Manchester. Today."

"I can't. Maybe next week," I said, and hung up. Like a death watch, I was filled with a fierce need to keep constant vigil near the corpse.

The state Fire Marshal and officials from the U.S. Bureau of Alcohol, Tobacco, Firearms and Explosives arrived to search the remains. Two days later, a huge yellow backhoe trundled down the drive.

As the backhoe began to tank over the debris, I hurried back to my pool, built at great expense to look like a rustic swimming hole. That first year the drainage hadn't worked; then the careful planting got too much shade and died.

This summer the daylilies on the bank were growing in thick, colorful clumps. I sat down in the sun and wrapped my arms around my chest; even a heavy sweat suit wasn't keeping me warm. Ten years ago, the boys had been skinny little kids playing Marco Polo at the shallow end. Later came the parties. Music blaring and girls in bikinis shaking out their long, wet hair, so young and untested. Their lives were just beginning, but two parts of mine were over. First my career. Now my husband and my home. As for me, I might still be in the sights of people who wanted me dead. Who gave Tom orders? Terrorists? Industrial spies? Agents for a rogue government? Again, I had an intense need to see a face.

At eleven o'clock, a high-level FBI investigator appeared. I had forgotten that he was coming today.

"Mrs. Streat? Jim Kirch." He showed me his card, a young man with a friendly smile and sharp eyes. Trained, no doubt, to interview victims too deep in shock to make sense.

"That's a lot more comfortable than it looks," I said, pointing to a teakwood chair. "Coffee?"

"If it's handy."

"Just inside." I got up and went for the pot and another mug.

As I sat down again, he gave me an appraising look. "I appreciate you seeing me today. Sorry about your house."

"Yes," I said, rejecting the impulse to say, "So am I." So far I had managed to keep anger about the bomb on hold.

"About this man Myers. We have some background from our British colleagues, some from our own sources, but we need your input."

"Of course."

"It appears that Myers had no police record. No known connection to terrorists. There was no reason to detain him at airports. He rented a gray Ford Taurus from a Hertz agency in midtown Manhattan. Parked it in the woods near the Hardwick cemetery. Carried a small raft to the river, inflated it, and came in."

"Do you know who he was, I mean, where he came from?"

"The FBI is working on a profile. So far it's very solid. Father was a high school football coach in California; mother was a pediatric hospital nurse. Myers was in Vietnam for three years. Long-range patroller, one of the toughest jobs there was in Nam. That's where he may have gone sour. After his discharge he ran guns to Africa, then hired out as a professional hit man. Our sources say he was one of the best in the business, with a reputation for leaving no traces. An expert in electronics, which would explain his access to a new class of devices."

"Those devices. He was *everywhere* with them. He got into so *many* different places, God knows how."

"As I say, he was an expert. And he may not have been working alone." Kirch took a sip of coffee. "To go on, his primary cover was a foundation in Zambia. He spent time there; he was well liked at the agricultural station at Mount Makula. He even supported a village. The great humanitarian. Not your usual cover." I nodded.

"It was one of the reasons I liked him so much. He talked about hen projects for the women. He really seemed to care about those people."

"Figures. We find criminals are apt to be good actors who believe in their parts. Very good at leading two lives."

I picked up my mug, holding it for warmth. "I can tell you one thing," I said. "Tom Myers was an incredible actor. A chameleon. At Heathrow he pretended to be a driver who could barely speak English. He had a mustache and dark makeup on his face. When he heard my godmother was with me, he took off. That was the first time he tried to kill me."

The agent took out a little pad. "Knew she was coming," he said aloud as he made a note. "Thought she was alone. Could have received bad information from an accomplice. Go on, Mrs. Streat."

"At dinner in Cambridge, that first night, he was wearing a big cast on his arm. He was very laid-back, very relaxed. He helped me get rid of a man who made a pass at me. Then he went out and killed Estes. Tried to kill me for the second time."

"Can you give me a time frame?"

"Roughly. At around ten o'clock he knocked Dr. Estes down. I assume he got rid of the bicycle. He sent a message to the college porter asking me to call a friend. He had to work incredibly fast."

"You went to make the call. What happened?"

"I saw his shadow outside the door of the booth. I scared him off by pretending to call the porter for help. I thought it was the man who made a pass at me at dinner. Or just that, a shadow. The hall was very dark."

"Anything else?"

I hesitated. The agent was drawing me out, wanting to hear the story from my perspective.

"The next day he followed me around Cambridge. He put on a tweed hat and walked like an old man. Tried to push me under a bus. He wasn't wearing that cast."

"An old trick, the cast. The mind believes what the eye sees, a man with a handicap, not capable of violence. After you left Cambridge, he told the porter at St. Paul's that his arm was giving him trouble and he was going to London to see his doctor. He followed you, planted the time-release chemical in the flat, doubled back to Cambridge, and killed Dr. Lineham. The next day he followed you here, a place he knew well."

"Very well." I kept my eyes on the bank of daylilies. "You said just now he might not be working alone. Do you have any evidence? That he was taking orders?"

The agent put away his notebook. "I can't be specific. I'll just say we're looking for a link to a criminal or terrorist network.

The sense is that Myers was no free agent, selecting victims at will. Terrorist cell or hired gun, I'd say he was part of a team in a high-stakes operation. The man had to maintain his reputation for jobs done one hundred percent and on time."

"And I was one of his few failures. Even so . . . the risk—to come here. He must have known I'd have security."

"True, but that type thrives on taking risks. 'Hey, look at me; see what I can do.' You were spoiling his record. There's a big, competitive underworld of guns for hire. Some even advertise."

"You make it sound like hiring a chimney cleaner."

"Same idea, but in a world most people never see. By now his handlers, whoever they are, will know they've lost him. Figure that the police and the FBI will be on his trail. The question is whether these handlers keep after you or write you off as not worth another try."

"What does that mean?"

"It means you have to be protected until we find them." He put his hands on his knees and looked at me. "Here's the situation, Mrs. Streat. We can't keep our agents in that trailer much longer. Besides, pretty soon it'll be too cold for you to live in a pool house. The feeling is that you should be moved to a safe house. As soon as possible."

The mug tilted in my hand. Coffee spilled onto the glass table.

"Not yet—I mean, it won't be cold for weeks. There's a heater."

He shook his head. "I know how you feel. It's a terrible loss. These things are never easy, but we find it's better to make a clean cut, not drag the process out."

"I see." Coffee was dripping onto the wood deck, making a dark stain. "Where would you send me?"

"I can't tell you that now."

"Oh." I stared at the spreading stain. These people hadn't saved my house. Now they wanted to bounce me around like a human volleyball. Cut me off from my boys.

"I've got to mop this up," I said, and and went into the pool house for paper towels.

The roll of paper stood on the tiny counter. I tore off a wad, trying to think ahead. I should have seen this coming. Jim Kirch was just carrying out orders. On the other hand, I mustn't let him put me in isolation. Not this week, anyhow. There was unfinished work I had to do.

When I went back, O'Hara was sniffing suspiciously at the agent's trousers. "Sorry to keep you waiting," I said.

"No problem. Great pool. Like an old swimming hole in the woods."

"That's what we were aiming for." I wiped up the coffee and crumpled the paper into a ball. He leaned down and reached for his briefcase.

"About this move. It should be within the next few days. There's a process that has to be followed, but your two agents will spell out the details."

"One minute." I picked O'Hara up and sat down. In the past few weeks I had lost the usual hang-ups about confronting authority. "I've been thinking," I said. "Your top priority is to find out who gave Myers his orders. Right?"

"Right."

"It just so happens I have some contacts who might be able to help."

"Give me names and we'll get right on it."

"I could, but that would never work. They'd run the other way from the FBI."

"What are you getting at? Anything to do with this investigation, we have to handle it."

"I understand. Very well. I realize I haven't a clue about things like cutouts and intelligence analysis. On the other hand, I made the link between my husband and a British physicist who was killed. I worked with the British police when another physicist was killed the next day."

"So I've heard, but that wasn't in our jurisdiction."

"No, but don't forget one thing. I identified Tom Myers. I went down and looked at his face and gave you a name."

Jim Kirch frowned. He fingered his plain blue tie. "You've been very helpful, no question, but we can't afford to take chances with your safety. By now you ought to appreciate that."

"I can. I do. I'm not asking for very long. It's a matter of a few calls. A few days."

"That's not the way it works, Mrs. Streat."

"The way it works can lead to mistakes. Like a house being blown up. If I can't get any results in ten days, I'll leave quietly. No foot-dragging. No fuss."

In the distance a machine coughed and started up. A neighboring farmer was mowing hay in our field. The agent walked to the end of the pool and back. He stood looking down at his feet, a man steering a tricky course in choppy waters. Finally he turned.

"Like I say, this isn't how it works. I should take this up the line, get a green light."

"But—"

"I've learned, the hard way, to respect humanint. I'll give you ten days, Mrs. Streat. If you need help from us, you have it. Ten days. No more," he said, and went away.

The smell of charred wood in the air was faint and acrid. I left the pool and went down the path to look at the remains of my house. A bit of twisted iron here, a fragment of steel there.

Two fieldstone chimneys stood watch above the rubble left by the backhoe. Stone lasted. Like graves. In colonial days, the house had been an "ordinary," a place where travelers could get food and hay for their horses. I was the intruder who had not kept faith with those early settlers.

With O'Hara at my heels, I went around to the terrace. The sun was warm, the river serene and uncaring. The fire had taken leaves off the nearby trees; the birds had either burned to death or found new places to live. Standing there, I was torn by a fierce biblical tooth-for-a-tooth rage against the bastards who had hired Tom to get their hands on a new weapons system. Hired him to steal a little notebook that could destroy my boys, destroy all those kids who used to play Marco Polo in my pool.

"Come," I said to O'Hara, and walked to the weeping willow where Lewis's ashes were buried; there still was no proper stone. O'Hara sat down, his eyes on my face. Any sudden noise sent him into spasms of shivering. He missed his toys. He would hate moving to a new place.

"Ten days," I said to him. Ten days, no more, to find the faceless cowards who had stripped me as bare as those leafless trees.

"Lorna? It's Emma. I'm back in Connecticut."

"Emma. My God, your house. I'd have called, but I thought you were still in Cambridge."

"I'm living in the pool house, I'm not sure for how long."

"It's the absolute worst. I don't know what to say. You put so much of yourself into that place. Such a great place."

"I know. Lorna, that talk we had before I left for Cambridge. About bugs in the office."

"I was waiting until you got back to tell you. My electronics wizard friend and I went in over the weekend and took the office apart. The bug was buried in the ficus tree, the one by the corner window. I couldn't believe it."

"I guess I'm not surprised. What did your friend say?"

"He went off the wall. He acted as if he'd stumbled onto DNA. He's heard rumors that Danny Peplow's company is developing a new device, but he doesn't know if it's gone beyond the lab stage."

"Danny's company?" Suddenly it was June. I was standing in Robina's elegant drawing room. Marge was carrying on about an MIT professor's lecture on listeners in closets. Danny had snapped at her, "Forget about that load of crap." A surprise because Danny was always so protective of Marge.

". . . God knows how we'd ever pin anything on Danny," Lorna was saying, "but whoever heard that tape may have figured both men had to be done in before your husband went into action."

"Someone with a lot to lose when Lewis started investigating. Was there anything on the tape?"

"Nothing. My friend figures it was erased after transmitting, another reason he went ballistic."

"Where is it now?"

"I put it in the office safe and told my friend I'd practice voodoo on him if he ever opened his mouth. You owe me. He's no good in bed."

I laughed. "Extra pay for hazardous work?"

"Big-time. Now that you know, I have to call the DA's office. Tell them the office was bugged."

I let out my breath. "The DA's office? Why tell them? They'll come barging in and ask a lot of questions."

"They will, but I can't sit on my hands any longer. Don't

forget, I've been sending copies of weapons projects to London. I sent one in February, blueprints of a new missile finder. The Navy may use it."

"All the same—"

"Listen. If there's the remotest chance anyone is sending our projects to Hong Kong, maybe on to China, that's criminal. I've got a responsibility to notify the authorities."

"I agree, I totally agree, but couldn't it wait for a few days?"

"Wait for what? I put it off until we could talk. We can't drag our feet on this."

I pushed back my hair. "You're absolutely right. We can't drag our feet, but I wonder if the DA's office is the best way to go."

"Why not?"

"The press, for one thing. Someone in the DA's office is bound to give them a tip. You know what will happen then. Airport murder of Chinese engineer linked to death of well-known CEO. Office bugged. Technology stolen. No arrests. Anything to get a sensational story."

"I get the point, but that doesn't let me off the hook. Any other ideas?"

"Back to Danny. What's the latest on the takeover?"

"Galbraith sent for Bill Talbot, but shaking the trees won't help. Your husband had the drive. The vision."

"You think it will happen?"

"Yes, but it wouldn't be the usual corporate deal. You know, buying up stock, maneuvering a board. Galbraith holds most of the stock. A takeover would mean twisting his arm, giving him a very pressing reason to sell."

"True. He doesn't need more money. The one thing he seems to want is a peerage. To sit in the House of Lords." I paused, working on a new idea. "I don't know how these things work, but a scandal about spies and stolen Galbraith technology wouldn't do him any good."

"And our Danny wouldn't be above using bugs and smear tactics to own this company."

"But not killing. He's got a very nice wife."

"That makes him nice? We're always hearing how Mafia dons love their wives and children. I know one of the Peplow managers. She says half the people who see him have to take a private elevator. When he goes by her, smiling that little smile, she feels a cold wind at her back."

"That bad?"

"That bad." She stopped. I could hear voices in the background. "Emma, sorry, there's an appointment waiting. This business about the DA. I've got a legal obligation to report any suspicion of stolen sensitive technology. The sooner the better."

"I know." I stared at the raunchy Guns N' Roses poster on the wall. I needed Lorna's input on the idea taking shape in my head—no, better to go ahead on my own. Lorna might throw cold water.

"Emma?"

"I'm here. Lorna, I need an enormous favor. I wouldn't ask if it wasn't serious."

"What favor?"

"Wait a week. Maybe less. I can't explain right now, but as soon as I can, I will. It has something to do with Lewis."

"Hold it, girl. There's a lot you're not telling me."

"I want to, believe me. I'd give anything to tell you the whole story, but I can't. Not yet."

"You're up to something. Whatever it is, I don't like it. All right. For Lewis, a week. No more."

"A week, no more," I said, and put down the receiver.

twenty-two

Saturday, July 18

The midmorning traffic on Interstate 95 near Bridgeport thundered along like water rushing over a dam. I winced as a double tractor trailer changed lanes a few feet ahead; my father had been killed in an accident a few miles from here.

Ed, the number one agent on my FBI team, shook his head. "Ought to be a law."

"It must be the worst stretch of road in the country." I sat back, pleating the skirt of my borrowed green cotton dress. Yesterday I had walked up and down beside the pool for hours, grappling with opposing forces: "You're out of your mind, Emma." But then: "If you want to know something and there's no other way, go to Danny." Lewis's voice as we left London like fugitives. "It'll cost you, but he has his methods. . . ."

Danny fit the job description of a mastermind. He had an underground information network. A company that could make electronic bugs. But . . . was Danny hungry enough to hire a dedicated killer like Tom Myers? If so, it was sheer madness to confront him like a mouse dancing up to a cat.

At eight o'clock last night I had reached Marge Peplow at home.

"Marge, it's Emma."

"Emma. Your house, your beautiful old house. I read about it in the papers. I was going to write. First Lewis, now this—"

"Don't get me started; it's been—well, don't get me started. Marge, I need to talk to Danny as soon as possible. It has to do with Lewis."

"He's watching TV, getting worked up about a government investigation. I'll ask him."

In a minute she was back. "Come down tomorrow morning at ten. He has a meeting at eleven," and she had given me directions.

Norwalk. Southport. Fairfield. At last, Greenwich. The quiet in the residential streets was startling after the noise on the highway. At ten on a sunny summer morning, BMWs and Volvo station wagons moved sedately past low stone walls and big houses set on small plots of land. The houses were large, with towering stone gateposts and lighting enough to protect a penetentiary. Marge's taste ran to beads and pink chiffon. Danny's money was blatantly new. Their house would be huge French Provincial with a Palladian window. Jack, the other FBI man, was looking at a grid map.

"Slow down, Ed. This is it."

"Are you sure?" I asked. The house facing a short circular drive was pure Victorian, with turrets and gingerbread detail and a wraparound front porch hung with pots of geraniums.

"Number thirty-two. How long will you be, Mrs. Streat?" Ed asked.

"Not over an hour. Maybe less."

"Right. Jack, you better get out here and walk around. Two men sitting in a car draws attention. I'll be right by the door, Mrs. Streat." They hadn't wanted to make this trip. It had taken a call to Jim Kirch to get the green light.

In an elaborate fenced yard, two small children were swinging, attended by a young woman. As I got out of the plain blue sedan, Marge appeared on the porch, a dumpy little person with sharp eyes and a big smile. Her pocketbook had always opened wide for my relief funds. I waved, telling myself to ignore the surface suburban trappings and remember that Danny was a man no one trusted. A man who had emerged from backstreets and was on the prowl to extend his empire.

"Marge." I ran up the wide painted steps and kissed her cheek. "Your directions were perfect. You're a dear to let me barge in like this."

"You're not barging in. I just hope Danny can help with whatever it is," and she led the way into a wide hall. The table and chairs were rosewood Gothic. Museum quality.

"I love your house," I said, meaning it.

"I bet you were expecting French Provincial. We started with a Victorian bureau years ago. Ahead of the curve." I shouldn't have been surprised. Marge wasn't behind the door when brains were handed out.

"Are those your grandchildren outside?"

"Katie and Dennis, and that's our daughter-in-law. They live around the corner. Danny, here's Emma. I'm going out to Monica."

The sunroom was filled with plants and old unpainted

wicker furniture. Danny was sitting in a comfortable chair, reading *The Wall Street Journal.* He put it down and stood up.

"Traffic bad? Sit here, why don't you? Coffee?"

"Thanks. I need it, after those trucks."

"That highway's a death trap. Milk? Sugar? Have one of Marge's muffins. Specialty of the house." Wary eyes above the cynical little smile.

"Nothing in the coffee." I could pretend to nibble at the muffin. Danny was wearing a loose shirt and slacks. At business meetings he always seemed too sharply dressed, dark hair too well cut.

"So, Emma. What can I do for you?"

I put my hands in my lap. My best hope was to get some kind of reaction out of Danny. Anger, denial, a threat—*anything* to move forward.

"After the service for Lewis, you said to let you know if you could help."

"I remember. You got a problem?"

"It's . . . complicated. The day before we left for that June meeting in London, a Chinese engineer from Hong Kong came to Lewis's office. He was knifed to death at JFK the next day."

"On a people mover. It was in the papers."

"His name was Nelson Bin. Whatever went on in that meeting upset Lewis. Really upset him. I tried to find out what was wrong. He wouldn't talk about it."

"Noticed he looked pretty bad in London."

"I know. Two days later he was killed. I'm trying to find out if someone wanted both of those men dead." Danny's expression didn't change, but I sensed I had his full attention.

"I assume the police are working on the case. What do they say?"

"Nothing. Nothing at all. The hit-and-run driver didn't

leave any traces. Neither did whoever knifed the engineer on the people mover."

"Give the police time. These cases can drag on."

"They can, but I don't want to wait for years. To be honest, I'm here because Lewis told me you have a great information network. Better than the CIA."

Danny gave me a quick look. "So what are you asking me?"

I swallowed, remembering the bug in the ficus tree. "I want to know what that engineer could have told Lewis. What could have upset him so much." The words came out in a rush.

Danny put down his cup. "Jeez, Emma, I'm not a mind reader. I wasn't there."

"No, but you could make a guess."

Danny shook his head. "Come on. Get real. You want me to make a guess?"

"Yes. I do."

He laughed. "Okay. Let's say the engineer from Hong Kong wanted to make some kind of deal. It happens. Something bad enough to make Lewis look like he'd been hung out to dry. Anything else?"

Outside the children were laughing as their mother pushed the swings. I stared at the headlines in *The Wall Street Journal.* The preliminaries were over and the clock was running. It was time to put my neck on the block. I twisted my wedding ring and leaned forward.

"One more thing. Last week a bug was found in Lewis's office. State of the art. Not on the market. Lewis's assistant says she has to tell the DA's office. It could be helpful to them."

"Could be."

"I asked her to wait a few days. God knows what will happen when they start looking under rocks. And if the press gets the story, it could turn into a blockbuster scandal."

"It could," he said.

I swallowed again and made the leap. "That doesn't bother you? I've heard your company make those kinds of bugs."

Silence. Danny took a pair of horn-rimmed glasses out of his shirt pocket and put them on. The little smile was far more frightening than outright anger.

"Emma. Spit it out. You think I bugged that office? Gave Lewis the shove to get my hands on his company?"

"Frankly, I wouldn't put it past you to bug that office, but to arrange two murders—" I stopped. Outside a child was screaming, a shrill howl of anguish. In seconds Danny was at the screen door.

"What happened? How bad is it?" he shouted.

Marge turned. "Dennis fell off the swing. Calm down, honey; it's just a skinned knee, no need to call nine one one."

Danny came back and sat down. "Kids screaming. Sorry. Dennis has to toughen up."

"It's a horrible sound," I said. My hands were shaking. He glanced at his watch.

"Getting late. Emma, you've got guts to come here and get this crap off your chest. Pretty crude, most people would get the shove, but I don't forget the time Ed Collins's trophy wife was making fun of Marge. You told her it was better to have a big heart than a size-eight figure."

"It was a pleasure. Barbara has a mean tongue when she's drinking."

"Mean when she isn't. Tell you what. It so happens I have contacts in Hong Kong. I'll look into this fellow Nelson Bin. Not just for you. I like to know what's going on out there. Particularly when shady dealings and murders are involved."

"I'd appreciate it," I said, trying to keep my voice steady.

Was the cat playing with the mouse, letting it run a few steps before pouncing? "How long will that take, do you think?"

"Depends. A week, a month. Maybe more. I may have to offer a reward. China can be tricky. Life is cheaper over there." He gave me a sharp look. "There's one condition."

"Which is?" My neck tensed.

"I don't like people meddling in my business. For any reason. You understand? If someone from Galbraith Tech or the police comes around asking questions, we never talked. You get no report on Bin."

"I won't mention your name to anyone."

"That's it, then." He stood up. "I'm off. Nothing gets done at these meetings if I'm not there to crack the whip. Come outside and I'll turn you over to Marge."

I got to my feet. "Thanks, Danny. Thanks very much."

"No problem." He went to the screen door. "Marge," he called. "I'm leaving. I'm sending Emma out to you." Suddenly he turned. "Did Lewis ever start an investigation?"

I hesitated. "I'm pretty sure he didn't. There wasn't time."

"Then here's a tip. A freebie. Go and check out George Galbraith."

I stared. "Check him for what?"

"Connections to high-tech companies in China. Companies that make weapons."

It took me a few seconds to catch his meaning. "George *Galbraith*? You're out of your—I mean, you're joking."

"I never joke."

"But Galbraith's lost interest. Besides, he would never steal his own—"

Danny opened the door. "Take it or leave it. If anything useful surfaces in Hong Kong, I'll be in touch."

As the car swung out of the Peplow driveway, I looked at my watch. My floundering bravado had lasted exactly half an hour. What would happen now? I was protected by my watchdogs, but Danny could get at my boys.

Southport. Bridgeport. Milford. I went back over every word, every sentence, probing for hidden meanings. Naïve to think that Danny was motivated by my kindness to Marge. Better to assume he was throwing sand in my eyes to keep me away from the DA's office—or fooling me into starting a false rumor about George Galbraith that would lower the takeover price.

As we reached the outskirts of New Haven, my eyes began to close. When I woke up, the car was starting down the winding driveway and the sky overhead was a mass of solid black clouds.

"Made good time," Ed said. "Looks like we just got ahead of a real bad storm."

I blinked and sat up. "Thanks, both of you. I know you didn't want to do this trip, but I appreciate it," I said, relieved to be safely back in my little cage.

Half an hour later the rain poured down in tropical torrents; lightning and thunder sent O'Hara under the bed, panting and shaking, beyond a reassuring pat. I made tea and tried to do mental gymnastics. Mind-boggling to picture an elderly title-chasing snob as an undercover criminal. Impossible—but George Galbraith had once been a brilliant innovator with the brains to start a great company. Tom Myers was proof that criminals were superb actors. Could Galbraith have fooled Lewis all those years? I was in deep waters, way over my head, but one fact stood out. Danny's tip might well be a classic red herring, but it had to be passed on.

It was nine o'clock in England when I called Upper Brook Street. The old butler answered.

"It's Mrs. Streat in Connecticut," I said. "I'd like to speak to Lord Rodale."

"I'll see if he is at home, madam."

In a moment Rodale was on the line. "Mrs. Streat. About your house. Another terrible blow for you. I'm extremely sorry." A concerned, deep voice.

"It—thank you."

"Well done, to identify Myers. Any more of these break-throughs and we'll have to put you on the force. Where are you now?"

"Living in my pool house. I'm calling because . . . several things have happened." As I talked, I could picture him frowning, trying to read between the lines.

"How much have you told your husband's assistant?"

"Not the truth about Lewis's death. Nothing at all about Estes or the notebook, but she knows there was a listener in her office. The thing is, she sends blueprints of Galbraith projects to London and she's concerned about stolen technology. Now she wants to bring back the New York District Attorney bunch. Have them do more investigating. I asked her to wait a few days. I wanted to talk to you before they take over."

"I see. How much did you tell the mysterious man you saw this morning?"

"Same as the assistant, nothing about the English end, but just as I was leaving, he asked if Lewis had started an investigation. I said I didn't think so. Then he said something strange. He said, 'Here's a tip. Go and check out George Galbraith for connections to high-tech companies in China. Companies that make weapons.' I tried to get more out of him, but I couldn't."

"Bit of a stretch. Is he a reliable source?"

"He's as street-smart as they come. Believe me. *And* he has an ear to the ground in Hong Kong, China, everywhere. Quite frankly, I think he may have reasons of his own to give me that tip, but I felt I had to pass it along. Do you know George Galbraith?"

"Slightly through the art world. Aside from being a crashing bore, I've never heard anything against him. How large is the London office?"

"It's just a few rooms in Berkeley Square. Galbraith only goes there once in a while. The manager is Hank Lausch, an old friend. You may have met him. He married Robina Fyfe. He has a shaky old secretary, Mrs. Dean. Those three, that's all. The security there is nonexistent. It used to drive Lewis crazy."

"Difficult, especially if the Chinese are involved. They don't leave money trails and brief cases. You may not know, but over here the decision to prosecute is made by the Director of Public Prosecutions for the Crown. There has to be a good chance of conviction."

"There's nothing you can do?"

"Nothing that comes to mind, I'm afraid." A pause. "I assume you still have tight security."

"Very tight. The FBI wants to move me to a safe house. I don't know where or for how long. Is there . . . any chance of a breakthrough soon?"

"I can tell you that we're following Lineham's money trail. Working closely with your people. The thought of that notebook in the hands of a rogue state is keeping everyone's feet to the fire." He cleared his throat. "Back to Galbraith. Frankly, it sounds to me as if someone was pulling your leg.

"It's possible," I said, beginning to feel foolish. "But I didn't—"

"On the other hand, I've just thought of someone who might be helpful. It wouldn't hurt to ask him a few questions."

"Oh? How long will that take?"

"Hard to say. It's a long shot. A very long shot, but if anything useful *should* turn up, I'll be in touch."

twenty-three

Tuesday, July 21

The weather turned rainy and damp. I came down with Mrs. Gates's streaming cold and lay in bed, coughing, eating apple-sauce and mashed potatoes. One night I dreamed that I was bending over a man on the people mover. Blood was dripping through the steel mesh and people were screaming. Suddenly the man was lying on the bank by the white gates. Lewis was with him. They were angry, arguing—but I couldn't hear what they were saying.

Caroline called from Cambridge, her righteous wrath over my departure defused by the fire. "I'm devastated for you, utterly devastated." Then: "By the way, all your Cambridge admirers have disappeared into the blue. First, it was that ghastly man, I've forgotten his name."

"Wininger."

"It seems he makes the rounds of these seminars, looking for available women. After you left, he began to bully a blond divorcée from Santa Barbara. She complained to Pat Dickinson.

He was asked to leave. Then the man with the cast went off to see a London doctor and never came back."

"He said at breakfast he was hurting. How's the course?"

"Too many people from the Chicago suburbs, but the instructor is a pet. Darling girl, I'll treat you to a tour of great houses next spring, the ones you pay the earth to stay in, not just walk around behind red velvet ropes."

"I'd love it," I said, knowing I wouldn't. Still, a lot could happen in a year. Less than two months ago, Caroline had been sitting on my terrace, lecturing me about getting a life. Now I was in limbo, cut off from the outside world. The balls I had thrown wildly into the air hadn't come down and the clock was running. At least there wouldn't be much to pack. Everything that defined me as a person—books, music, clothes—gone. Mrs. Gates could tell the world that I was away having a rest cure, no way to know when I would be back.

Robina called. "We hear your house was blown up by a Save the Planet fanatic."

"A what?"

"A fanatic crusading against high tech. Is that true?"

"Really, where people get these stories."

"It's the price you Americans pay for being so violent. Look, my dear, come over. Soon. I'm expecting my brother from South Africa. He'd do very nicely for you in the short run. Charming but penniless."

I laughed. I hadn't expected Robina to keep in touch. "I wish I could. By the way, do you know a Lord Rodale? Andrew Rodale?"

"Just the way one does. I went to school with his ex-wife. Half the women in London want to be the next Lady Rodale, but one hears he's sleeping with his neighbor in Wiltshire, Lucy Bellew. Her husband Rupert died a few years ago; Rupert was my several-times-removed cousin. Andrew collects sporting paintings and keeps a string of racehorses with his ex-mother-in-law in Newmarket. My brother thinks he works undercover for one of the secret services."

"He doesn't know which one?"

"Heavens, no. Will that do you?"

"That'll do me."

"Be careful, my dear, if you meet him. I hear he's a tiger between the sheets."

Donald the hopeful lawyer called. "You need to get out. See people. I'll take you to dinner at the Yacht Club."

"Sorry, I'd love to, but I've got a rotten cold." Donald didn't have the look of the Regency rake in a Georgette Heyer novel, a glint of amused humor in steely gray eyes. Donald's neck was too thin; his voice was nasal.

As I lay in bed I thought about Rodale and the dreary house with no flowers and with dog pee on the carpet. What were his favorite books? Dogs? A mistake to let curiosity about Andrew Rodale ruin me for other men.

One night I dreamed we were together in Venice, leaning over a balcony. He was wearing a blue cotton shirt with the sleeves rolled up. He turned and touched my neck. "You're beautiful. You need someone to look after you." Then we were dancing. A warm, languorous dance. We both had learned to cope with physical flaws—his leg, my voice—but suddenly his limp was gone and I was singing an oldies song. Singing that I had stars in my eyes. Singing that love never made a fool of me.

I was in the shower trying to clear my sinuses when the phone rang. I wrapped myself in a towel and picked it up.

"Andrew Rodale here. Something's come up. I'd like your thoughts." My heart gave a treacherous leap.

"Of course." At last, a breakthrough. The computer wizard had found a suspect. . . . He was under surveillance . . . in custody. . . . I wouldn't have to move.

"After we talked, I went to see my great-uncle. He's a wise old bloke who used to have strong ties in Hong Kong. He did some discreet digging. What he came up with may interest you."

"Yes? What?"

"In 1940 Galbraith joined the Royal Scots as a private and went from his native Glasgow to Hong Kong. In 1941, after General Maltby surrendered to the Japanese, Galbraith escaped to unoccupied China. He joined the BAAC, the British Army aid group that maintained links with the prison camps in Hong Kong."

I pulled the towel tighter. "George Galbraith? In China? He always told Lewis he knew absolutely nothing about that part of the world. He didn't like it. He wouldn't let Lewis open an office out there."

"There may be a reason. After the war ended, Galbraith went back to Hong Kong. He made his first fortune in black-market pharmaceuticals, mainly penicillin, some of it bad. The Chinese called it 'bad powder.' Several of the British died, including my great-uncle's friend Lady Fenwick. Long ago, but memories don't fade about certain things in certain circles. Why Galbraith will never get a peerage, no matter how many paintings he gives to the nation."

"Oh." So the old boy network still had power.

"My great-uncle pressed more buttons. It seems that Galbraith had a black-market partner, a Chinese soldier. Member of an important criminal triad. This man joined the communist revolution in the early days and rose very high in the military. He's now running a large weapons factory in Guangdong Province, if you follow."

"I follow," I said. "But I can't believe Galbraith would send his own technology to China. Risk being found out. I mean, the disgrace. The *scandal*. No more invitations to fish and shoot with dukes."

"Be that as it may, human nature is complex, as we both know. For some, there's no such thing as too much money. Taking risks can be an addictive form of gambling. And never forget the power of blackmail."

Water was dripping into my eyes. I wiped them with a corner of the towel. This was unexpected, to say the least. I had firmly convinced myself that Danny's tip was nothing but a self-serving trick.

"I've consulted up the line," Rodale was saying. "The feeling is that Galbraith can't be questioned officially, but it could be done with a light touch, along the lines of 'This is the story, sir. Can you shed any light?'"

I dropped the towel. "Question him? Ask him if he's a . . . a criminal? George Galbraith is proud. He has a battalion of lawyers. He'll hit you with a dozen lawsuits if you accuse him of something he didn't do."

"We're not ruling that out, but remember what's at stake. The longer it takes us to get answers, the harder to locate that notebook."

I coughed. "Sorry. Where would you have this talk? Who else would be there?"

"Bit of a cobble, but my thought is to meet Galbraith privately. Sound him out, leaving room to retreat. An old friend, Lucy Bellew, has a place near mine in Wiltshire. You may have heard of Elsham, a hundred rooms, famous gardens. Since her husband died, she's been running it as a snob appeal hotel, charges hair-raising prices. She's agreed to invite Galbraith to come and look at a Claude landscape she wants to sell. A private sale with several other bidders."

"I see." According to Robina, Andrew Rodale and his neighbor Lady Bellew were lovers. He was clearing his throat.

"Today is Tuesday the twenty-first. I realize it's very short notice, but I'd like you to fly over and be at Elsham Friday night. If I draw a blank with Galbraith, he'll go off with a painting and no harm done. On the other hand, if there's smoke in the woodwork, you'll be there to tell your very pivotal part of the story."

Fly over . . . tell your very pivotal part of the story. I sat down on the edge of the bed, telling myself not to lash out. We were working for the same end. He was following a lead I had given him. All the same, it was *outrageous* to think he could jerk me across the ocean on a moment's notice. I had a cold. Nothing to wear. No wish to meet his mistress.

"Mrs. Streat?"

I counted to ten. "It *is* very short notice. I really don't see how I can leave, but I should tell you one thing."

"Yes?"

"My husband had to deal with Galbraith for years. This is a very proud man. He'll never in this world admit to doing anything wrong."

"Our sense is that if he's made aware—convinced—that there could be a high-level investigation, he'll prefer to answer questions in an unofficial setting. Behind closed doors. He wouldn't like this part of his life story resurrected."

"Even so—there must be another way to find out if he's still involved with a Chinese partner."

"Indeed. Look. If you have a better plan, I'd be glad to

know." The edge in his voice was unmistakable. He hadn't actually said: "*You* started this," but the meaning was clear. I stood up and kicked the towel into a corner.

"I *don't* have a better plan. I *did* call and give you Galbraith's name. It's extremely inconvenient, but I'll fly over for Friday night. Just for one night." There was no missing the edge in *my* voice.

"Fair enough. Ian will organize the details, square them with your security. If anything new comes up, I'll be in touch."

"Good. Do that." I put the cell phone down. Standing at a window in the London flat, I had watched a fly struggle to free its feet from wet paint. Like that fly, I was caught fast in my own trap. Now, if Rodale's freewheeling plan went wrong, his informant, Mrs. Streat, would be there to share the blame.

part four

twenty-four

Friday, July 24

England

The early evening sun cast long shadows across the flat Wiltshire field patterned with bales of hay. A baling machine stood
deserted in the far corner. A century ago, farmworkers carrying
pitchforks would be trudging home between the hedgerows.

My driver turned his head and spoke over his shoulder.
"Nearly there, Mrs. Streat."

"How much longer?"

"Five minutes, thereabouts." Henn was ex–Metropolitan
Police, a member of Rodale's security team. A middle-aged
man, wearing a gray chauffeur's uniform, driving a comfortable
old Bentley. I stretched and rubbed my eyes.

"I must have slept most of the way."

"Nasty thing, jet lag."

"It is. Very." I had flown from JFK last night with a zealous
young woman who followed me down the aisle to the toilet,
mounted guard at the airport hotel, then handed me over to
Henn.

We were passing through a village; the low houses on either side of the street were built of soft, yellow stone. Vintage post-card England, with a pub named The Fallen Sparrow. Mossy graves behind an ivy-covered church. Women with string shopping bags, wearing long cardigans, stood in front of W. Morris Greengrocer.

I sat back, resisting the impulse to check my makeup and brush out my hair. Rodale's young halo-haired PA had taken care of my itinerary. There had been no contact with Rodale until just as I was leaving the pool house: "Sorry not to be in touch before, but it's been nonstop. I'll meet you at Elsham. Fill you in on the latest developments."

Picking up the brochure Henn had given me, I began to skim:

> *Welcome to Elsham, home of the Bellew family . . .*
> *recorded history of the house goes back to the*
> *thirteenth century . . . title bestowed by Queen*
> *Elizabeth after a ruinous three-week visit with a*
> *hundred retainers . . . main block of present house*
> *built in 1757 by Robert Adam . . . in 1767*
> *Robert Bellew made his second Grand Tour through*
> *Europe . . . brought back two shiploads of sculpture,*
> *tapestries, paintings, china.*

"We're there, Mrs. Streat," Henn said. "The estate begins at the high wall."

"You've been here before?"

"The wife and I came last spring. It's one of the finest places in England. She wanted to see the gardens; I had a beer in the buttery. Cost me an arm and a leg, it did."

We were turning through high iron gates topped by gold

finials. The avenue was shaded by rows of ancient oaks. Henn eased the car over a rattling cattle grid and onto the grass verge. He picked up a mobile phone.

"I'm on the avenue," he said. A pause. "Right. I'll tell her." He put the phone back and turned his head. "Lord Rodale's been delayed." I dropped the brochure.

"Delayed? Where is he? He said he'd be here to meet me."

"He rang Mercer a few moments ago. He's been held up in London."

"Oh. Who's Mercer?"

"My partner. The regular butler was given a short holiday. Mercer is taking his place."

"I see." I sat back. This was bad news. I had no wish to meet Galbraith by myself. "Did he—did Lord Rodale say when he'll get here?"

"He hopes to be down in time for dinner. Unless there's another delay," and the car left the verge.

As open spaces appeared between the ancient trees, Henn slowed.

"Elsham," he announced with pride.

I stared out the window. There, in the distance, stood a monumental stretch of gray stone embellished with balustrades and pediments, flanked by massive wings, A blue and white flag flew from one of the towers. In an epic film, men in costume would be galloping across the wide park. I crossed my legs and began to swing one foot. On my way to the airport, I had made a quick detour to a Madison Avenue boutique and bought black leather trousers and a new black dress.

The avenue ended in a sweeping court. Henn stopped in front of a double flight of stone stairs leading up to a massive open door.

"I'll fetch your bag from the boot."

"Thanks." As I got out, the sound of shrill barking shattered the air. A procession of black and tan Jack Russell terriers came streaming through the door. Their tails stood up like little flags, their eyes popped with excitement.

"Jamie, Biddy, Digger, down! *Down*, I say!" A woman came running after them, followed by an old black Labrador. "Mrs. Streat? I'm Lucy Bellew, welcome to Elsham. They jump, but they won't bite."

"Don't worry, I have a Jack Russell at home," I said, patting the dog who was joyously clawing my knees. Lady Bellew was small and pretty, with fluffy brown hair and wide-set light blue eyes. Good legs. She was wearing a short green linen skirt and a white shirt.

"They're usually allowed into this part of the house one by one, not such a rat pack. I hope you had a good drive down?" A breathless voice, as if her mind was constantly dashing ahead of her tongue.

"It was fine."

As the dogs and Lady Bellew led the way up to the huge door, a young black man in a white jacket appeared.

"Oh, this is Mercer, Mrs. Streat. He'll do about your bag and I'll take you straight to your room. Drinks in an hour, not much time for a toes up, I'm afraid." She glanced at me, a quick, assessing look. I could see myself through her eyes: Great hair. Amazing blue, those eyes. Admirable clothes.

In the enormous rotunda, a painted ceiling was supported by towering alabaster columns. A mass of pale pink and dark red dahlias stood on the round center table.

"Lovely arrangement," I said.

"Thank you, they take a frightful lot of time, but the bob-a-nobs—the public, that is—seem to like them. Shall I give you the guided tour as we go?"

"I wish you would." The lucky bob-a-nobs could buy tickets, walk around behind a frayed velvet rope, and leave.

"The hall is by Robert Adam. The portraits on the stairs are Kneller and Van Dyck. The po-faced lady in red velvet was a Yorkshire wool heiress who paid for a new roof at the turn of the century, the eighteenth century, that is." I glanced around as we went up a curved staircase that seemed to be suspended in space. Kneller. Van Dyck. Caroline, art collector and admirer of famous houses, would be in heaven.

"This is the West Wing," Lady Bellew said as we started down a long hall. It was painted a deep apricot color; the tall cabinets were filled with Sèvres tureens and compotes.

"We're rather small numbers tonight," she went on. "You, Andrew Rodale, George Galbraith, a Mrs. Dearborn: She's a collector, the wife of one of your senators, her daughter is with her. Oh, and there's Gordon Taylor from New York, he's rather a fixture here, the one art dealer I can trust. He's in charge of the sale tomorrow. I've never liked that Claude, so dull, I'm praying George Galbraith will pay a huge price."

"I hope he does," I said. How much had Rodale told her about his precarious plan? About me?

"Quite frankly, I'm not sure Andrew knows what he's doing. Rather peculiar, a security type pretending to be a butler. Still, it's only for one night. I've put my foot down about gunfire in the garden, mad chases through the shrubbery."

"Men and their games," I said lightly.

"Exactly, but I had no choice. Andrew was endlessly kind after Rupert dropped dead at a pheasant shoot. Friends are forever trying to knock our heads together. Oh, I almost forgot. Andrew said to tell you that Robina and Hank Lausch are coming."

I glanced at her, hiding surprise. "Oh. I see."

"I've put them near you in the West Wing so you won't be

alone. Robina and my husband are—were—distant cousins. She knows every inch of this house and the value of everything in it. I gather you know them."

"Hank for years, Robina just since they were married. I didn't realize they'd been invited."

"Not until yesterday. It was distinctly awkward. Andrew had me ring Robina and tell her I might sell a piece of majolica she covets—that obsession with majolica seems to take the place of children. Anyhow, *that* brought her on the run."

"I can imagine."

"I've put on a perfectly frightful reserve price, I really don't want to part with it. With any luck, Hank will be firm and put his foot down. We were all *enormously* relieved when Robina found herself a rich American and swept him off his feet. I adore Hank, he's a sweetie, but not much between the eyes, would you say?"

"But Hank has no—" I stopped in front of a breakfront cabinet and choked back the word "money." Lady Bellew was wrong. Hank was no rich American with a family fortune behind him. His salary in New York had been respectable, nothing more, and I happened to know that what he was paid in London wouldn't cover the cost of Robina's clothes.

"Hank *is* a dear," I said, feeling my way. "But I thought Robina had the money."

"Not she. The Fyfes are experts on living off their family and their wits, the old game of pay your gambling debts and let the tailor starve, but to be fair, Robina's life hasn't been easy. Her mother had ghastly delusions of grandeur. Rupert always said the countess was certifiably mad."

"Mad?"

"Not foaming-at-the-mouth mad, but certain in her bones

that the world owed her the best of everything. When the world didn't jump to oblige, she'd fall off her perch. Not easy for her children."

"No, not easy," I said, wanting to hear more.

"In any case, I stopped asking Robina after the maids told me she smoked in bed. I was absolutely livid."

"I don't blame you. A fire here would be horrible."

"My worst nightmare. When I married Rupert I was selling horses for a bloodstock agency. I never expected to be a glorified custodian, but one finds that looking after an old house becomes rather a sacred trust."

"Yes. It does." Had Rodale told her about my house?

"For me, Elsham is a seven-hundred-year-old grande dame who has seen a great deal of life. Nothing that goes on inside these walls could shock her; it's all happened before." She paused and opened a door.

"Here we are, then. Lady Honoria's room. My husband's great-grandmother. She's the beauty in the Sir Thomas Lawrence portrait over the mantel. Her lovers used to come through a little hidden door just down the hall, painted to match the walls. One was a famous Prime Minister; one can see him slipping through the door in his nightcap, clutching his candle."

I laughed. "I've always wondered what was behind those hidden doors."

"Dark little passages, mostly. Ways for servants to get from wing to wing without being seen. Architects like Robert Adam liked to do their work where it showed."

Lady Honoria's room was immense; the huge bed was hung with crimson damask curtains. Far above our heads, naked gods and goddesses cavorted on the painted ceiling. There was a silver biscuit box, fruit on a plate, new magazines, but sleeping here would be like spending the night in a museum.

Lady Bellew went to the dressing table and shifted a vase of flowers a few inches. Straightened the lace runner. "Tell me. Have you known Andrew for ages?"

"We met in London a few days ago. I gather he has a place nearby."

"The next village. *His* place is a little jewel, Palladian, a few big rooms, no kilometers of leaking roof and dry rot in the attics. An old bachelor uncle left it to him, that and all the money. Have you seen his house in town?"

"Once."

"A *mausoleum.* Frightful. Nothing's been touched since his mother died. Every woman he knows longs to have a go at it."

"He won't let them?"

"Can't be bothered. He's too madly consumed with hunting down criminals."

"I've heard he was divorced."

"For years. They married much too young. Rose was sweet, dreary, and she never stood up to him. He needs a woman who can send him writhing to his knees. Rose is far happier now, letting herself go and raising King Charles spaniels. Two nice daughters with good jobs."

"His leg. How did he hurt it?"

"A booby trap in Derry. All the ligaments and muscles were torn." She paused. "Andrew said your husband died a few months ago. I'm so sorry. Do you have children?"

"Two sons in college. What about you?"

"Two. My daughter's married, lives in Wales. My son is kicking up his heels in Australia, dreading the day when Mum can't cope."

"I don't blame him. It boggles the mind, how you keep this up."

"My ladies from the village clean in the winter, go through room by room. Violet, my housekeeper, is a treasure; her father was head gardener with twenty under him. Now we have six," she said, plumping a pillow on the gilded Regency chaise. "If you'd like tea, just ring the bell; it's the old-fashioned pull by the bed."

"No thanks. No tea."

"We're not frightfully dressy tonight, drinks in the Green Drawing Room. We've had people seriously lost, so my clever son made maps, like a museum; there's one on the dressing table. Oh, here's Mercer with your bag. Eight o'clock, then," she said, and disappeared. A charming babbler, probably good in bed. Spacy, but no fool.

The temporary butler had the tall, graceful look of a Jamaican. He wouldn't be likely to drop glasses or spill soup.

"Where shall I put your bag, Mrs. Streat? There doesn't seem to be a closet."

"Try the armoire." I touched the loose flowers, needing to feel my way. "Henn told me you're his partner."

"Right."

"Lord Rodale said he'd be here to meet me; tell me about the plans for tonight."

"He's on his way. He asked me to give you this." Mercer reached into his pocket and pulled out a gold coin. It was embossed with a Russian double eagle and hung from a thin gold chain. I took it in my hand.

"What's this for?"

"It's called a safety line. You wear it around your neck. If you press the coin, it sends a signal and I'll know where you're at."

"My aunt wears one that connects her to a hospital, at least she says she wears it. But why would I need this here?"

"Just a precaution. No violent types in the house that we know of, but I can't be everywhere, not in a hundred rooms."

"You certainly can't. Has Mr. Galbraith come yet?"

"An hour ago. He's in the East Wing. If you need anything, just ring for the butler." He grinned and left, a handsome young security agent who was enjoying his part and playing it with exuberance.

In the distance, a church bell rang. In the village, people were eating, watching television, drinking at The Fallen Sparrow. A quiet, peaceful place, but back in the London mausoleum Rodale's assistant was working around the clock to find a gang of dedicated criminals. Agencies at opposite ends of the world were listening for key words in the ether. It was hard to imagine how tonight's talk with Galbraith could move the process, but it was important to be flexible. Stay in the background. Let Rodale call the shots.

After a moment, I went to the window and looked out at the axis of formal gardens. The little lake and a miniature Greek temple, the essence of the elegant eighteenth century. This was Rodale's world. Lady Bellew was his kind of woman. I was the outsider who hadn't even known that Robina had no money.

A stream of water rose from the fountain in the lake. I stared at the graceful pattern of drops and thought about Lady Bellew's announcement: "We were all *enormously* relieved when Robina found herself a rich American and swept him off his feet."

Rooks were flying about in trees that bordered a walk between a row of double yews. I watched them, grappling with this startling new set of facts. If Hank had no money and

Robina had no money—Lady Bellew was family; she must know—then who in God's name was paying for a house in Eaton Terrace and a country place in Hampshire? *And* the best clubs in London. *And* a Rolls-Royce and a Jaguar. A collection of early Italian majolica worth a fortune.

The resident pack of Jack Russell terriers raced along the walk between the yews, sending the rooks into the air. I stared down, trying to ignore the queasy feeling in my stomach. Kind, guileless Uncle Hank had spent weekends horsing around the pool with my boys. Kind, guileless Hank was always ready to lend a helping hand. But . . . Hank had access to papers in the London office. He knew about Lewis's early morning walks. He knew my plans.

I pressed my hands to my stomach. Not Hank. Not *Hank*— but on the morning of July 10 Caroline had called from New York asking me to change my flight. I had scribbled a fax to Hank with the new time and place for Wheeler to meet me. Inserted it into Ned's machine and sent it winging off to Hampshire. There had been no reason to say that Caroline would be with me. "One person," Tom had kept saying at the Heathrow Horizon Hotel. "Only one person." Could that small omission have saved my life?

The dogs disappeared. The rooks settled back into the trees. I turned from the window, still clutching my stomach. If I touched the coin on the safety line, Mercer would come. I could tell him that I had a migraine coming on. I would have to lie flat in bed. Not leave my room.

The coin lay on the dressing table. I picked it up, took a deep breath, and put it down. Granny Metcalf had believed that courage must be exercised like muscles. I could hear her voice: "Face your fences squarely, Emma. Finish what you start." Avoiding Hank tonight was not an option.

From high on the wall above the carved mantel, Lady Honoria's beautiful painted face stared down at me disdainfully.

"Up yours," I said to the dead beauty, and went to take clothes out of my bag.

twenty-five

I brushed my hair until it stood out in a coppery mass around my face. Zipped myself into the new black dress with a long skirt and wide shoulder straps. Put on the tacky safety line. Picked up the map and shut the door. There were no locks.

I was late. The hall was empty and silent. The Lausches must have gone ahead. As I marched through the Portrait Gallery, the eyes of ruffed and wigged ancestors seemed to follow me. Then came the Tapestry Room, then the double-cube Red Drawing Room with paintings by Canaletto and G. Poussin. By now my eyes were getting used to the grand scale. At last, the Green Drawing Room.

In the distance, the other guests had gathered at long windows that looked out on an Elizabethan knot garden. Squaring my shoulders, I crossed the faded, buckling parquet floor. Appearance was key, the performer going onstage, but right now I felt alone in a jungle, listening for snapping twigs, moving branches.

"There you are." Lady Bellew, wearing short, floating blue silk, left the group and came forward to meet me. "What a heaven dress. Now. This is Roger Hamphill, a neighbor, Sir Roger, to be precise, but you mustn't talk to him, he's next to you at dinner. Champagne?"

Mercer was passing a tray of tall champagne glasses with studied skill. As I took a glass, Hank turned and saw me. His round face beamed.

"Emma. For God's sake. I thought you were in Hardwick picking up the pieces."

"I was, but my art-collecting godmother heard that Lady Bellew was selling a Claude landscape. She asked me to come over and look at it." During a quick bath in the eight-foot-long tub, I had worked out a halfway believable reason to be here. Hank shook his head.

"Bad luck. Galbraith wants it. Why he came down from Scotland."

"Oh Lord, oh well, I don't think Caroline really cares. She was just trying to get me out of Hardwick," I said, aware that George Galbraith was standing a few feet away, looking down his nose at me. An aging giant with veined, mottled hands.

"Good evening, Mr. Galbraith," I said, smiling.

"Mrs. Streat." The courtly bow, a sidelong glance from those pale blue eyes. "You're looking well. Is this—er—your first visit to Elsham?"

"Yes, it is."

"Henry Lausch told me about your house. A sad loss."

"It was. Very sad."

"What brings you here tonight? I—er—wasn't aware that you are a collector."

I kept smiling. If he called my bluff I could reach Caroline on her last night in Cambridge. She would jump at the chance to bid against him, a despised rival. "As a matter of fact, I'm here for my godmother. I think you know her. Caroline Vogt."

His lips tightened. "Ah. Mrs. Vogt," he said abruptly, and turned to Sir Roger.

"Emma." Robina was coming towards me, walking in her unique way, hips slightly forward. She was wearing a white silk dress and a necklace of pale green carved jade that must have cost the earth. She raised her eyebrows.

"I couldn't believe it when I saw you walk across the room. You should have let us know you were coming. We could have brought you down."

"It was very last-minute. My godmother sent me here to look at a Claude. Maybe make a bid."

"Rather a lot to ask, I'd have thought, after what you've been through."

"Not really. She's the closest thing I have to a mother."

"Waste of your time. Galbraith will get it. Did she set a limit?"

"A limit? Yes. Of course." I glanced around, feeling trapped, and caught Lady Bellew's eye. She moved towards us.

"You two already know each other; you can talk later. I want Mrs. Streat to meet Gordon Taylor and the Dearborns." Under the vague manner, Lady Bellew was keeping a firm hand on the mysterious crosscurrents running through her house. "Delia Dearborn is studying native Peruvian dances in London, so clever of her," she chattered, steering me towards a waiflike girl wearing a black tank top and black lipstick. Suddenly Lady Bellew stopped. I followed her look.

Rodale was crossing the room, tall and imposing in formal black evening clothes. I took a quick sip of champagne. Lady Bellew waved him over.

"Andrew. At last."

"Sorry to be late, Lucy. Good evening, Mrs. Streat." He glanced at my necklace and then at the dress, a man who liked women and knew how to please them.

"Good evening, Lord Rodale."

"Good flight?"

"Fine."

Lady Bellew glanced at her watch. "Time to start moving the troops. I know you Americans love a long cocktail hour, but here it's two glasses of champagne and in we go. You'll have to make do with wine at dinner, Andrew."

He nodded. "Right, but move the troops slowly, will you? I need a word with Mrs. Streat."

"Not too long a word." Lovers who understood each other very well? He turned to me.

"Have you had a good look at the Claude?"

"Not yet."

"It's over on that wall," and we moved towards a small painting of trees and meadows and a distant tower.

"I'm telling everyone I came to bid for my godmother," I said, tilting my head to one side as if making a study. "You weren't here, so I had use my own judgment."

"Sorry about that. I was leaving when a call came in about funds shifted from Hong Kong to an offshore bank in the Bahamas. It might have come in handy tonight. Turned out to be useless."

"I see." I made a circle of thumb and finger and looked through it like an art expert. "Lady Bellew says she won't miss this and neither would I. Why are the Lausches here?"

"Because Lausch knows how the security works—or doesn't work—in that office. My plan is to take Galbraith and Lausch into the library after the men finish their port. Begin by saying copies of a project may have been stolen."

"Yes, but before then there's something I have to tell you. It could be important. It came to me when Lady Bellew said—"

"Later," Rodale said under his breath. Galbraith had come from behind and was joining us.

"Good evening, Rodale. I hear you outbid the Americans for that early Stubbs. Are you deserting the sporting genre?"

"Not at all, but I've always liked this particular Claude."

Mercer was passing by with his tray. I gave him my glass, afraid I might break the fragile stem. I *had* to be wrong about Hank. Robina always kept him on a very short leash. It would take enormous talent to lead a double life under her nose.

The dining room was vast, with pale neo-classical plaster-work. The long polished table in the center was bare except for an ornate silver centerpiece. Lady Bellew led us to the far end of the room where a smaller table was set between rococco pier mirrors.

"Tomorrow night we'll be rather grand, forty for dinner, then a recital in the Red Drawing Room. Mr. Galbraith, you're here beside me. I want to hear all about Scotland and Malcolm's place. Duncan Liddell tells me that if anyone plugs in a razor, let alone a computer, every fuse in the castle blows."

Hank was on my left, Sir Roger on my right. As two young maids in black dresses and white aprons brought soup, I turned to Sir Roger, a cheerful-looking man with red cheeks and a white walrus mustache.

"It amazes me, how you manage to keep these huge places in your families."

He nodded, pleased to be on safe conversational footing. "We all have to compete for the public these days. I let a bit of fishing; Lucy has guests and the public, but I think she rather likes it. To be frank, after Rupert died, we never thought she'd turn out to be such an organizer. A charmer, my late wife thought, but head in the clouds, forever babbling on. We were wrong, I'm glad to say."

Roast lamb and braised vegetables followed the soup. I pushed food around on my plate. The senator's wife was telling art expert Gordon Taylor about a visit to the Matisse Chapel in Grasse: "Nobody realizes how much Matisse owed to the nuns who took care of him." Two innocent bystanders, oblivious to the growing tensions in this civilized setting. Once I had asked an Olympic downhill racer what was in his mind as he stood at the starting gate, about to plunge down the icy slope.

"Focus," he had said. "Looking ahead. Getting a line."

The maids were removing the Worcester dinner plates. Lady Bellew was turning from Galbraith to Gordon Taylor. As we switched partners, Hank shook his head.

"Hell of a blow, losing that house. All the good times. It was pretty special."

"I know."

"Enough said for now." He picked up his wineglass. "By the way, what happened to you after the ambassador's reception? We thought you were going back to Cambridge. Robina called St. Paul's the next day. The porter told her you'd fallen down some stairs and gone home. How's the arm now?"

"My—it's nearly well. Just a few twinges." I dug in my poles and pushed off down the slope. "Hank, I meant to ask you at that reception, but there wasn't time. Wasn't Wheeler supposed to meet me the morning I arrived in London? Take me to Cambridge?"

"That's right. The Heathrow Horizon. Don't tell me he went to the terminal."

"He didn't, but a very peculiar driver came up to me in the lobby. He barely spoke English. When he heard there were two people, my godmother and me, he turned and ran."

"We don't use an agency, just Wheeler and sometimes Ron. Good Lord. What did you do?"

"Hired another car, but that driver wasn't just cruising the lobby looking for single women. He asked for me at the desk. He gave me your name. He knew I was going to Cambridge."

"Can't understand that."

"Neither can I, and I want to know why the man went berserk when he heard there was someone coming with me. He couldn't get away fast enough. I mean, what was he planning to do? Kidnap me?"

"You didn't report it to the hotel?"

"I wanted to talk to you first, but there never seemed to be a chance. Now that I know you didn't send him, I'll get to work. Notify the police. Give them a report and a description. There may have been other complaints. In fact, I may talk to my friend Nick at the embassy—you met him at the reception. Ask him to put me in touch with Scotland Yard. What do you think?" I kept my eyes on Hank's face. He was frowning.

"Haven't heard of any kidnappings lately, not like the old days, but I don't like the fact that the driver knew your name. And mine. Look. Call your friend Nick by all means, but I've got a contact at Scotland Yard. An Inspector Munro. Helped us with a break-in at Eaton Square. Nice fellow. I can try to reach him."

"Would you?"

"First thing in the morning."

I nodded. Genuine concern or great acting? I must press on.

"Something else," I said, keeping my voice steady. "Wheeler and I talked about this on the way from Cambridge to the ambassador's reception. He was really upset when I told him what happened. He said his wife got a message on the machine telling him *not* to meet me."

"Hold it. Wheeler says he got a message not to meet you?"

"That's what he said."

"You faxed me on a Friday. To Hampshire. Right?"

"Right."

"I got to Hampshire in the late afternoon. I read it. Two minutes later I put a message on Wheeler's answering machine: 'Meet Mrs. Streat Sunday, same time, but meet her at the Heathrow Horizon, not the terminal.' Couldn't have been clearer."

"He got that, but then there was a second message saying not to meet me at all. He figured you must have decided to come yourself."

"Not like Wheeler to make a mistake. I never sent a second message."

"And I sent just that one fax."

Mercer was refilling wineglasses. Lady Bellew was discussing Scotland with Galbraith. Across the table, Rodale was talking to the young dance wannabe. The lines around his eyes fanned out as he smiled; his neck was tan against the white starched shirt. I studied Hank's face. He was rubbing his chin, looking puzzled.

"Makes no sense. People are in and out of the house, maids, guests, but the fax machine is tucked away in my little office off our bedroom. You know the place. Just a cubby hole. No one is allowed to touch my desk except Robina. She tidies up, keeps me organized, bless her. We'll ask her about it."

The maids under Lady Bellew's watchful eye were passing a chocolate souffle and cream. "The cream is from our cows," Lady Bellew said brightly to Gordon Taylor. Robina was sitting across the table talking to Galbraith, tilting her smooth dark head. Hank was still rubbing his chin.

"Look, Emma. You'd better come up to London with us after

the auction. I'll get hold of Inspector Munro. Would that work for you?"

"I think so." I closed my eyes for a second, hearing Sergeant Johnson's voice on a hot July morning: "One little lead can get the case rolling. . . . People remember something that didn't seem right, but wasn't important at the time."

"No one is allowed to touch my desk except Robina," Hank had just said. Harmless words—with enormous implications. Through Hank, Robina had access to the London office. To the company flat. To my travel plans. And—Robina was cold-blooded enough to hire a Tom Myers to do her dirty work. Greedy enough to make money by selling stolen technology. Hank wiped his mouth.

"That's settled. We'll have that dinner you missed when you went off after the ambassador's reception. Robina was in a snit about losing you to the embassy chap. She likes to know everything that's going on. Run the show."

"Yes. She does." Robina and I were friends. We went out to *lunch.* She had kissed me after Lewis's service.

Lady Bellew was standing up. "Attention, please, everyone. There are two big groups coming here tomorrow. Ladies from the Garden Club of America for a tour and lunch. In the evening, a dinner and recital to benefit our local orchestra. We're open to the public from ten until four but never fear, no one will come wandering into your rooms. Now, ladies, coffee in the Morning Room. Roger, will you see to the port?"

The Morning Room was comfortably small. A bright fire burned in the iron grate. A portrait of Lady Bellew in an eighteenth-century pose hung over the mantel; she was wearing a large white hat and four terriers posed proudly at her feet.

After sitting down at a low table under the portrait, she began to dispense coffee from two silver pots.

"Real or decaf, Mrs. Streat?"

"Real, please." I looked at Robina. "Shall we go over here?" I asked, moving towards a love seat across the room. She shrugged her shoulders and followed.

"I'm perishing for a cigarette but Lucy is so paranoid about fire. Ridiculous. One might almost think it's *her* family place. As for that Dearborn woman, if she says one more word about the Matisse Chapel I'll throttle her."

"Poor Gordon Taylor got the brunt at dinner."

"Ghastly woman, but I gather she's part of this peculiar bun fight over the Claude. How on earth did your godmother hear that Lucy might sell a painting?"

"News spreads fast. The big dealers know what Caroline wants. I gather you're here for a piece of majolica."

"Who told you that?"

"Lady Bellew."

"Poor Lucy." Robina crossed her legs. "She does her best, but she must be in serious trouble with Inland Revenue. Her own fault, of course."

I took a sip of coffee. "Actually, I have to admire her," I said. "I was feeling very sorry for myself, no roof over my head. Almost worse to be holding up the weight of centuries." Robina must have gone at night to the cluttered little office on Berkeley Square. Let herself in with a copy of Hank's key. Found the blueprints. If I was right, her luck had run out when Nelson Bin went to see Lewis. From then on it must have been a desperate race to cover her tracks.

". . . Rupert—my cousin—was rather a dear. He would have *given* me the majolica and said it belonged in the family. By rights, of course, the place should have come to me." I glanced at her. Had Robina inherited her mother's delusions of grandeur?

"I thought there was a son," I said. "I only hope he wants all this. Mine certainly wouldn't."

Across the room, Mrs. Dearborn was telling Lady Bellew how much she loved the BBC programs. "So educational. We have nothing but violence and sex at home." The waif daughter looked sulky. I took a deep breath and plunged down the slopes for the second time in an hour, forcing myself to make the leap between guesswork and action.

"By the way, Hank's asked me to come up to London with you tomorrow. He wants me to talk to an Inspector Munro at Scotland Yard."

"Oh? What about?"

"It's about the fax I sent Hank on the tenth changing my flight. Wheeler was supposed to meet me, but a very threatening driver came instead. If he's a public menace the top people at Scotland Yard should know about him. They have ways of finding cars. Tracing calls."

Robina's eyebrows went up. "He didn't hurt you, did he?"

"No."

"Then I can't imagine why the sleuths would bother. Not after all this time." She touched the jade necklace. I put my cup down on a small lacquer table.

"All the same, I want them to find out who sent the driver and why he rushed off when I told him my godmother was with me. Find out who gave Wheeler a message telling him not to come."

Robina touched the jade necklace again. "No need to make a fuss. There's a perfectly simple answer. Hank, poor lamb, is apt to be a bit careless about faxes. He probably mixed up the messages," she said, and began to stir the last drops of coffee in her cup. Her hand was steady, but there were brilliant red circles on her white cheeks. Telltale color for a woman who had enormous control. Dear, gullible Hank had just put a noose around his wife's throat—and we both knew it. I sat still. Not Danny. Not Galbraith. Not Hank. Not a network of terrorists. Lady Bellew was looking at us.

"You two seem very cozy. More coffee? Oh, Mercer, there you are. Mrs. Streat and Mrs. Lausch need more coffee."

Mercer picked up the silver pot. As he came towards us, I touched the coin on the safety line.

"Mercer, I need your help. I have to call my son in the States before it gets too late. Is there a phone nearby I can use?"

His expression changed. "There's one in an alcove off the rotunda, Mrs. Streat. I can show you."

"Thanks." I stood up. "Be right back," I said to Robina. "You met my son Jake at the service, not the one with red hair. He's being a saint, giving me a hand with the ghastly insurance people."

"Of course." Robina smiled, a small twist of the lips.

"Thank God you got the message," I said to Mercer as we went down the long hall. "I have to see Lord Rodale. Right now. Where is he?"

"The men have finished their port. Lord Rodale is taking Mr. Galbraith and Mr. Lausch to the library."

"You'll have to stop him. This is important."

"He'll want a reason, Mrs. Streat. What shall I tell him?"

We had reached the rotunda. I turned and faced him.

"There's no time to explain. Just tell him Lady Robina is the criminal everyone's looking for."

"I'm to say Lady Robina is a criminal?" Mercer hesitated, a young professional on shaky ground.

"Yes. Lady Robina. After you get hold of Lord Rodale, come

back to the Morning Room and tell me my call has come through, my son is on the line, whatever. I'll try to keep her talking."

In the Morning Room, Lady Bellew was still sitting at the low table. Mrs. Dearborn had switched gears and was describing an estate auction at Sotheby's. I looked at the love seat. Looked again. Robina had gone.

I ran. Mercer was almost out of sight when I reached him.

"She's *gone*. Oh God, let me think. She wouldn't go off in her car without money. She'd have to go back to her room. Get cash and credit cards. A coat."

Mercer shook his head. "She may have just gone to the cloakroom."

"I tell you, she'll make a run for it. She knows a dozen ways to get out of the house. She knows it like the back of her hand."

"Mrs. Streat. Are you sure—"

"Don't just *stand* there. Find Lord Rodale. I'm going to the West Wing."

twenty-six

At nine thirty the house was dim and shadowy, lit by a few small bulbs in wall sconces. I ran back through the Red Drawing Room, the Tapestry Room, the Portrait Gallery. The portraits were dim and colorless; the furnishings had lost their shapes. As I went, the rich food churned in my stomach. One sentence hammered in my brain: *She's not going to get away.*

At last, the stairs that led to the West Wing and the long hall with breakfront cabinets. In my room, the rosy nymphs cavorted on the ceiling, holding out apples to goddesses. A water carafe stood on the table by the curtained bed. My new white T-shirt lay neatly folded on the linen pillows.

I stood still, catching my breath, my back to the door. I must find the Lausches' room and keep Robina there—by force, if necessary. A plate of fruit stood on the table by the Regency chaise. There was a knife with a gold handle, no, too small for a weapon. A spray bottle of cologne would be better. I would aim for the eyes—

"You and that bogus butler." Robina's voice in my ear. "You didn't call your son." As I jumped, she whipped a cord around my wrists, pulling them together. Her face was a few inches away. The red circles had spread over her cheekbones.

"I don't know what you're talking about," I said, clamping down on visceral fear.

"Lies. You aren't here to bid on a painting." She reached around and tore off the safety line. She was holding a Swiss Army knife, blade open, a few inches from my chest. The fingers of the other hand opened and closed in spasms. I tried to move my wrists. Oh God, I should have waited for Mercer. I should have locked the door.

"You'd better undo that cord. I told Mercer about you. He's on his way."

"No use, my dear. Turn around," and she prodded me forward. As we reached the hall, I stumbled, playing for time. The knife pricked my spine.

"Robina, don't be a fool—"

"Say another word and I'll slit your throat," she said calmly, and opened the little hidden door, painted to match the walls. Pressed a switch.

In the dim light I could see a flight of steep stairs and rough unpainted walls. The unfinished part of the house that guests never saw. The air was musty and smelled of mice.

"Up." We began to climb. It was hard to keep my balance with hands tied behind my back. Black dots pulsated behind my eyes. Stupid, so stupid to have rushed off alone.

"Faster." She pushed another light switch. We started down a long hall lined with little cubicles of rooms. Behind me, Robina was breathing hard. Instead of Caleche, I could smell the sharp, acrid odor of fear. A good sign. She might still be open to reason.

"Listen," I said, trying not to gasp. "It's not too late to go back. You never killed anyone. Tom Myers did all the killing, not you."

She gave the cord a vicious twist. "That overpaid bungler. He couldn't get rid of you. He couldn't find the notebook. All my work for nothing." The knife jabbed into my back, a small knife, but sharp enough to hack me to death. If she left me bleeding in one of these rooms no one would find me until my body began to smell. My boys—my poor boys. I tried again.

"*Think,* Robina. Kill me and you'll spend the rest of your life in prison. Raped. Beaten. A pariah. No one will lift a finger to help you."

"In here." She opened a door and pushed me forward. I had a quick glimpse of a room filled with old-fashioned glass cases framed in wood. "When Lucy told me you were coming I took a can of petrol from the garage and put it in the cupboard. First you, then the house. It should have been mine. By the time there's smoke I'll be back in the Morning Room. I'll go outside with the others. No fingerprints."

"*Robina.*" Like a hooked fish, back arching, I tried to get my hands free.

"Stand still. This won't take long." As she reached around me to open the cupboard door, I threw myself backwards. She staggered under my weight. The knife cut my cheek as she went down, crashing into a glass case.

I ran for my life. Along the hall, down one flight of stairs, another hall. Hands still tied, tripping over my feet. Blood was running down my cheek, dripping onto my neck. Once I lost my way and found myself in a room filled with broken china and chairs without legs. At last, the first flight of unpainted stairs. I opened the door and fell headfirst into the hall. Mercer was standing outside my room, knocking. He turned and saw me. I struggled to my knees.

"She took me to the top of the house. She's going to set the house on fire." In seconds he was beside me, helping me up.

"Lady Robina?"

"I told you. She has a knife. She's got gasoline, I mean petrol. My hands."

"Hold still." The cord fell to the ground. "I'll go for Lord Rodale."

"No, no, for God's sake don't leave me alone." I clutched at his white jacket, babbling wildly. "She might come back. She tried to kill me, she's somewhere in the house."

"I won't leave you. Can you walk?"

"She tried to burn me alive, she's going to burn down the house—yes, I can walk."

"I'll bring Lord Rodale to the rotunda. You fetch Lady Bellew."

Nothing had changed in the Morning Room. The portrait of Lady Bellew and the dogs still hung over the mantel. The fire burned brightly in the grate. Lady Bellew was showing Mrs. Dearborn a small silver box. She saw me standing in the doorway and gasped. The box fell to the floor. Mrs. Dearborn shrank back and screamed.

For a few seconds I stood still, seeing myself in their eyes. A few minutes ago this woman had been sitting on the love seat, smiling, sipping coffee. Now there was blood running down her face. Her dress was torn. A Lucia di Lammermoor gone mad. Lady Bellew stepped forward as if to shield her guests.

"What on earth—"

"There's been an accident. Lord Rodale wants you in the rotunda."

"Mrs. Dearborn—Delia—stay here. I'll be right back." A hostess whose party was suddenly destructing.

Rodale was standing beside the center table with the dahlia arrangement. He took a step towards me. "Christ," he said under his breath. Then he turned to Lady Bellew. "Robina's gone bonkers. She attacked Mrs. Streat, then took her up to the attics."

"*Robina?* She was perfectly all right a few moments ago. The two of them were sitting together having coffee."

"She tried to kill Mrs. Streat. She may try to set the house on fire."

"*Fire?*" Lady Bellew's hands went to her face. "Find her. Stop her." The rising voice of panic.

"Lucy. Pay attention. Get everyone together, all the maids and the guests. Put them in the Green Drawing Room. There are doors to the garden in case you have to get out."

"She couldn't. She *couldn't.*"

"We'll need the fire brigade. A doctor. Have Roger ring them. He's a magistrate; they'll pay attention to him. Mercer and I will go up and look for her." The deep voice, taking charge. "Can she get out of the West Wing through the attics?"

"Oh God, let me think. I don't *know;* there are so many doors; she knows every inch of the house."

"Who've you got for men living on the place?"

"Just Maddox in the stables."

"Get Maddox on the line. Tell him to go to the garage and watch the cars. When the fire brigade comes, send them up. And Lucy, not a word to Lausch. If he wants to know where Robina is, tell him she's with me. Roger will help you. Hurry."

"Maddox and Roger," she said under her breath, and ran, the blue silk skirt floating behind her.

Rodale turned to Mercer. "Find two big torches. Come up to the landing, Mrs. Streat. One look at you and the maids will have hysterics."

The landing was wide. The po-faced wool heiress gazed blankly ahead, oblivious to looming disaster. I sat down on the stairs and touched my face. The trickle of blood had stopped.

"Can you tell me what happened?" Rodale was standing a few steps below me. I stared at his hands gripping the banister and tried to concentrate.

"It was all so fast. At dinner I asked Hank about the fax I sent him. About sending the driver to the Heathrow Horizon. Suddenly—it *wasn't* Hank. Someone else saw that fax. It *had* to be Robina. I talked to her in the Morning Room. She knew I knew. There were red circles on her cheeks."

"And?"

"I left her. I asked Mercer to find you. When I went back she wasn't there. I thought she must have gone to her room to get money. She came up behind me and tied my hands. She had a knife. We went to the top of the house. She was going to set me on fire and run back and be with the others. The house would burn to the ground. No fingerprints."

"Good God."

Doors were opening below. The maids, two in black dresses, two in white aprons, scurried around the marble columns. A house infected with fear, the inhabitants running like animals in a forest fire. Lady Bellew appeared.

"Where's Mary? Don't act like sheep, you're perfectly safe, the fire brigade is on the way. Come along to the Green Drawing Room, all of you."

Rodale took my arm. "Go down and stay with the others. Where the hell is Mercer?"

"Sorry, sir. Dead batteries." Mercer was hurrying up the stairs holding two flashlights. I stood up.

"I'm going with you," I said.

"Get someone to look at that cut—"

"No. She knows every inch of the house. She even turned on lights."

"We're wasting time. Go to Lucy."

I didn't move. "Will you *listen?* I *know* where she took me. You don't. It's like a maze up there, dozens of rooms. While you're tramping around getting lost, she'll get away. She may be gone by now."

A pause. Rodale nodded. "You stuck out the foot that tripped her. Come."

twenty-seven

The little door in the hall was half-open. We started up the flight of wooden stairs framed by rough boards. The dim lights were still on. As we climbed, I stumbled. Rodale took my arm.

"All right?"

"All right." We were reaching the first narrow hall and the row of cubicles.

"Maids' rooms," Rodale said under his breath. As we went by, I thought of young girls carrying coal, slop jars, tea trays, from morning to night. Their rooms up here would be icy in winter, airless in summer.

Another flight of stairs. We went carefully in near darkness, eyes straining, listening. At the top of the next flight of stairs we stopped.

"Which way?" Rodale asked.

"I think—down here." Dear God, don't let her get away or burn the house down and I'll never ask you for anything again.

Mercer opened the door to a storeroom filled with china

pitchers and night jars. An old harp with the gilt falling off. Methodically, he swung his light around every cluttered space. No figure crouched in the shadows. No one rushed out at us, hands clawing.

The next passage ended in the vast echoing space under the long roof beam—a great beam that had been there for seven hundred years, centuries before the Pilgrims landed on Plymouth Rock.

"We need more lights. Dogs," Mercer muttered to Rodale as we went down another hall.

"Not those damn terriers. We may have missed her; she may have doubled back another way." His voice was sharp with frustration. He walked to a bricked-up wall. "The West Wing ends here. We must have missed something."

"We have," I said to him. "We've missed the room she took me to. There were glass cases, like a museum."

"The Science Room. Every family had an amateur scientist in those days. It must be down that hall where we had to make a choice."

I bit my lip. "Oh God, I was so sure I could find it."

"She can't go far. We'll send out alerts, put out roadblocks—"

"Sir. *Sir.*" Mercer had gone ahead. Now he was running towards us. "Smoke, sir. Coming from under a door." I raised my head. A faint smell of smoke was drifting down the hall. Fire, so harmless in a chimney, so deadly in a cupboard doused with gasoline. Rodale swung around and handed me his light.

"Take this. Send the firemen. Hurry."

The way back was endless. I tried to run. The heavy light wobbled in my hand. Halfway down a flight of stairs I dropped it. Once I lost my way and ended up in a storeroom filled with broken lamps and chairs with legs missing.

At last, the final set of stairs. I flew down them and out into the hall. Three firemen were coming towards me. They were wearing helmets and boots and carried extinguishers. I pointed to the small door.

"Up there. People. Smoke."

"Come on, lads," and they went thudding up the stairs.

The door to my room was open. I stumbled to the chair in front of the dressing table and collapsed.

Men hurried by in the hall. "Hoses on the walls were inspected last month," one shouted.

"We need small extinguishers."

"Get Dr. Bentham."

I laid my head on the glass-covered tabletop. I should keep running, find the Green Drawing Room, but my legs were cramping in painful spasms. Disconnected pictures raced through my mind. Little stick men moving around in front of my bombed house. Impossible for these firemen to put out flames ignited by gasoline. In a few minutes the fire would go roaring down the stairs at Elsham, crackling the irreplaceable Knellers and the Van Dycks. Destroying the po-faced wool heiress whose money had saved the roof.

No smoke drifted into the room. After a while I raised my head and stared at myself in the mirror. Blood was trickling down my cheek again. Dirt streaked my face. The cord, a curtain tieback, had made red welts on my wrists.

Men were going back and forth outside my door.

"It was them thick walls what saved the house," one said.

"Going to be a job, getting a stretcher down those stairs."

"A body bag will do. A lad's gone to fetch one."

"Who was she?"

"A guest, is what I heard. Done herself in. Must have tried to take the house with her."

I closed my eyes, feeling deathly sick. Robina had fallen against the glass case, but to set the fire she *must* have walked into the cupboard and used her gold cigarette lighter. Would the agony last for seconds? Minutes? Buddhist priests on the evening news had sat motionless as they went up in flames.

Without knowing I had moved, I found myself standing in front of the Victorian armoire. Reaching in, I threw the empty bag onto the floor. Pulled out the white shirt, the shiny new black raincoat. Sweaters and shoes. Oh God, the layer between the will to live and madness was thin, so horribly thin.

"Mrs. Streat?" A middle-aged woman wearing a flowered apron came hurrying through the door. She was carrying a small tray. "I'm Violet, the housekeeper. M'lady sent me with brandy." She put the tray on a table and handed me a glass. "No danger now, but oh dear, your face. Dreadful, what I heard Mercer telling m'lady. Lady Robina, of all people to start that fire, and I was the one showed her the cupboard in the Science Room. People like to see what's at the top of the house and she was always one to go poking her nose in cupboards, acting like the place was hers."

I swallowed and choked. Brandy. Fire in the throat. Violet picked up the broken safety line and put it beside the decanter.

"Pretty little thing. You'll need to get it mended. Oh dear, oh dear, I was the one told her about old Sir Gilbert, how he did experiments to see how long people could breathe in that cupboard. A boy in the village died before they put a stop to *that*. Seventy years ago, it was, but to set a fire, bring down this old house—fair turns my stomach. Never know, do you?"

I didn't answer. As Violet bustled around the room, turning

on lights. I concentrated on the portrait of Lady Honoria. Violet followed my look.

"Very fine, Her Ladyship, but I'd never have a wink of sleep in this room, all those little chaps on the ceiling staring down at me." She paused for breath. "My head's awhirl. We must get you out of that dress. Clean your face and tuck you into bed."

I dug my nails into the palms of my hands. "I'm leaving," I said.

Violet put down the T-shirt. "Leaving?"

"Now. For London. I need a car and driver."

Violet pulled at the straps of her flowered apron. Looked at the pile of clothes on the floor, the open bag. "I'll fetch m'lady. You put your feet up and rest while I get m'lady. Ah, here she is now."

Lady Bellew was wearing a long tan cardigan over the blue dress. She had the look of a woman who was needed in three places at once. A woman trying to keep her head above a rising flood of disasters.

"Mrs. Streat. I can't tell you—frightful, absolutely frightful, that this should happen to you at Elsham." She turned to Violet. "We must get her straight to bed."

"She's asking for a car, m'lady. She's packing. She wants to leave."

"Leave? Now?" Lady Bellew looked at the clothes scattered on the floor. "Good heavens, you've had a terrible shock; you can't rush off alone. Where would you go?"

"To London. I need a car and driver."

"But if you have no hotel room—you might go round and round for hours."

"I'll find one. I can't stay here."

"Yes, well, we'll arrange something, but your dress, your face, you mustn't go off like this." She leaned down, picked up my black sweater, and wrapped it around my shoulders.

"A cut like that can go septic," she went on. "I've brought Dettol, but Dr. Bentham must see it. Violet, what was I— you'd better go down. Send Mary up here. Have Betty make coffee and sandwiches. There's beer in the old butler's pantry," and Lady Bellew disappeared into the bathroom, still talking. As with Violet, extreme shock was affecting her tongue.

"Poor Gordon is coping with Mrs. Dearborn. The daughter is loving every moment, fancies herself in a Gothic melodrama, which in a ghastly way she is. *Jane Eyre,* complete with mad-woman and burning house. Here," she said, holding out a wet linen hand towel.

"The blood. It'll be ruined."

"Heavens, that's the *least.* Mary will be here in a moment, she'll help you. I must get back to the library. The men are at each other's throats." I stared at her, hand in midair.

"At each other's throats?"

"Oh God, oh God." She pressed her hands to her face. "The ambulance is coming, not that there's anything they can do. It's Hank. He refuses to believe she's dead. He wants to talk to her. He says Andrew is telling lies, something about Robina stealing papers from Galbraith." I let go of the towel.

"What about Galbraith?"

"*He's* in a blind *rage,* calling for his car and driver. He's accusing Andrew and me of luring him here under false pretenses; he's going to sue us both for trying to trick him, no matter how long it takes or what it costs him. And he *can* ruin us, you know. He *can.*"

I stared at her, jolted out of numbness. I had tried to warn Rodale: "George Galbraith is proud. He has a battalion of lawyers. He'll hit you with a dozen lawsuits if you accuse him of something he didn't do."

Lady Bellew was still talking. ". . . why I ever let Andrew talk me into this . . . this . . . but it was supposed to be a private sale, a chance to have a quiet little talk with Galbraith. Now the ghastliness with Robina. I don't *understand.* Do you?"

"A little. Not much."

"I admit I didn't like her, none of us did, but we'd known her forever. She was *family.* Sorry, I'm losing my mind; I must fly. What did I do with the Dettol?"

"It's here. I put it on." Robina was dead, but her poison was spreading. It had to be stopped. I pushed back the chair. For the third time, I looked down at the treacherous icy slopes stretching below me. "I'm going with you to the library," I said. Lady Bellew dropped the scissors she was holding.

"You can't. You're in shock. You almost died."

"There's no choice. I know Hank and Galbraith. I've known them for a long time."

"No, no, you've been incredibly brave, but when the adrenaline wears off you'll collapse in a heap."

I stood up and put my arms into the sleeves of the black sweater. Collapsing could wait.

"It's something I have to do for my husband," I said, and turned towards the door. Ma had loved an old Negro spiritual. The choir sang it at her funeral. "One more river . . . There's one more river to cross."

twenty-eight

Like a great ship, the house struggled to right itself after disaster. Men hurried through the rotunda, talking in clipped half sentences: "Dr. Bentham's gone up . . . need to keep a team on duty all night. . . . The Super's been called from headquarters." The machinery of disaster sliding into place.

Lady Bellew led me down a short hall lined with marble busts of Roman dignitaries. As she opened a door, I could hear Galbraith's angry voice, the voice of a man who was never crossed.

"Oh God." She put her hand to her head. "Oh God, he's still at it, hammer and tongs."

The library had linenfold wood paneling; the walls were lined with books behind gilded grills; across the room, a pair of doors opened to a dark terrace. Like figures in a fixed tableau, Galbraith and Rodale were standing on either side of the fireplace, arms behind their backs, the stiff parade ground posture. Hank sat slumped in a leather chair beside the desk, staring at the floor.

"Mrs. Streat." Andrew Rodale walked towards us. He had taken off his coat. The white dress shirt was torn; his hands were covered with red blisters. He looked at Lady Bellew. "She should be in bed."

"I told her about Hank and . . . the other. She said she's known them for a long time. She said she had to come."

"Right." A pause. He turned to me. "Not easy, but try to understand. We've told Lausch that Robina committed suicide. Not how. I realize it's far too soon, but it needs to sink in that she was leading a double life. Stealing."

I put my hand on the nearest chair. "You can't expect him to take that in. Not so soon."

"Granted, but the case is now out of my hands. The police are coming. He'll be questioned. He may be suspected of covering up for her. Later there'll be an inquest."

"But that's—"

"He needs to be prepared for the worst. You managed to get through to Mrs. Estes. See what you can do."

Hank hadn't moved. I went to the chair and took his hand. Impossible to tell him that Robina had tried to kill me. Or that she had married him to tap into the Galbraith millions.

"Hank," I said. "I'm so sorry."

He looked at me, the defiant glare of an angry child. "Rodale keeps saying she killed herself. He's lying. She was fine at dinner. You were with her in the Morning Room. *You* know she was fine."

I swallowed. "Rodale isn't lying. Robina wasn't fine. She was out of her mind with fear."

"Fear? Robina? She doesn't know the meaning of the word. I want to see her." He rubbed at his eyes. "Jesus, Emma, what's this crap about stealing projects? What's Rodale trying to hang on her?"

"Listen." I kneeled down and took his arms in both hands. "Please *listen.* Robina is—was—breaking into your office. Copying blueprints of Galbraith projects and selling them. It was a criminal offense. Tonight she knew she'd been found out. She couldn't face the disgrace."

"I have to talk to her. Where is she?"

"She's dead, Hank. The police are coming. They may ask you questions about her."

"Lies. Leave me alone." He pushed my hands away and closed his eyes. I sat back on my heels, feeling helpless. Cruel to inflict more pain. Worse to let him sink deeper into denial.

A silver-framed picture of the Queen and two corgis stood on the desk nearby. I stared at the Queen's stern face. She was wearing a flowered scarf that tied under her chin, a woman who had been trained to handle loss with dignity. I leaned forward and tried again.

"Hank. We've known each other a long time. We've always trusted each other. Just tell me this: Who paid for your houses, the clubs, the majolica? Was it you or Robina?"

He opened his eyes. "You know damn well it wasn't me. She had money from her Fyfe grandmother. She got it a few months after we were married. That's when she bought the Eaton Terrace house."

"Not with her grandmother's money. Robina's family had no money. There was nothing to inherit."

"I just told you, her grandmother left it to her."

"There *was* no money in the family. Ask Lady Bellew. She'll tell you the same thing. Robina's money came from making copies of Galbraith Tech weapons systems. Selling them illegally."

"For Christ's sake, I'm not a fool. I lived with her. I know where the money came from."

"She was clever, Hank. She fooled everyone. She did great harm."

"Crap. Nothing but crap. Admit it, Emma. You never liked her."

I shifted on my heels and took a deep breath. "Just one more question. Did Robina help you with the business?"

"You know she did. Right from the start she pitched in."

"So she *could* have made a duplicate key for the office. Gone there at night."

"Key? She'd have no use for a key. She never goes to the office."

"But she *did* help you at home. Organized your papers."

"What are you getting at?"

"We talked at dinner. I asked you about the fax I sent to Hampshire. You said it was in the little office by your bedroom. You said Robina was the only other person who could have seen it."

"What if she did? She was helping me. She loves me. She's always helping me."

I dug my nails into my palms. "Hank. She *did* see the fax. She sent that message to Wheeler telling him not to meet me. She sent a driver to kill me. I was a threat and she wanted me out of her way. Tonight she realized she was going to be exposed. She couldn't face the scandal." I stopped. Hank's round face was crumpling like a child's.

"You're all against her. Leave me alone."

"For now, but I'm here to help. Remember that." I stood up. Hank's pain was just beginning. I must try to be with him when he heard about Lewis.

There was a small fire in the grate. A log fell with a flurry of sparks. Rodale and Galbraith were still in the same place, hands behind their backs. Galbraith cleared his throat.

"Let me say this before I leave. There is no substance to what we've just heard in this room. None whatsoever. For the sake of her family, I trust that Lady Robina's death will be treated as an unfortunate accident." He stared at Rodale, the icy look. "Rodale, I hold you and Lady Bellew responsible for bringing me here under false pretenses. Steps will be taken."

Rodale's expression didn't change. "There were no false pretenses, sir. The painting is for sale. An auction was planned."

"That may be, but you have used the event to meddle in my concerns. Unwise, to say the least."

"Not at all. You can understand that when technology leaves this country illegally, questions must be raised."

"Indeed, but you have no evidence against me or my company."

"There is evidence, sir. Your former CEO, Lewis Streat, suspected that projects were being copied and sold from your London office. Passed along to an engineer in Hong Kong."

"Facts, Rodale. I want facts. Who is this engineer? Has he been questioned?"

"Unfortunately, he was knifed to death in June. Lewis Streat died three days later. An intensive investigation of these two deaths has been under way."

"In that case, I trust whoever is responsible will be found and punished. That's all. I believe my driver is waiting." He took a step towards the door. In a moment he would be on his way to London, the old fox going to ground in his den. I looked at Rodale. His eyes had narrowed, the hunter looking through his sights.

"One thing before you leave, sir. In 1945 you had a profitable black-market business in Hong Kong. You had a Chinese partner. He now runs a large weapons factory in Guangdong. It's possible that blueprints of your weapons projects have gone to this former partner in China. Possible that the Hong Kong engineer was the conduit."

"Nonsense." A vein began to throb in Galbraith's forehead.

"Then tell me this. When did you last have any contact with your former partner?"

Galbraith drew himself up to his full height. "A thoroughly scurrilous suggestion. Actionable. My lawyers will meet with yours."

"Very well, but the question must be answered. I will make my report. The inquiry will go on, but at a far higher level. I think you take my meaning."

Silence. For a moment the two men stood there, motionless, each taking the other's measure.

Finally Galbraith nodded. "As I suspected. Nothing but a tempest in a teapot. Four years ago I received a letter from this partner. He asked for copies of my latest weapons projects. If I refused, he would inform Scotland Yard about our black-market connection of sixty years ago. An empty threat, under the circumstances."

"You didn't turn that letter over to the authorities?"

"Certainly not. I know how to deal with blackmail. His letter was placed in a file. I can assure you that my files are never touched. By anyone." He turned. "Mrs. Streat." He stared down his nose at me, the look designed to shake the strongest nerves.

"Yes?" I stood straight.

"Mrs. Streat, I fail to understand your part in this farce. What's more, if your husband suspected that there were irregularities in the office, he should have alerted me at once. It was irresponsible of him to leave London last June without a word of warning. Highly irresponsible."

My head jerked back as if he had hit me. I could see Lewis

walking across the lawn to look at the thermometer. See myself standing in my sunny kitchen, washing lettuce as he sat at the kitchen table, his face grim, talking about trouble in London. Trouble that began with a murder on a people mover and was ending in a library thousands of miles away. Ending with one little letter that should have been sent to the authorities. Or shredded. Or locked in a safe. I faced Galbraith, fists clenched.

"How dare you; how *dare* you hide your head in the sand. Robina *lived* off your money. Your stupidity. She hired a professional killer. He murdered my husband and Dr. Estes. He blew up my house." My voice was fading, but the words came out with the force of a scream.

Galbraith stared down at me. "Control, if you please. You have no evidence."

"There *is* evidence. A notebook with formulas for a new project has been stolen. Formulas for a new use of laser that can replace all our weapons. Lord Rodale and hundreds of experts are working around the clock to find it."

"I've heard quite enough. Good evening." He moved forward.

I raised my hand and shook it in his face. "Listen to me. Until that notebook is found the whole world is in danger. Why? Because an arrogant old man thought he could never make a mistake. Thought nobody would *dare* touch his files. Thought he could play *God.*" It was over. I touched my throat, turned on my heel, and walked towards the open doors.

The terrace was dark, with a low stone balustrade. I stood there, holding on to a marble statue, afraid to move. After a while I let go of the statue. Somehow I must find my way back to my room, but I seemed to be immobilized with cold, as if waves of ice-cold water were running up and down my spine.

"There you are." Rodale's voice. His arm went around my shoulders. "It's over. You've been very brave."

I turned and pressed my face into his white shirt. It smelled of sweat and starch and soot. "She—she smelled like an *animal*. She could have run away. She hated me so much. She hated me for years and I never saw. We had lunch together and I never guessed—"

"Steady. We'll never know what was in that twisted mind."

In the court nearby, brakes screeched on gravel. Doors slammed. A man called: "Open the door, Jed. They're bringing her out." I shuddered and kept my head pressed into Andrew Rodale's shoulder.

"You're very cold." He began to rub my back, but there was nothing sensual in his touch. This was protection. Comfort. Suddenly there were lights around us. Voices.

"Oh God, Andrew. I've been looking for you everywhere." Lady Bellew was coming from the house. "It's started, there's a man from Global News on the line. They're sending a van." I didn't move. Rodale shifted his weight from one leg to the other. He kept his arm around me.

"No need to panic, Lucy. The police will keep them out."

"The Dearborn woman is in a frightful flap. I told her that she and the ghoulish daughter can leave with Gordon Taylor. Dr. Bentham has given Hank a sedative and I had him look at Galbraith. All we needed."

"What happened?"

"He was standing there when you left, then he sat down. It was like a giant tree falling in the forest. A touch of angina, Dr. Bentham said, but he's had his pills."

"He's fit to be taken to London?"

"Dr. Bentham says you can take both men. Mercer's fetching your car. You'll have a medical person with you, just in case. No need for an ambulance." I raised my head. Rodale's arm tightened.

"Lucy," he said sharply. "Stop nattering and pay attention. Mrs. Streat's at the end of her rope. Get her straight to bed. Have Dr. Bentham see her."

"I *told* her when the adrenaline ran out she'd collapse in a heap. Let me think. My daughter Edie's room is in the East Wing, just down the hall from mine. Small and cozy, if she doesn't mind girl clobber."

I shook my head and tried to break free. "London."

Rodale touched my face. "The house is safe. You're safe. Lucy will look after you."

"No." My legs were giving way. There was something I had to tell him, something important, but my brain was shutting down.

He took hold of my shoulders again, half-carrying me towards the doors. "Bed. I have a plan. I'll ring you tomorrow."

twenty-nine

There should have been nightmares. Hands clawing at my throat. A smell of smoke. Instead, I woke to bright sunlight in a small white room. A young girl's room; there was a bookcase filled with Pony Club trophies and a collection of Beatrix Potter china animals. I had been tucked into bed with hot water bottles, hot tea, sleeping pills. Like Eileen Grady, the Irish security expert, Lady Bellew knew how to put victims back together.

After a moment, I pulled myself up on the pillows and made a tentative check. The cut on my cheek was tender but not painful. My eyes were heavy from the pills, but the rest of my body felt free and weightless. I lay still, letting the changes take hold. No more FBI watchdogs. No need to keep secrets from family and friends. I must get up and call my neglected boys. There *would* be graduations. Weddings. A grandchild to hold on my shoulder, warm little body in a fuzzy sleep suit. Later I would have to think about Robina—but not yet.

The white curtains stirred in the morning air. Outside the window, a terrier was barking shrilly.

"Help! Go away! Help!"

I sat straight, as if yanked up by a string. A young woman carrying a camera was standing on the grass, surrounded by the resident pack of terriers. She kicked at them and they began to leap at her foot, delighted with this game. A policeman in a black helmet came hurrying around the corner.

"There's a sign, madam. No visitors allowed on this part of the grounds."

"Just one picture and I'll leave."

"You're in the wrong place, madam. Come along," and they moved off, attended by the playful pack. I let out my breath. Just a tourist trying to photograph an off-limits part of the house.

"Mrs. Streat?" The door flew open and Lady Bellew appeared. Breathless, wearing yesterday's green skirt and a yellow blouse.

"That woman. Did she see you?"

I shook my head. "A policeman came. She was screaming her head off, kicking the dogs."

"It's the press; the place is crawling with them. We're open to the public today, so they're buying tickets and pretending to be tourists. One just came into the kitchen and tried to grill the maids."

"About the fire?"

"About *you.* There are *wicked* stories in the papers this morning. 'Suspicious Death of Society Figure.' 'Earl's Daughter Dies in Stately Home.' That wretched Dearborn girl was interviewed on the morning news. I saw her. She sat there, looking anorexic, telling the world how Mrs. Streat and Lady Robina disappeared after dinner. Half an hour later Mrs. Streat came back with a torn dress and blood running down her face. Lady Robina was found burned to death in the attic."

"My God. They think *I* killed her? Is that what they think?"

"I rang Andrew for help, but he's at some high-level meeting. Useless. I've sent for more constables. Oh, I could *kill* that girl with my bare hands."

"I should have gone to London."

"No, no, you couldn't have managed, the state you were in. We'll survive, but today will be like a comic opera. Two buses with your American Garden Club ladies arriving for lunch, reporters popping up behind every bush—but nothing matters except the house is still standing and you're alive. You were so *brave.* I'll never forget how you stood there in the library facing Galbraith. And you were the one who cornered Robina. Did you know about her when you came here?"

"God, no. She was the last person. In fact, the idea first came into my head when you told me she had no money. Suddenly all the loose ends came together. She knew about my plans. She was always asking questions, keeping tabs on me, what I was doing, where I was going."

"She was obsessed about money. I remember when she came out of the schoolroom, so cool and collected. She began to gamble, cards, horses, her first husband divorced her after she nearly ruined him, but to be so twisted and hide it for so long—there must have been signs, but we never saw them."

"She was clever. And everyone was looking for terrorists."

"She was *evil*—thank God the madness isn't on *my* side. How are you feeling?"

I pushed back the covers. "I have to get home. I had a flight at noon today, but I'll never make it."

"Don't fret; Andrew will cope. The least he can do, after putting us through this nightmare. I should never have listened to him—our friends keep trying to marry us off, but they're wasting their time. That one-track mind—we'd kill each other in a week. Here's Violet with your breakfast," and she was gone.

"Good morning, Mrs. Streat." Violet came in carrying a large tray. She put it on my lap and stood back, folding her hands over the printed smock. "Had a good sleep, did you?"

"Very." So Lady Bellew and Rodale were *not* lovers.

"Half-dead, you were, by the time we got you settled. Now these dratted reporters. One burst into the orangerie just now while Betty and I were setting the tables for lunch. Bold as brass, asking questions about you. I've brought scrambled eggs and toast and a lemon tart. The Garden Club ladies are having them for a sweet. I thought you might fancy one."

"Thanks. Thanks very much." I held on to the sliding tray as a tan and white Jack Russell jumped onto the bed.

Violet reached for him. "Digger, down. *Bad* dog."

I laughed. "Let him stay. My dog sleeps in my bed at home."

"The greedy little beggar follows the trays. Here's a bell. Just ring if you want more coffee."

"This is fine. You must be very busy."

"Better than standing around crying our eyes out," and she, too, departed.

The house was very quiet. I drank coffee, trying to think ahead. By now Nick Yates must have seen the news. After my shower, I would call him. Explain what had happened. Ask him to get me back to my two stone chimneys.

I thought about Andrew Rodale, the compelling combination of physical and mental toughness. Unattainable, like my first love. At age fifteen, I had yearned for a boy who never glanced my way. Last night Rodale and I had worked together as partners. He had held me, comforted me. He had said he would call, but now he was knee-deep in meetings, moving on. It didn't matter.

"Mrs. Streat?" It was Violet, carrying a cordless phone. "Lord Rodale wants a word," she said, and disappeared.

I took a deep breath and put the phone to my ear.

"Good morning," I said.

"Good morning." The deep voice. "Lucy sounds back to normal, giving me hell for turning Elsham into a press orgy."

"They're all over the place trying to get a look at me. Two women fighting each other like alley cats. Guests at Elsham. I should know by now that trouble doesn't have a sell-by date."

"The facts will be out before long. How are you feeling?"

"No nightmares, but it's hard to make the leap from terrorists to one greedy woman. Someone I thought I knew."

"A lethal mix, brains and no morals. It'll take time to work out how she and Myers operated." He paused. "I've just come from a high-level meeting. Now our concern is to find the notebook. Otherwise we'll be running in place for years, waiting for a lethal new weapons system to surface."

I shifted the receiver to the other hand. "About the notebook. I came down to the library to tell you, but with all the drama it flew out of my head."

"Understandable. Tell me what?"

"This. Robina said they never had the notebook. She said Tom never found it." I waited for the predictable reaction.

"Bit of a stretch, that. What exactly did she say? When?"

"She was pushing me up the stairs. She said Tom was an overpaid bungler. He couldn't kill me. He couldn't find the notebook and all her work was for nothing."

"Hard to believe anything she said last night, given her state of mind."

"I'm not sure. She was half-crazed with anger, but she was making sense. Besides, why bother to lie if she was going to kill me?"

"I can tell you we've checked every nook and cranny in Cambridge. The Estes house. The Cavendish Lab. No notebook."

"But if Robina *wasn't* lying, if Estes *wasn't* carrying it in his vest pocket that night, he must have hidden it *somewhere*."

"In that case, it may never be found. My sense is that Samuel Estes was a true eccentric. A genius. Chances are he'd have put it in a place where no one would ever think to look."

"So there's nothing you can do."

"Nothing that comes to mind. Nothing short of a miracle." He cleared his throat. "Last night I said I had a plan."

"I should have gone back to London."

"No. You were falling apart." He cleared his throat. "When we met for the first time, at the House of Lords, I had the distinct feeling that you didn't like me."

"I didn't. I wanted to meet someone at Scotland Yard, not go out to dinner. You tried to pick my brains and walk away."

"You gave me a hard time, but I was impressed by what you were doing for your husband. Far more than most wives would or could. I wanted to see you again, but you were part of the job. Off-limits." A pause. "Do you know Venice?"

"Venice? Not well. One *Traviata* years ago at the old La Fenice."

"A friend of mine has a palazzo on the Grand Canal, near the one Wagner loved. I often go there at the end of a case to relax and clear the mind."

"A change, certainly."

"In fact, I'm leaving tonight for three days. It should be longer, but there's a new job coming up. If I remember, you were to fly home today."

"I was, but now I have to get new reservations and a way to escape from—"

"Wait. Let me finish. I want you to come to Venice with me."

I jumped. Coffee spilled on the sheet. "Come with you to Venice? Tonight?"

"You need to avoid the press for a few days. We need to talk about Robina. A shock like last night can have serious after-effects. Best to get the poison out of your system before you go home."

"I—give me a moment." I held Digger by the collar. With the other hand, I smoothed the white linen sheet. A palazzo on the Grand Canal. Light on a lagoon. Exotic beauty with a hint of dark depravity. Endless time to talk—and make love in a huge, carved bed. In my dream, this man had leaned over a balcony in Venice and stroked my neck. There were a dozen reasons why I should go home to the empty pool house—but extreme fear had a way of changing priorities. And there was still the matter of the missing notebook. Had Estes been carrying it when he was hit? If so, where was it now?

"Mrs. Streat?" Rodale was waiting for an answer.

I stared at Digger's quivering nose. How many other women had Rodale taken to this palazzo? Did it matter? I wasn't a yearning teenager. He had made it clear that this was no long-term commitment, just an invitation to share a few days with a complex man who put work ahead of women. A man who went to Venice to replace violence with beauty.

"I'll come," I said. "What time do I leave here?"

"Henn will be at Elsham at noon. He'll take you straight to Heathrow. We'll get the seven o'clock flight to Marco Polo. I'll line up a water taxi." A fine example of British understatement. Digger's nose was an inch from the tart.

"Don't even think it," I said sharply.

"You've changed your mind?"

"No." I shifted the tray. "As a matter of fact, I've just had a thought. I realize it's out of the way, but could Henn take me to Cambridge and then to Heathrow?"

"Very much out of the way. Why Cambridge? To see your godmother?"

"She'll have left by now. Actually, it's about the notebook."

"You want to go to Cambridge to look for the notebook?" A wary tone of voice.

"Just an idea. It may turn out to be nothing."

He cleared his throat. "Look here. It's quite extraordinary, what you've done. You seem to have a talent for finding these unlikely connections, a talent that can't be taught in any police academy. Having said that—"

"Yes?"

"For God's sake, don't get a taste for detecting. Give it a pass. Lie back and rest on your laurels."

thirty

Saturday, July 25

In Cambridge, the city of bells and gowns, the Great Saint Mary's bell rang the hour of three as Henn pulled into Trinity Lane.

"I'll park down by the King's College gates, out of the way. How long will you be, Mrs. Streat?"

"An hour, maybe less."

At the door to the Porter's Lodge, I hesitated, then walked through the two courts and down to the terrace overlooking the Backs. A few weeks ago, I had watched a punt sweep gracefully through the green water of the Cam. Then I had turned, gone to a phone booth, and called Dr. Estes. The beginning of my mission—but there was one more river to cross.

As I went back to the Porter's Lodge, a gardener was planting clumps of early chrysanthemums in the herbaceous borders. He nodded as I went by.

"Fine afternoon."

"Very fine," I said, and walked slowly through the narrow

passage between the kitchens and the great hall. At the opening night dinner, Caroline had told me to stand up or the bench would bite the backs of my knees. A young instructor had passed by us on his way to the dais. He had sneezed, then reached into his gown for a handkerchief. After Harvard commencements there had always been an epic search for Pa's glasses.

In the Porter's Lodge Mr. Bennett was leaning on his hands, listening to a young woman who had locked her key in her room.

"I'm always so careful, I can't think how it happened."

"When the other porter comes I'll attend to it." He turned and saw me standing there. "Yes, madam?" The heavy eyebrows met in a straight line. This was a face that spelled trouble. Disappearances. Police coming to the college with questions. I gave him my warmest smile.

"Hello, Mr. Bennett. I've come back to ask you a question."
"Yes?"

"It's about the night Dr. Estes was killed. A young man with a beard brought you a gown. He thought Dr. Estes was carrying it when he was hit."

"Yes?"

"Where is that gown now, do you know?"

"Dr. Estes' gown?" A wary look. "After he died, I rang Mrs. Estes. She said she had no use for it. She asked me to give it away. I put the hood in the Senior Combination Room to be used in an emergency."

"What about the gown?"

"The gown was very worn, frayed at the seams, too shabby for Oxfam." The telephone rang and he picked it up. "Porter speaking. . . . You left an umbrella in the Chesterfield Room? What color umbrella?"

The same brown paper parcels still lay in the dented bicycle basket. I waited. As Mr. Bennett put down the phone, I leaned forward.

"You say that the gown was very worn."

"Beyond repair. I put it in the dustbin behind the kitchens."

"The dustbin? How long ago was that?"

"Five days, that would be. Now, if you don't mind—"

"Wait. Where does that collection go?"

"To the nearest landfill." He turned and reached for a key on the board. I put my hand on the counter. A dustbin. Five days ago. Oh God, I had been so *sure.*

"Mr. Bennett, just one more question. The gown. Did you happen to look in the sleeves? Or the pockets?"

Mr. Bennett drew himself up. "I *beg* your pardon?"

"I'm asking because Dr. Estes was doing research for my husband's company when he died. My husband told me Dr. Estes always wrote his first calculations, equations, whatever you call them, in a little notebook."

"Indeed."

"The notebook has disappeared. People are looking for it everywhere. The thing is, my father was a professor at Harvard. He used to put glasses and notes in his gown. It must happen all the time, people putting things in their gowns."

"Quite." A slight smoothing of ruffled feathers. "Come to think of it, I did turn out the pockets in case of valuables. There was a handkerchief. Eyedrops. A small notebook. Brown leather, very worn. I had a look inside. Nothing but petty cash accounts. Bus fares, paper from WHSmith."

"Are you sure?"

"Petty cash accounts. At the back, a few pages of numbers scribbled down. Messy little scrawls. Nothing your husband's company would ever want. The notebook went into the dustbin with the gown. Now if you'll excuse me, this young lady is waiting to get into her room."

The court outside was peaceful. The gardener was trimming blue lobelias in a window box. White clouds, looking like a Constable painting, rose high above the line of massive chimneys. I went to Staircase D and leaned against the stone arch.

Two young men came running down the narrow stairs. Students taking possession of their rooms again, or maybe another seminar was starting today. They smiled at me and went on. One had the same color hair as my son Steven. I closed my eyes and thought about Lewis. His love for me and for his sons. His concern about a new weapons system. At last, requiem for Lewis. He would understand about Venice, want me to go on with my life.

It was getting late. I began to walk back through the court, swinging my arms, remembering an old hymn, one of Granny Metcalf's favorites:

> *Grant us wisdom,*
> *Grant us courage,*
> *For the facing of this hour . . .*

As a child, I had sung it at the top of my lungs. Belted out the words without a trace of comprehension. In the past five months my courage had been well exercised, even by Granny's standards. I had been stripped of my husband and my home. I had nearly died, but trees toppled in windstorms came back with strong new growth.

In the Lodge, the porter was talking on the telephone. I smiled at him as I went by, remembering Rodale's high-handed advice: ". . . don't get a taste for detecting. Lie back and rest on your laurels." But talent was a rare commodity; it should be encouraged, not wasted. On the plane to Venice, I would tell him casually, over a glass of wine, that Whitehall could relax. Agents could stop their round-the-clock search. His baby-faced assistant could get a full night's sleep. Emma Streat, untrained maker of connections, had traced the missing notebook to a hill of rotting orange skins and potato peels.

The old Bentley was parked under the walls of Clare College Chapel, a few feet from the place where Dr. Estes had been struck down. In a few hours I would be on my way to Italy. By next week Rodale would be deep in another search. I would fly back to my family. But before leaving Venice I must call Caroline and tell her that I had followed her advice and gone off with a new man.

"What's his name?"

"Andrew Rodale. Lord Rodale."

"Oh God, not one of those penniless peers. They'll do anything for money."

"Don't worry. I'll hang on to my purse."

I walked faster. Tonight Rodale would bring the same concentration to making love that he brought to his work. It wouldn't be easy for me to find the first notes, but the man was an expert. He would never put a foot wrong in bed and I was ready to give again, full measure. *Con brio.*

Henn was leaning against a wall, reading a newspaper. I stopped and looked up at the towers of King's College Chapel. Tonight the boys choir would sing at Evensong:

> *Lighten our darkness. . . .*
> *By thy great mercy defend us from all perils*
> *and dangers of this night . . .*

And all the days to come. There was a saying that a life nearly lost must be lived fully and well.

As I came up, Henn turned and saw me. He smiled and folded his paper.

"Time we were off. If we're late Lord Rodale will have my head. Ready?" He opened the car door. I got in and put my bag on the floor.

"Yes. Ready."